JENNA'S PROTECTOR

Guardian Hostage Rescue Specialists: CHARLIE Team

ELLIE MASTERS

Editors: Roxane Leblanc, Erin Toland

Published in the United States of America

JEM Publishing

This is a work of fiction. While reference might be made to actual historical events or existing locations, the names, characters, businesses, places, and incidents are either the product of the author's imagination or are used fictitiously, and any resemblance to actual persons, living or dead, business establishments, events, or locales is entirely coincidental.

~

PAPERBACK ISBN: 978-1-964261-22-5
HARDBACK: ISBN: 978-1-964261-23-2

Dedication

This book is dedicated to my one and only—my amazing and wonderful husband.

Without your care and support, my writing would not have made it this far.

You pushed me when I needed to be pushed.

You supported me when I felt discouraged.

You believed in me when I didn't believe in myself.

If it weren't for you, this book never would have come to life.

Also by Ellie Masters

The LIGHTER SIDE

Ellie Masters is the lighter side of the Jet & Ellie Masters writing duo! You will find Contemporary Romance, Military Romance, Romantic Suspense, Billionaire Romance, and Rock Star Romance in Ellie's Works.

YOU CAN FIND ELLIE'S BOOKS HERE:
ELLIEMASTERS.COM/BOOKS

Military Romance
Guardian Hostage Rescue Specialists

Rescuing Melissa

(Get a FREE copy of Rescuing Melissa

when you join Ellie's Newsletter)

Alpha Team

Rescuing Zoe

Rescuing Moira

Rescuing Eve

Rescuing Lily

Rescuing Jinx

Rescuing Maria

Bravo Team

Rescuing Angie

Rescuing Isabelle

Rescuing Carmen

Rescuing Rosalie

Rescuing Kaye

Ashes to New

Heart's Insanity

Heart's Desire

Heart's Collide

Hearts Divided

Hearts Entwined

Forest's FALL

Hearts The Last Beat

The LaRouge Triplets

Asher

Brody

Cage

Billionaire Romance
Billionaire Boys Club

Hawke

Richard

Contemporary Romance

Cocky Captain

Romantic Suspense

EACH BOOK IS A STANDALONE NOVEL.

The Starling

~AND~

Science Fiction

Ellie Masters writing as L.A. Warren

To My Readers

This book is a work of fiction. It does not exist in the real world and should not be construed as reality. As in most romantic fiction, I've taken liberties. I've compressed the romance into a sliver of time. I've allowed these characters to develop strong bonds of trust over a matter of days.

This does not happen in real life where you, my amazing readers, live. Take more time in your romance and learn who you're giving a piece of your heart to. I urge you to move with caution. Always protect yourself.

Grab the First Book in The Guardian Hostage Rescue Specialists Series for Free

https://elliemasters.com/RescuingMelissa

ONE

Carter

I FLIP THROUGH THE CASE FILES OF THREE GIRLS WHO HAVE disappeared, frustration gnawing at me. No leads, no witnesses, no resources. Just broken homes, pretty faces, and troubled pasts—girls nobody would miss.

A runaway, a druggie, and a thief.

The system failed them, and now they're gone.

Sitting at my dingy, rusted government-issue desk, I rub my temples, trying to ease the headache that's been building all morning. The budget constraints are suffocating, making it nearly impossible to gather the resources I need for this case.

Correction. There's no *nearly impossible* about any of this. It's simply, *exhaustingly impossible*.

Leaning back, I pinch the bridge of my nose and blow out a frustrated breath. All I have are empty leads and fruitless dead ends.

The office around me is a testament to the lack of funding—cracked linoleum floors, flickering fluorescent lights, and walls stained with years of neglect. The musty smell of old papers and dust fills the air, mixing with the faint scent of stale coffee from the pot that's been sitting for hours.

Max, my loyal German Shepherd, sits by my side. His expressive eyes watch me intently. I reach down and scratch behind his ears.

"At least I've got you, buddy."

He wags his tail in response, a small comfort amongst the chaos.

I grab my phone, needing to talk to someone who can help me make sense of this. I dial my brother, who works for an organization with extensive resources—resources I don't have but would kill to utilize in this case.

Sadly, that is not the way of things.

"Hey, troublemaker, what's the crisis this time?" My twin brother picks up, his voice dripping with its usual sarcasm.

Max's ears perk up at the sound of Blake's voice. An eager whine escapes his dark muzzle, followed by a quick thumping of his tail—Max loves Blake and hasn't seen him in a while.

"Another one's gone missing. Fifteen years old. No leads. I'm hitting a wall here."

"Man, that sucks. Look, I don't know if this will help or not, but I was talking to the team the other night, telling them about your disappearances, and I might have something for you." Blake's voice is steady, but concern weaves through each word.

"Might?" I sit up straight, suddenly alert and eager for any scrap that might give me a direction on where to go next. "Shit, that's a whole lot more than I have right now."

"You need to talk to Forest."

"Forest?" I frown. "Forest, who?"

"Dude, I've told you about Forest. The creator of Guardian Hostage Rescue Specialists?" When I don't respond, Blake continues. "The dude is otherworld smart. Operates on a whole other plane of existence than us mere mortals."

I won't say it to Blake, but that's a bit over the top, even for me.

"Hero worship much?" I don't do that kind of shit.

"Whatever, dude," Blake continues, non-plussed. "He overheard my conversation with the guys and said he might have some information that could help."

"Shit, I'll take whatever he has." I sigh, feeling the weight of my frustration. It's not the solid lead I need, but it's better than the shit-for-nothing I've compiled on the girls' disappearances. "Give me his contact info, and I'll call him. Thanks."

"I'm not saying it'll help, but Forest doesn't poke his nose into something without a reason."

"Would be wonderful if this was a case you guys were working instead of me. Got hit with budget cuts again. I've got piss-poor resources and a lack of staff."

Which is all to say: I've got Max.

My dog.

Sure, there are other detectives, but like me, they're buried under a mountain of paperwork. We have receptionists who answer the phones and track down information as they can. The beat cops are tired, stuck in a job that should make them heroes, but their contributions are devalued under a wave of public opinion and outcry over a few unfortunate events and bad apples that have left their stain on our profession.

"You know the Guardians only take on certain cases—hostage rescue and human trafficking. We're not really into the missing person's gig." Blake chuckles, a hint of sympathy in his voice.

"You sure about that?" I can't help but challenge him. "All of your cases are about those who've been taken—aka missing. You literally work missing persons."

"Not gonna split hairs with you—*again*, but you always have an open invite to join us. Better resources, better support… Or you can keep being dissatisfied with what you've got."

I grit my teeth, the familiar argument bubbling up. "Yeah, yeah. I know. Just—give me Forest's info."

"I'm serious. We could use someone like you." Blake's tone softens. "Guardian HRS is always hiring good men. Think about it."

"I don't have all the fancy-schmancy SEAL training you have. I'm just an average Joe, doing what I can to protect and serve."

"Team skills can be taught. Your detective nose, however, that's a true gift. Honestly, we could use someone with your abilities."

"I'll think about it," I mutter, already dreading the empty promises of my current job. "Thanks, Blake."

Max nudges my hand, sensing my frustration. He looks up at me with his expressive eyes. I swear the mutt can read my mind.

"Don't worry, boy. We'll figure this out."

I dial Forest's number.

He answers on the second ring.

"Carter Jackson?"

"Yes."

"I take it you spoke to Blake." The man's voice is deep. Not a baritone, but octaves lower. He sounds like boulders grinding against each other.

"He said you have something for me."

"I do, but first, I need you to promise me you'll be discreet."

"Of course. What is it?"

"There's someone you need to talk to, but I hesitate to give out her name."

"You have a lead?"

"Maybe. Jenna was never forthcoming about what happened, but I've got a sense about these things."

"Jenna?" Surely, he can't mean…

"Jenna Marlowe. I think you know her."

Holy fucking shit, do I know Jenna Marlowe. Just the mention of her name makes my stomach clench and heart race.

"I do."

"Well, she may or may not be connected to these cases in a way that could be crucial."

I lean back in my chair, processing his words. "Tall, long black hair, alluring green eyes?" He can't mean my Jenna.

Not that she's mine. I've yet to work up the courage to ask her out.

My days begin and end at Jenna's café. They begin with a stout coffee—that I don't particularly like—and end with a pathetic run-in to grab one of her savory sandwiches for my evening meal.

Always takeout.

"Yes, Lover Boy," Forest chuckles. "That's her. She has a past that might be connected to these disappearances. It's not an easy story, and it's something she goes to great lengths to keep hidden, but her insight could be invaluable. More likely than not, she's going to hate I said anything at all, and when you do bring it up..." He pauses, and it's as if the world stands still.

There's something in her past? Whatever it may be, Forest's tone hints at trauma.

"When you do bring it up, she's not going to like it. Just be—*gentle.*"

"You're telling me she knows something about this case?" Disbelief and desperation churn inside me.

"She might. And, Carter, I'm not kidding about the being gentle part. She's been through a lot. If you can get her to open up, it could make a difference."

"Could? How?" I can't believe Jenna could provide any insight.

She's just a gorgeous woman who runs my favorite coffee shop. I go there every day, not for the coffee I can barely stomach, but to see her. The thought she could be involved—even in the remote past—in something so horrible is beyond me.

"Why would you think Jenna has anything to do with my case?"

"A few years ago—" Forest's tone shifts, becoming more serious. "I found Jenna on a dark highway. She was scratched and bruised. Naked. Severely traumatized and physically injured. I brought her to the Facility: it's a place where we reintegrate those we've rescued back into the world. We provide trauma counseling, therapy—other services. She never divulged details from that night to anyone but me. One of those details is… sensitive."

"Sensitive?" I lean in, feeling the weight of his words.

Forest hesitates, his voice lowering. "Jenna did what she had to do to survive. She was in a situation where she had no choice, and it ended with… With an incident. That incident was never investigated. It needs to stay that way."

"I hear you, but what does she have to do with my case?" The impact of his words hits me, but I keep my expression neutral, nodding slightly.

"Jenna has information that could be crucial to your case, but you need to understand—pushing her for details about that night or trying to bring up what she's been through will only hurt her. The details of what happened must stay buried. Focus on what she can give you now, in the present."

I let out a slow breath, the gravity of the situation settling in. "I get it. I'll tread carefully."

Forest's voice softens just a bit. "Good. Jenna's been through hell, but she's strong. She'll help you if she can."

"Do you think she can?"

"There are several parallels that should not be ignored."

"Such as?"

"I'm ninety-nine percent positive that what happened to her is linked to the fate of those girls you're trying to find. Anyway, after a stay at the Facility, we gave her a new identity. New life. Helped her finish high school. Gave her the skills to live on her own. A business loan to open up that coffee shop."

"New identity?" What happened to Jenna that made her need a new identity?

"She wanted no ties or connections to that past. If you haven't figured it out already, you know why I say you need to be *gentle* with her. I violate a lot of trust in saying anything at all."

"Then why speak to me at all?"

"Because it's important, and I know Jenna. She survived something horrible. She would want to help others—in the same situation. I'm operating on an *ask forgiveness later* premise telling you any of this. I don't care if she gets pissed at me. She'll forgive me, eventually, but I wanted you to know she may not be receptive to the idea I spoke to you. I've seen too much and lived through too much. This is worth violating a bit of her trust."

"Alright. I'll talk to her. Thanks for the info." The weight of this new information presses down on me.

"Good luck, Carter. And be careful."

Max barks, sensing the end of the call. He stands, tail wagging, ready for our daily routine.

"Alright, boy, let's go see Jenna." I grab my keys, eager to have a reason to stop in and see Jenna but nervous about how the interaction might go.

Max and I head out to the truck with Max in the lead. Tongue lolling, tail wagging so hard his butt wiggles, Max jumps into the passenger seat with practiced ease. He knows the routine well and gives a little bark as we drive toward Marlowe's Café.

This is his favorite part because Jenna always has a treat for him.

Climbing out of my truck, I stand outside Marlowe's Café. The crisp morning air bites my skin, leaving a trail of goosebumps in its wake. My breath forms little clouds as I exhale.

Still early, barely past the ass-crack of dawn, the town is quiet at this hour. Early risers are still cocooned in their homes, but Max and I have been up since four in the morning.

I scan Main Street, the familiar storefronts seemingly frozen in time. This place feels different today—heavy with the weight of what I need to do.

Max trots alongside me, his nose twitching as he sniffs the air, ever vigilant and curious.

Always eager.

Fiercely loyal.

I push on the door to Marlowe's Café. The bell above the door jingles, slicing through the low hum of conversation and the clatter of dishes.

The rich aroma of ground coffee and fresh pastries wraps around me like a comforting blanket. The warmth contrasts sharply with the chill outside, enveloping me as I step inside.

Jenna is behind the counter, her back to me as she steams milk for a cappuccino. Her hair is pulled back in a loose bun, a few stray strands escaping control. The soft hum of music plays in the background, adding to the cozy atmosphere of the most perfect place on the planet.

I pause, taking in the sight of her. Jenna moves with an understated and innate grace. Her every action is fluid and purposeful. The woman is a natural beauty. She tries to hide it under baggy clothes and messy hair, but Jenna is runway-model gorgeous.

My heart spikes high above baseline the moment I see her. It does that every time I see her. In addition to the kick of adrenaline, there comes a clenching of my gut.

Her slender fingers expertly handle the steam wand. The way

she tilts her head and nibbles on her lower lip as she concentrates sends a jolt of warmth through me. I can't help but admire her effortless elegance.

The loose strands of her hair catch the light, framing her delicate features and highlighting her high cheekbones.

Her presence is magnetic, drawing me in every time I see her. I come here every day, usually a bit earlier than now—that call with Forest has me running late—but not for the coffee. I come to catch a glimpse of her. It always starts my day with a smile.

She turns slightly, giving me a full view of her long, dark lashes and the soft curve of her lips.

My heart skips a beat, and then it races ahead.

The vulnerability in her eyes contrasts with her outward strength. The depth makes me desperate to know everything about her.

I step further into the café. Max trots beside me, tail swishing and blissfully unaware of my unease. He's smitten with Jenna, always eager to see her and get his daily treat. Max whines softly, and I give him a reassuring pat to soothe his excitement.

He doesn't understand my hesitation.

"Easy, boy," I whisper. "We'll get your treat soon."

Max nudges my leg with his nose, reminding me to keep moving.

It's hard to believe Jenna carries a haunted past—a past Forest says might hold the key to my current case. It's hard to see how, but I'm desperate.

Jenna turns, her gaze meeting mine. For a moment, everything else fades away. Her smile is like a ray of sunshine, warming me from the inside out.

"Morning, Jenna." I manage to keep my voice steady.

"Morning, Detective Jackson." She laughs, her eyes sparkling. "And Max, I know you want this." Reaching under the counter, she pulls out a treat.

Max gives a happy *woof*, his butt wiggling feverishly as Jenna hands him the treat. I watch the interaction, a pang of longing hitting me hard.

I want to be the person she looks forward to seeing every day, not just another customer engaging in meaningless small talk.

I take a deep breath, steeling myself for a difficult and uncomfortable conversation.

Someday—I'm going to ask her out. But today, I must dredge up painful memories she's worked hard to forget. I hate that my first real conversation with her will be about this case.

The guilt is eating me alive.

The weight of Forest's words hangs heavy on my mind, but I push them aside for now, focusing on the woman who has unknowingly captured my heart.

Max looks up at me with expressive eyes as if sensing my internal conflict. I sigh and give him a reassuring pat.

"Let's do this, buddy."

Three teenage girls are missing, and I swear on everything I hold dear that there won't be a fourth.

TWO

Jenna

Before the morning rush gets going, the bell above the door jingles, cutting through the low hum of the coffee shop I call home.

I lift my gaze from the steaming espresso machine to greet the newcomers.

My regulars, Frank, Doris, and Mav, step inside.

"Morning, Jenna." Frank's gravelly, deep voice bellows, his silver mustache twitching like a hairy caterpillar on his lip.

"Morning, Frank." My reply is light and breezy, warm and sincere. "Your usual?"

"The blacker, the better." He rubs his hands together as if to wring out the chill from his bones.

"I've got you." I fill a cup with our strongest brew and slide the steaming mug across the counter toward Frank. "Here you go, strong and bold, just the way you like it."

"Wouldn't have it any other way." He winks as he takes the mug and inhales the dark aroma of a perfectly brewed coffee.

Doris grips his arm and walks beside him. Her silver curls bounce with each step. Mav, their grandniece, a schoolteacher with an infectious laugh, trails behind them, her nose buried deep in a book.

Not one of those e-readers, but a genuine book.

Her voracious appetite for literature knows no bounds.

They stop in every day like clockwork. Mav brings them here for a caffeine hit, then drives Frank and Doris to the senior center. She then heads to the elementary school to spend the day with a classroom of kindergartners. I couldn't do it, but she thrives in that environment.

"Morning, Jenna." Mav peeks up from her book, likely coming to the end of a chapter or paragraph. I've learned to give her time to find an appropriate place to stop before barraging her with questions.

"What can I get you?"

Mav, who loves all the frills in her coffee, never orders the same thing twice. She's on a quest for the perfect combination of sweet, cream, and caffeine.

"I'll have a large caramel macchiato with extra caramel drizzle, both in the cup and on top of the foam. Could you add a shot of vanilla syrup, too? And extra frothy with whipped cream on top."

"Gotcha."

Mav's order does not disappoint and reflects her penchant for a sweet, indulgent treat first thing in the morning.

"Oh, and if you have them, sprinkle some cinnamon and some chocolate shavings on top."

"You know I will." I quickly scratch down her order before I forget, then turn to Doris. "And what will you have today, Doris? Are we taking it boring black like the love of your life? Or dressing it up with all the frills like your grandniece?"

Doris responds in a manner I've come to love. She's balanced in all things. Not too plain nor too extravagant.

"Oh, love, you know me, always somewhere in the middle. Let's go with a medium cappuccino today. Just a touch of sugar and a dash of cinnamon on top, just a little something to brighten the day."

"I've got you covered. Have a seat. I'll bring them to you once they're done."

Mav's order will take a moment to prep. Doris isn't too steady on her feet, and I don't want her waiting while I create Mav's masterpiece.

Doris is a wonderful woman. She's welcoming to strangers and someone I'm glad to call a friend. She's the mother and great-aunt I never had, all rolled into one bundle of joy and delight.

I love her approach to coffee and life. She enjoys simple pleasures with a hint of something special.

But not too fancy.

"You spoil us too much," Doris chides gently. Her eyes crinkle at the corners, indicating a life well-lived and full of smiles.

"It's no trouble." I feign nonchalance while my hands move on autopilot, crafting their orders with the precision born out of countless repetitions.

And then, out of nowhere, a memory crashes over me like icy waves against jagged rocks—cold, dark, and suffocating.

I strike, the letter opener sinking into flesh, warm blood spilling over my fingers. His eyes widen in shock, then go lifeless.

The steam wand hisses, and I froth the milk for Mav's cappuccino; the sound drowns out a past I want to forget, but those memories always lurk, invading my thoughts at every turn. There's not one day when they don't intrude on my life.

As hard as I try to drown them out, they find chinks in my armor where they slip in, resurface, and steal my breath.

While I work, Frank steers Doris toward their special spot near the door. Mav is already there, tucked into the special nook, nose buried back in her book.

It's a cozy little booth with a great view of Main Street.

Not too pretentious. Not too plain.

It's just right.

As I lose myself in the routine of my job, the memories subside, replaced by the gratitude that fills my heart. The simple act of serving brings normalcy to my world.

Surrounded by the delicate aromas of coffee beans and pastries baking in the back, I carve out a new life for myself one day at a time—a life far removed from the one that nearly devoured me whole.

The air is thick with the stench of sweat and fear…

I push the intrusive thought away and repeat the mantra I created for moments like this: *I won't let the memories win. I will breathe and enjoy the freedom I fought so hard to have. I will focus on the present—forget the past—and embrace the life I've built.*

A flicker of determination ignites in my eyes as I bus orders for Mav and Doris to their table.

"Thanks, Jenna." Mav cups her drink and takes a sip. The froth sticks to her lips, and she darts out her tongue to lick them clean. "You always know how to start our day right." Her voice is a modern marvel, a melodious tune that brightens the darkest corners of my soul.

"I can't let my favorite people down." I note Frank's half-downed cup and nod. "I'll bring you a refill."

"Thanks, Jenna." Frank gulps his coffee and sets the empty mug on the table. "Best damn coffee in town."

"Thank you." I turn to leave, but Doris's next words catch in my throat.

"Did you hear?" Doris's voice pierces the relative quiet, heavy with concern. "Another girl's gone missing. Vanished into thin air."

My hands grow still as their conversation flows around me. Its chilly tendrils sink into my skin and hitch in my breath.

"Terrible." Frank sips his coffee, his brow furrowing. "This town used to be safe." He shakes his head and stares into his mug.

"Seventeen, they said. Can you imagine?" Mav glances up from the page she's reading.

Yes.

Yes, I can.

A shudder wracks my body, and I turn away under the pretense of grabbing a cloth from the pocket of my apron.

He lunges at me, ripping the lingerie off in one swift motion. I'm exposed, vulnerable, and terrified. He pushes me down onto the bed, his hands rough and demanding…

My past rips through the walls I've built over the years. Terror grips me hard and renews my greatest fear: that one day, I may find myself taken once again.

Swallowed by shadows.

I scratch absently at the invisible tattoo on my wrist—a tattoo I didn't place and am too scared to get removed.

"Jenna?" Frank reaches for my arm. "Are you okay?"

"Y-yes." I clutch the cloth to keep my hands from shaking.

Miraculously, my voice remains steady despite the torrent of emotions raging through me. I offer a soft smile and wipe down the spotless table.

"I was just wondering if I took the pastries out of the oven."

"You sure?" Doris's eyes fill with genuine worry and meet mine. "You look like you've seen a ghost."

Not a ghost.

Just my past.

"Yes, I'm just going to go check."

She and Frank welcomed me to this town with open arms and few questions. They seemed to sense I was running from something and knew I wasn't ready to talk about it.

I'll never be ready.

These people and this place are my anchors.

I shouldn't let their comments about another missing teen get to me.

It's a good day.

Business is steady.

My customers are happy.

The café hums with life.

I'm happy to kickstart their day with lattes, laughter, and light-hearted banter.

That's what I need to focus on.

Focus on the positive and bury the negative.

Unfortunately, a part of me is always a little bit afraid.

Afraid of being noticed.

Afraid of being found.

Afraid of being taken.

Their conversation continues, weaving through both the mundane and the tragic.

I can't shake the feeling these disappearances are more than random strokes of bad luck. There's a pattern—I feel it—and it's one I know all too well.

It's a constant battle… Fighting the pull of my memories, suffocated by the weight of my fears, and forced to live with the fact I'm Jenna Marlowe, a barista with eyes that have seen too much darkness.

Danger could slip through that door as easily as my morning regulars.

The only light is that I'm no longer seventeen.

No longer prey.

No longer naive.

No longer vulnerable.

Speaking of regulars—I try to shift my thoughts—one regular is running late. He's the brightest spot of my day.

My sweater keeps slipping off one shoulder and I pull it back into place. Loose-fitting clothes are a strategic choice. They create a barrier between me and the world, a gentle reminder that I'm no longer strutting my stuff in the suffocating grip of haute couture, where every stitch and seam screams perfection, and every flaw is magnified a thousand-fold.

My friends finish their morning caffeine infusion and say their goodbyes. I glance at my watch, noting that Detective Jackson, who is usually prompt, is late.

"See you later, Jenna." Frank waves as he holds the door for his girls.

"Stay safe," I call out as they leave.

I spend the next few minutes tidying up, refilling stock, and checking inventory.

The chime over the door suddenly rings. My breath catches, and my hands still.

I don't need to look up to know who it is. My pulse quickens at the familiar rhythm of Detective Carter Jackson's gait as he slowly strolls from the door to stand on the other side of my counter.

Max, his German Shepherd, sits obediently by his side, tail thumping against the floor, eyes bright—nose going a mile a minute as he checks out all the wonderful smells in my coffee shop.

"Morning, Jenna." Carter's deep, rumbly voice sends shivers down my spine.

It's delicious and decadent all at once. He leans against the counter, his presence filling the space, his eyes locked on mine.

"Detective Jackson," I greet him, a smile playing on my lips. "And good morning to you too, Max."

I lean over to give Max a treat from the jar I keep behind the counter for our four-footed friends. Max accepts it gratefully, all lips and slobber but no teeth. His tail wags so hard that his entire body shakes.

I turn my attention back to Carter. "The usual today?"

"You know it," he chuckles, the sound warming me from the inside out. "I don't know how I'd start my day without your perfect brew."

My cheeks flush at the compliment. "Well, I aim to please. Double shot espresso, no sugar, a splash of cold water, right?"

"Spot on." His smile is disarming, his eyes crinkling at the corners. "I'm impressed you remember."

"I remember everything about you—I mean, about your order." I stumble over my words, mentally kicking myself for the slip. "I only meant—I know what you like."

"You do?"

"You like your coffee strong and straightforward with a bit of a twist, Detective."

"Please, call me Carter."

"As you wish, Detective."

If it weren't for my past, I would've jumped his bones already. I just think a man of the law would have problems sleeping with a murderer.

As I prepare his drink, his gaze on me is intense and unwavering. We do this dance every morning—the banter, the lingering looks, and the unspoken words hanging between us.

My mind wanders, imagining what it would be like to have those strong hands on my waist, those lips on mine…

"Here you go." I hand him his espresso, and our fingers brush against each other.

The contact is electric, sending sparks up my arm. I quickly pull away and wipe down an already spotless counter.

"Thanks." He takes a sip, his eyes never leaving mine. "Perfect as always. You're a lifesaver."

"Just doing my job." I try to keep my tone light, but I sense a heaviness in the air, a tension that wasn't there before.

He doesn't move away from the counter, his fingers tapping against the smooth surface. Max sits patiently, watching us with intelligent eyes.

It's like Carter wants to say something but holds back, either unsure or reluctant to say whatever is on his mind. The wheels turn in his head, evident in the slight furrow of his brow as he searches for the right words.

"Is there something else I can help you with?" I try to keep my voice steady—my heart pounds. Anticipation and nerves coil in my stomach.

Is he going to ask me out?

"I..." He trails off, his gaze dropping to his cup momentarily before meeting mine again. "I was wondering if we could talk." He clears his throat, looking uncomfortable. "Somewhere private."

My breath catches in my throat. *Private?*

"Um, sure." My voice wavers with a surge of excitement mixed with nerves. "Just let me grab Malia and ask her to watch the front."

He nods, his expression unreadable. There's something in his eyes, a flicker of emotion I can't quite place.

My heart races, hoping this might be the moment I've been waiting for.

I untie my apron with shaky hands and hang it on a hook behind the counter.

"Malia, can you watch the front for a moment?" I call out to my part-timer, who's in the back room checking inventory.

"Sure thing, boss." Malia's energy is infectious. She doesn't walk to the register. She bounces.

I'm going to have a *private* conversation with the man of my dreams.

THREE

Carter

Jenna leads me to a small office tucked away at the back of Marlowe's Café. The aroma of freshly ground coffee beans gives way to the musty scent of old ledgers and paper.

Max follows us, his nails clicking softly on the worn wooden floor. His tail wags gently, and his nose twitches constantly, drinking in the new scents. His head tilts slightly as if processing the lingering sweetness of pastries, the sharp tang of cleaning supplies, and the unique scent that is purely Jenna.

As we enter the cramped space, Jenna's fingers trail along the edge of an old oak desk, her touch almost reverent. She turns slowly, her green eyes meeting mine with curiosity.

"What did you want to talk about, Detective?" Her voice wavers, barely above a whisper, so unlike the confident barista who greets me every morning.

I'm about to hurt her in the worst way possible.

Jenna kneels to scratch behind Max's ears, a small smile playing on her lips as my loyal companion leans into her touch. The simple gesture, so full of warmth, makes what I'm about to do even harder.

"I need your help." The words come out more abruptly than I intended, my usual confidence faltering in her presence.

"My help? What do you need my help with?" Her brow furrows, confusion evident in her emerald eyes. She tilts her head slightly.

"I'm working a case." I scratch the back of my neck.

"A case?" She crosses her arms, her confusion deepening. "What could I possibly have to do with any of your cases?"

"It's a kidnapping case. The missing girls. Have you heard about them?"

Recognition flashes across her face, followed by something deeper, more visceral.

"I… Yes, I have. Some regulars were talking about another girl going missing just this morning." Her voice wavers slightly, a tremor that most people wouldn't notice.

I'm not most people, not when it comes to Jenna.

"It's horrifying," she says. "But I don't see how I can help you." She absently strokes Max's fur as he sits contentedly at her feet, his presence a soothing buffer between us.

I take a step closer, careful not to invade her personal space but wanting to convey my sincerity.

"I need to ask you something. I wouldn't be asking if it wasn't important."

"What is it?" Her voice is barely above a whisper, her fingers now clutching at the fabric of her shirt over her belly. It's a subtle gesture, one I wouldn't have noticed if I hadn't spent months cataloging her every movement.

I swallow hard. I'm about to drag her back into a past she's tried to leave behind.

"It's about your past." I keep my voice low and as gentle as possible.

The warmth in her eyes vanishes instantly. Her posture straightens as if bracing for a physical blow.

"My past?" The words come out in a whisper, but the tension in the small office makes it feel like a shout.

A fierce, protective instinct surges through me. I want to shield her, to take back my words and pretend this conversation never happened.

But I can't.

The missing girls are counting on me.

I force myself to continue, hating every word. "I know what happened to you."

The transformation in her expression is heart-wrenching. Disbelief morphs into shock, then raw fear. Her breathing quickens—a subtle change that nonetheless screams of rising panic. Max whines softly, picking up on her distress, and presses closer to her legs.

God, her eyes tell a story of pain and fear, making me want to gather her in my arms and never let go.

But I can't.

I'm here as a detective, using her trauma to solve a case. The guilt of it sits heavy in my chest, a weight I'm not sure I'll ever be rid of.

"Why are you digging into my past?" She steps back, eyes wild with a mix of fear and rage.

"I didn't dig into your past. I reached out for help, and your name was mentioned." I raise both hands in a placating gesture, my heart breaking at the pain I've caused her.

Her gaze darts around the small room, reminiscent of a trapped animal searching desperately for escape. Max whines softly, picking up on the tension, his tail tucked between his legs.

"How?" she chokes out, her voice barely above a whisper. "How is my past related to any of this?"

I meet her gaze, my eyes filled with concern and an ache that goes beyond professional duty. "I was told you might have insights that could help me find these girls. That could help me stop whoever's behind this."

"No." Jenna wraps her arms around herself. "I buried my past for a reason."

I take a deep breath, steeling myself. "If there was any other way…" I trail off, running a hand through my hair in frustration. "I've exhausted every lead. These girls, they're running out of time. Without your help, they might be lost forever."

Jenna's eyes flash with anger, but beneath it, a flicker of something else exists.

Understanding?

Compassion?

Resignation?

"Please. These girls need your help."

"No one knows about my past," Jenna whispers. "No one except for…" Her words trail off as understanding dawns. Her eyes snap open with disbelief and betrayal. "No. He wouldn't. He promised…"

Her raw, emotional pain hits me like a physical blow. Her eyes glisten with unshed tears, and her hands tremble as she clutches the edge of the desk, knuckles white. The haunted look on her face reveals the depth of her reopened wounds.

Max whines again, pressing his body against Jenna's legs, his brown eyes darting anxiously between us.

"I'm not here to spill your secrets, Jenna." I keep my voice steady despite the turmoil inside me.

I take a step closer, breaching her personal space. The urge to wrap her in my arms, to shield her from this pain, is almost overwhelming.

Tears spill down her cheeks. The sight of them stings worse than if she'd slapped me. "Do you have any idea how hard I've worked to put that behind me?" Her voice breaks. "Do you know what it's like to live with those memories, those scars?" She absently scratches the inside of her wrist.

Max nudges Jenna's hand, and she strokes his head, her eyes never leaving mine.

"I was told you have a unique perspective. You've seen things, experienced things that could be invaluable in cracking this case."

"How?" she asks, shaking her head in disbelief. "How did you find out?"

I take a deep breath. "I was talking to my brother, Blake. He works for the Guardian Hostage Rescue Specialists."

Recognition flashes in her eyes at the name.

"I needed help with this case, and when I told him about it, he mentioned it to his team. Forest Summers overheard that conversation and he told Blake to have me reach out."

Her eyes squeeze shut, and when she opens them again, her steely determination takes my breath away.

"My past is in my past for a reason. Right where I intend to keep it. I'm sorry, but that was years ago. I can't help you."

"Jenna…" Her name comes out as a plea. Every nerve in my body screams that I'm losing her.

Without thinking, I take her hand in mine. It's small and delicate, but there's strength there too. Max whines again, pressing closer to Jenna as if trying to offer comfort.

Her eyes widen in surprise at the contact, but she doesn't pull away. Those eyes, once so guarded, now reveal a world of pain and fear. They're piercing, wounded, beautiful, and filled with an ache that makes my heart clench.

"I know you have to find them," she says softly, "but… Not me. Please, isn't there someone else? Anyone else who can help?"

"I know it's asking a lot. I know it's painful, but the tiniest detail could break this case wide open."

For a long moment, Jenna is silent, her internal struggle playing out across her face. Max looks up at her, his tail giving a tentative wag as if encouraging her. For a long moment, the only sound in the room is our breathing and the soft panting of the dog.

Finally, Jenna's shoulders slump slightly. Her voice is small and vulnerable. "I can't promise anything. But—I'll listen. That's all I can offer."

"Thank you." I give her hand a gentle squeeze. "That's more than enough. We'll take this at your pace, I promise."

Jenna's hand is still in mine, and our fingers are now intertwined. We're holding hands, but not in the way I would like.

Her skin's warmth against mine is comforting and distracting, but her pulse, quick and erratic, shows her distress.

"What did Forest say to you?" Jenna asks, her voice barely above a whisper.

I swallow hard, knowing my next words will cause her pain. "He told me he found you. You were…" I hesitate but press on, "running from something. You were bruised, hurt."

Jenna's breath catches—a small, pained sound. Her hand trembles slightly, and it takes every ounce of willpower within me to resist the urge to pull her into my arms.

I'm acutely aware of how long I've been holding her hand. This prolonged contact between us should feel awkward, but it doesn't. Her skin is soft, and her hand fits perfectly in mine. I don't want to let go, afraid she'll pull away if I do.

Jenna's hair, black and silky, cascades down to her waist. A stray strand falls across her face, and I clench my hand to keep from reaching out and tucking it behind her ear. Her eyes, those mesmerizing green eyes, flood with fear, pain, and suffering.

The scent of her—the richest blend of coffee, vanilla, and something uniquely Jenna—envelops me. I could spend all day simply breathing her in.

Her breath flutters against my skin when she speaks, sending shivers down my spine. It's intoxicating, and I have to remind myself this is a professional interaction.

"I'll help you." Her voice is stronger now. "But I need you to promise me something."

"Anything," I reply, perhaps too quickly.

"This stays between us. I don't want my past to get out. It's a small town, and I don't need any rumors circulating. I don't want people to know what—what happened to me. I don't want to be treated like a victim."

"I promise." I nod solemnly, squeezing her hand gently.

The relief that washes over me is tempered by the weight of what I'm asking her to do. I'm in awe of her strength and her willingness to revisit her trauma to help others.

It makes me admire her even more, if that's possible.

"Thank you," I say, my voice rough with emotion.

Jenna nods, a small, sad smile touching her lips. Then, I realize I'm still holding her hand, my thumb unconsciously tracing circles on her skin. I should let go and maintain professional distance, but I can't break the connection.

Instead, I find myself lost in her eyes, struck by the depth of emotion I see there. The air between us feels charged, heavy with unspoken words, and brimming with possibility.

For a moment, I forget about the case, the missing girls, and everything except the extraordinary woman in front of me.

But I can't forget.

Not really.

This isn't about me or my feelings for Jenna. It's about finding those girls, about stopping whoever is behind their disappearances.

With a reluctant sigh, I step back, giving her some space. "We should get started. Whenever you're ready, of course." My voice is huskier than I intend.

Jenna nods, taking a deep breath as if preparing for battle. And in a way, she is.

"Let's get this over with." Her voice is steady despite her fear.

FOUR

Jenna

We sit in the small office, the air thick with tension. Max sits quietly at my side, his presence soothing. His ears perk up, and he watches us intently, sensing the gravity of the conversation.

"What do you want to know?"

"If you could tell me what happened to you, maybe I can find something that ties in with my case. Forest told me a little but left out a lot more."

"There's not much to tell." My voice is steadier than I feel.

"Take your time." Carter nods, his expression one of solemn determination.

"I was seventeen, a runaway, and living on and off the streets." I take a deep breath, gathering my thoughts. "Or rather, I bounced between living on the streets and living in an abusive home. It wasn't pleasant."

"Seventeen?"

"Yeah."

"So young."

"Not for that industry."

"What industry?"

"A modeling agency approached me, promising fame, magazine

covers, and money. So much money. They offered me housing, training, and a way to finish school. It was the answer to all my problems. At first, it was everything they said it would be—glamorous and exciting. But then things changed."

Carter hangs on my every word, his eyes filled with empathy and understanding. Max nudges my leg gently, giving a little whine. I reach down, absently petting him, drawing comfort from him.

"The glamour slowly twisted into manipulation—then exploitation. I had no idea what I was doing, or what was happening to me. It was insidious."

"How did they do that?"

"The grooming process was gradual but relentless. They started by building us up, telling us how beautiful we were and how we had the potential to be stars. They taught us how to walk, talk, and behave in a way that would make us irresistible to men. They called it 'charm school,' but it was really a way to break us down and mold us into their perfect playthings. We trained to be models and hostesses for private events where wealthy men would gather. It was all about making the men feel special. We were encouraged to flirt."

"Flirt?"

"Yes. We got tips if we flirted well and were punished if it seemed as if we were unwilling to make the guests feel desired. I was young and naive, and the attention initially felt like validation."

"Punished? What did they do?"

"Along with the grooming came threats. We were told things would happen if we didn't behave or comply. They reminded us how easily we could be replaced. They threatened to send us back to the lives we had run away from, back to the poverty and abuse."

"That's horrible." Carter's brows pinch together.

"The threats were so ingrained that we began to believe them. We became terrified of making a mistake, of stepping out of line. The constant fear created a sense of dependence and obedience that was hard to shake."

"What were the punishments?"

"They withheld food, gave chores… The physical abuse was subtle at first but escalated quickly. A late arrival to class meant a sharp slap across the face. A misstep during a walkthrough resulted in being locked in a dark closet for hours. The worst was when one of the girls broke down crying during a fitting session; she was dragged out of the room and came back with bruises all over her body."

"They physically abused you?" He starts to say something more but thinks better of it. His lips press into a stern line.

"The staff justified these actions by saying it was all part of our 'training' to become perfect models. They claimed it built character and discipline, but it only instilled fear and compliance. We learned to hide our pain and do whatever it took to avoid their wrath."

"They took advantage of you."

"One of the girls, Sophia—she and I became close friends there —anyway, she was always a bit of a rebel, constantly getting into trouble. She tried to slip out once. Sophia was… promiscuous. Unlike me, she wasn't a virgin. She told me she wanted to *get some.* None of the guards would touch her. Or the men at the fancy parties. Long story short, she didn't make it to the nearest town before the guards caught her. When they brought her back, we were all forced to watch her punishment."

"They made you watch?"

"To make a point. They stripped her and whipped her in front of us. Her screams echoed through the facility, a chilling reminder of what awaited anyone who dared to defy them. Afterward, she was locked in solitary confinement for days, with only bread and water to survive on."

"At any time, did you think about escape?"

"Never. We were there to learn, and they had rules we had to follow. It was just the way things were. I knew any attempt to break the rules would result in punishment. That fear kept us in line, but not once did I feel like I was a captive. I was grateful for what they were doing for me. Their emotional control was that strong."

"You did say insidious."

"It was nothing compared to the mental manipulation. The staff would praise us one moment and degrade us the next. They told us we were special, chosen for greatness. They played mind games, isolating us from each other and making us compete for their approval. They had us believing we would be nothing without them. The constant gaslighting and brainwashing made it impossible to think clearly. And then…" I hesitate with this last part.

"And then, what?"

"They hooked us on drugs. Cocaine mostly; said it was to help us stay slim. There was more."

Much more.

"Is there a name? An address?"

"Elite Essence is what they called themselves. I never knew the address."

"Were you ever told you could leave?"

"And go where?" I shrug. "They took me from the street. I wasn't abducted like the girls in your case, but my father had no idea what happened to me. I could go back to him or back to living on the streets. Despite the hardships at the estate, it was better than returning to an abusive home. Never was there any reason to think things weren't on the up and up. I was excited by all the things they told me. I went willingly. We all did."

"You mentioned flirting with the men. Did you have to…" Carter's jaw tightens, and his grip on my hand grows firmer, offering silent support. Max's ears twitch, and he moves closer, his body language alert yet calming.

"No." I shake my head vigorously. "They were very careful about that. It was nice, to be honest."

"Nice? What does that mean?"

"They protected us from the men who got too *handsy*. The men didn't touch us. They weren't allowed."

"Not allowed?"

"Like I said, we were protected from things like that. It had something to do with an old club way back when. The men could look but not touch. It made it more—civilized."

"Civilized?"

"They wanted us to feel safe. Said as much at the outset. The men couldn't touch us; we were supposed to report it if it happened. On the other hand, we were encouraged to flirt and do whatever it took to make them feel special. There was nothing about sex, which is why it never occurred to me that..." I choke up at this part, then shake my head as if that could erase the memories.

"I never felt exploited. Uncomfortable, for sure. At least at first, but then it became a game."

"Game?"

"To see who could get the biggest tips. The best gifts."

"Gifts?"

"If a man favored a girl, he could give her gifts."

"Jenna, I hate to ask, but the more specific you can be..."

"I didn't see the trap until it was too late. They began taking me to these private parties, introducing me to clients who were powerful and wealthy. The men at these events had a way of looking at me that made my skin crawl. Their eyes were predatory, and I felt dirty being a part of it, but I kept telling myself it was just part of the job. I was there to make them feel special and get as big of a tip as possible. Gifts as well. I refused to accept what my gut was telling me."

"What happened at those parties?" Carter leans in closer, his expression intense.

"At first, it was just mingling. I was still in training and didn't understand what was happening. The clients would make suggestive comments, but I brushed it off. I was told to be polite, smile, and make them feel special. And like I said, they never touched me during those parties, just watched."

I pause, the memories flooding back. Max whines softly, sensing my distress, and nudges my leg again. I reach down to scratch his ear.

"Then came the night of the final private party. This time, it was different. They said I was ready to take the stage. I thought they meant to walk the runway and model for real."

FIVE

Jenna

"AND WHAT DID THAT MEAN? TO WALK TO THE RUNWAY FOR REAL?"
Carter's eyes probe for details, but he does it in a way that makes me
feel safe.

As if any of this is helping, but somehow, it feels good to finally
talk about it with someone other than Forest.

"Reliving these memories isn't easy."

"I know, but Forest thinks there's a connection and a way you
might be able to help me. I wouldn't ask if it wasn't important."

I take a deep breath. "That night, besides serving, I was told I
would model for the clients. They paraded us around in barely-there
lingerie. It was a fashion show but with a twist. As we walked up and
down the runway, the men placed bids. I thought they were bidding
on the merchandise—th-the lingerie. We were given numbers to
wear on our garters. I didn't realize they were bidding on me. I
thought…" I choke up at this point.

"When did you realize what was happening?"

"My gut was screaming at me that something was *off*, but I
ignored it. Sophia figured it out. She told me we had to get out.
That they planned to sell us. I didn't believe her. I should have."

"You can't blame yourself for what happened. They manipulated you. Used you."

"Yeah, but Sophia was always suspicious. I didn't believe her until they brought me to the man who placed the winning bid on the lingerie I thought I was modeling… That's when everything changed."

"I'm so sorry. I can't even imagine."

"He told me to strip. I thought he wanted the garment. He leaped to his feet when I hesitated and said I belonged to him. I was stunned. Shocked. He ripped the lingerie off me. It still didn't hit me until he touched me. They weren't supposed to touch us, but he touched me. And *they* allowed it."

I take a shaky breath, feeling the weight of the memories. Max lies down at my feet, his head resting on his paws, his eyes watching me closely.

"Whatever you tell me stays in this room. Forest made me promise. How did you escape?"

I swallow hard, the memories still fresh and raw despite the years. "I felt so stupid. Sophia warned me. Over and over, she said it wasn't right. After these parties, some girls didn't return to the dorms, but I didn't listen. I didn't want to believe her. But then, as I stood there, naked, with that man's hands on me, I had to do something."

Max sits up a little straighter as if sensing the importance of this part of the story.

"What did you do?"

The room fades away, the present slipping from my grasp as I'm pulled back into that night. I'm no longer sitting here, safe and sound—I'm back in that suffocating room, the walls closing around me…

THE AIR IS STALE, FILLED WITH THE PUNGENT SMELL OF SWEAT AND cigarettes. The fear that grips me is so palpable that I taste it, a bitter, metallic

tang that forces bile into my throat. His breath is hot against my skin, a grotesque contrast to the coldness of his eyes. Each exhale sends a shudder through me.

He pushes me onto the bed, his hands rough and demanding, bruising my flesh as he holds me down.

"Please, don't," I beg, my voice a whisper. But he ignores me, his grip tightening as he forces himself on me. Tears stream down my cheeks, the saltiness mixing with the bitter taste in my mouth.

"Stop fighting," he growls, his voice a low, menacing rumble. "I paid good money for you."

I fight back, kicking and clawing, but he's too strong.

I try to scream, but no sound comes out. My throat is dry, my voice stolen by the sheer terror that consumes me.

The physical pain is overwhelming, but it's the emotional agony that consumes me. I feel violated, broken, and utterly helpless.

Eventually, he finishes. The man pulls away, a twisted smile curling on his lips, a glint of sadistic anticipation in his eyes. It's not disgust—it's the cruel satisfaction of knowing he owns me, as if he's savoring the years of torment he's planning.

"I was told you knew how to behave, but you're a wild animal. That's okay, because I look forward to breaking you."

He storms out of the room, slamming the door behind him. I lie there, trembling, my body aching from the assault.

My limbs feel like lead. My heart is a heavy stone in my chest. The room spins, and I drown in a sea of despair.

Somehow, a small voice inside me whispers, urging me to move, to get out.

THE ROOM COMES BACK INTO FOCUS, THE PRESENT RUSHING BACK IN. I find myself sitting across from Carter, the weight of that night pressing down on me. His jaw is tense as I take a deep breath, trying to steady myself.

"He took my virginity. Ripped it from me the way he tore the lingerie off my body."

"I'm so sorry."

"Something inside of me died that night," I say softly, my voice barely above a whisper. "Part of me will always be back in that room, forever trapped in that moment."

Carter reaches out, gently touching me, offering silent comfort. I cling to that touch, drawing strength from it as I continue my story.

"I imagine security must have been tight. How did you escape?"

"There weren't many guards in that part of the estate. They were all at the event with the other girls. I knocked the guard out and ran."

"You're fearless, Jenna. Not many people could have done what you did. It's a miracle you got away. How did you knock out one of the guards?"

I take a deep breath, steeling myself for another flood of memories.

∼

I check the door. Locked. The window's next. It, too, is locked. I need something to pick the lock.

I search the room, pull out drawers, and find a small metal letter opener. It's not much, but maybe enough. I use the letter opener and try jimmying the lock.

Footsteps outside the door have me diving back onto the bed. I hide the letter opener under a pillow. The lock clicks and the door opens. It's not the man who bought me, but a guard.

"What are you doing?"

"Nothing. Just—waiting."

He turns to leave, but I can't let him go.

"Um, do you have a cigarette?"

"A cigarette?"

"It calms me."

By some grace, he considers my request. He hesitates but then pulls out a pack from his pocket. He lights a cigarette and hands it to me.

∼

I can't tell Carter what happened next. He's a cop.

But as I sit here, the memory tightens its hold on me, dragging me back to that night. I still feel the weight of the cigarette between my fingers and the tremor in my hand as I bring it to my lips.

~

"Thanks." I smile seductively at the guard. "Can you stay a moment? I'm scared." He looks uncertain but sits down on the edge of the bed.

Something comes over me—madness perhaps. Somehow, the letter opener is in my hand, and I stab it into his neck. The sudden gush of blood is horrifying. His eyes widen in shock. His hands fly up to his neck, trying to stem the flow of blood, but it's too late.

I jump off the bed, throw the letter opener aside, and run for the now—open door. The hallway is empty. I sprint down it, my bare feet slapping against the cold marble floors. The sound echoes through the corridor, seeming to amplify my desperation.

I spot a staircase leading down and take it, my legs threatening to give out with each step. At the bottom, there's a massive wooden door.

But it's locked.

~

My mind replays how my heart pounded as I grabbed the letter opener from under the pillows… How it felt sinking into the guard's neck.

I force the memory away, and the present rushes back in. I manage a small smile, feeling relieved that I made it through that part of the story without having to confess to a murder.

"I just did what I had to do to survive. I found a service stairway and headed down. Somehow, I made it to an exterior door. It was locked, but I broke a nearby window and climbed out."

"I can't even imagine what that must have been like… But you did what you had to do. You survived." His voice softens, making me feel like a hero rather than a murderer. Not that I told him about that part.

"Sliced my hands to shreds, my feet too, but I couldn't stop. It was pitch black, and I had no idea where I was. But I kept moving."

Max shifts slightly, his head resting on my foot, grounding me. I pet him absently, drawing strength from his presence.

"Outside, I hid between rows of expensive cars, making my way to the edge of the property. It didn't take long before they discovered I was gone. I ran as fast as I could, not caring where I was going, just needing to get away. I crossed the lawn and plunged into a field. The bushes scratched my skin, and my feet bled from the glass and sharp stones. I tripped several times, but I got up and just kept running."

Carter's grip on my hand tightens, his eyes urging me to continue.

"They sent dogs after me. I could hear their barks, their growls, the snapping of their teeth getting closer."

Max whines softly, sensing my distress. Carter's jaw is clenched, his anger palpable.

"I came across a road. The dogs were nearly on me. The men were a bit behind but closing in fast. A fancy car approached. It stopped. The man inside didn't ask questions. He popped open the passenger door and told me to climb in. The moment I did, the first dogs came into sight."

Carter's eyes fill with a mix of horror and admiration. "And then what happened?"

"The man drove off. He didn't press for details; he just drove. The dogs and the men chasing me disappeared in the rearview mirror. That man was Forest Summers. He took me to the Guardians. They helped me put my life back together and taught me how to hide and how to live without being discovered. That's how I escaped. It wasn't easy, and I was lucky. But I got out. No one can know any of this."

"I promise," Carter says, his voice low and fierce. "I'd never tell anyone."

I take a shaky breath, feeling the weight of the memories lifting slightly. Max gives a small whine, and I draw comfort from his steady presence.

"That's not what I mean."

"What do you mean?"

"That man paid millions for me. He will come for me if he discovers where I am."

"I'll protect you. I just… I need your help."

"Other than what I've told you, I don't know what else I can do."

"Can you tell me more about how they target girls? How they targeted you?"

"They target vulnerable girls—runaways, those with troubled family backgrounds, or those simply looking for a way out of their current lives. They lure them with promises that seem too good to be true, and once they have them, the real nightmare begins. That was me. If it's the same operation that took me, they canvas the streets for pretty girls. The girls that are missing… Are they pretty?"

"They're all beautiful, and all with tragic home situations."

"Then that's your connection."

"Can you tell me anything else about how they approached you? Their selection process?" His eyes never leave mine, his attention unwavering.

"They're meticulous. They study their targets, learn their routines, and their habits. They look for girls who won't be missed immediately or have a history of running away. Once they have enough information, they make their move. They promised the stars and groomed me for weeks before I agreed to go with them. Worked like a charm. I was everything they were looking for. Young, malleable, desperate, and looking for love and acceptance. Validation that I was worthy of more than my father's fists." I pause, the memories flooding back. Max lifts his head, sensing the tension in the room.

"And the parties?"

"The parties are where they do most of their business. High-profile clients, people with money and power, come to these events to '*shop*.' It's disgusting, but it's how they operate."

"And how do they keep their operation hidden?" Carter's jaw tightens, his anger palpable.

"They have connections. Corrupt officials, law enforcement on the take, and anyone who can help them stay under the radar. Those officials were their most lucrative clients. It's a well-oiled machine designed to avoid detection."

"I need to identify these connections. I'll start with the modeling agency. Can you give me their name?"

"Elite Essentials, but good luck with that."

"What do you mean?"

"When I was at the Facility, I tried to look them up. Sophia was also there that night—at the auction. She didn't get out like me. I thought I would find her… Free her."

"I have a few tricks up my sleeve. They may have changed the name, but I doubt they changed how they operate."

"All I can say is these people are careful and have a lot of money."

"Thank you." Carter leans forward, determination etched on his face. "This really helps."

I look into Carter's eyes, seeing the depth of his desperation. "I don't know how any of that can help you, but I've told you everything I know."

"Jenna, I know this is hard, but your insights are invaluable. I need to ask something else." Carter squeezes my hand, his grip strong and steady.

"What more could you need?" I furrow my brow, feeling the weight of his words. "I've told you everything."

"I need to profile these people. Your experience with them— how they think and operate—could be the key to predicting their next move. Anything you can remember about those men will help me find them."

I shake my head, feeling the pull of my past trying to drag me back under.

Carter's eyes soften, and he moves closer, his voice gentle yet insistent. "But you know their behavior, their tactics. You've seen their faces."

"I have."

Max nudges my leg again, his big eyes full of concern. I stroke his head, drawing strength from his unwavering loyalty. Carter watches me, waiting for my response.

"Please," he continues, "help me."

SIX

Jenna

My heart thunders against my ribcage, a wild beat echoing the storm of emotions churning within me. I draw in a deep breath to anchor myself. Tension ripples through each vertebra as I straighten my spine.

"I should get back out there." The words come out steadier than I feel. "Malia can't handle the lunch rush alone."

"Thank you. I mean it." Carter's eyes, warm and earnest, lock onto mine.

"What now?" My fingers twist the hem of my shirt, betraying my nerves.

"I want to bring in a sketch artist." Carter's chest rises with a deep breath. He leans in, his presence both comforting and overwhelming.

"Why?" The question escapes before I can stop it, sharp with fear. He doesn't need a sketch artist, but I've already shared too much. I need space.

"I'm hoping we can identify some men from those parties." Carter's voice is low and intense. "If I can get sketches, I can run them through facial recognition databases. It might help find a pattern or link to the current disappearances."

My stomach lurches, twisting into knots. "I don't know if I can help with that."

The lie tastes bitter on my tongue. Every face, leering smile, and predatory gaze is seared into my memory, and the thought of revisiting those images makes my skin crawl.

"You're the only one who has seen these people up close." Carter's tone is gentle but firm.

"I'll try." The words are barely a whisper. I swallow hard, feeling the sting of unshed tears.

I don't want to try.

I don't want to remember.

I don't want to visit a single moment from my past.

"I hate to ask more from you, but it could help." Carter's hand finds my shoulder. His grip is warm and reassuring.

I yearn to lean into his touch, to let his strength seep into me. His presence is a comfort, something solid I desperately need right now.

A soft whine draws my attention downward. Max nudges my leg, his brown eyes pools of concern. Kneeling, I bury my fingers in his soft fur, drawing strength from his unwavering presence.

Rising to my feet, I meet Carter's gaze. My voice is stronger now, bolstered by Max's silent support.

"Okay. When do we start?"

"As soon as possible. I need to schedule the sketch artist. I'll let you know."

"Then it's a date." The words slip out before I can stop them, a bitter reminder of the fantasies I've harbored. I force a smile, trying to mask the ache in my chest.

"I suppose it is." Carter's eyes soften, and a flicker of something unreadable passes over his face.

"If there's nothing else, I do need to get back out there."

Carter's gaze lingers, a flicker of something—regret? longing?—passing through him.

"Sure. I'm sorry to have taken up so much of your time." He opens his mouth as if to say more, then presses his lips together, the moment evaporating like mist in sunlight.

Would a real date have been too much to hope for? I nod, pushing the longing aside.

"Well, I guess that's it. Let me know when you… When you need me." I brush past him, the warmth of his body a fleeting comfort.

The scent of his cologne clings to me, a bittersweet reminder of our closeness. As I step back into the café, the cacophony of clanking dishes and murmured conversations washes over me. It's jarring, this abrupt transition from the intimacy of our conversation to the mundane bustle of everyday life.

The espresso machine hisses. Its familiar sound grounds me in the present. Yet, I feel as if I left a part of myself behind in that small room—the part that dared to hope, to dream of a future with Carter Jackson.

For a moment, I imagine what it might be like to spend more time with Carter—not as a victim or a witness, but as someone he cares for. The thought is both thrilling and terrifying.

But he's right.

As much as I want to pretend that part of my life never happened, I can't ignore the fact that I might be able to prevent others from suffering the same fate. The weight of this responsibility settles on my shoulders, heavy yet somehow empowering.

My phone buzzes in my pocket, startling me from my reverie. I pull it out, my heart stuttering as I read the name on the screen: Forest Summers. The man who helped me escape my personal hell, the leader of the Guardian Hostage Rescue Specialists.

With trembling fingers, I open the text. It's short, but it sucks the air from my lungs:

~

Forest: *I'm sending a Detective to talk to you. I think you can help him.*

Me: *Two minutes too late, Forest.*

Forest: *Sorry.*

~

A HUMORLESS LAUGH ESCAPES ME. FOREST SUMMERS BROUGHT MY past into my present with all the subtlety of a freight train.

And just like that, the past I've tried so hard to outrun catches up with me, pushing me into the arms of the man I've secretly yearned for since moving into this town. A man who, moments ago, I foolishly thought might be taking a step toward something more.

The bitter irony isn't lost on me. As I tie on my apron, preparing to lose myself in the familiar rhythm of brewing coffee and serving customers, I can't help but wonder: Is this a new beginning, or just another chapter in a story I thought I'd finished writing?

I turn away as Carter leaves. The soft jingle of the bell above the door marks his departure.

The hiss of the espresso machine jerks my thoughts back to the coffee shop. I breathe deeply, letting the freshly ground coffee's rich aroma fill my lungs. The rhythmic clink of cups and saucers, the low murmur of conversation, the scrape of chairs against the hardwood floor—these sounds envelop me, grounding me in the present.

I move behind the counter, my hands automatically reaching for the portafilter. The routine is comforting—measure, tamp, lock, brew. The machine whirs to life, and I lose myself in the sultry dance of creating the perfect shot of espresso.

A customer approaches, and I plaster on a fake smile. It feels fragile, like a mask that could slip at any moment, but it holds.

"What can I get you?" My voice is steady, betraying none of the turmoil beneath the surface.

As I work, I can't help but reflect on the foolishness of my dreams. Carter now knows my past. He sees the damage underneath. The spark I felt between us was clearly one-sided. He's not interested in me beyond his case, and that totally sucks.

The lunch rush begins in earnest, and I throw myself into the work.

Each latte becomes a canvas, each perfectly pulled shot of espresso a crafted masterpiece, and every friendly interaction with a regular customer a comforting anchor. These small victories remind me I've created something real here, something good.

It may not be the life I dreamed of, but it's mine. And for now, that has to be enough.

The rest of the day passes in a blur, my mind trapped in an endless loop of our conversation. I serve customers on autopilot, my smile a brittle mask hiding the turmoil within.

As I lock up for the night, exhaustion settles into my bones. The short walk home is a haze of streetlights and shadows, my thoughts as murky as the twilight around me. My apartment, once a sanctuary, now feels like a cage of my own making. My phone suddenly buzzes with an incoming text.

CARTER: I've secured a sketch artist. I'll pick you up tomorrow morning at 9 AM and take you to my office.

I stare at the message, my heart pounding. Tomorrow, I'll have to face my past again. I respond with a simple "*Okay*," and set my phone down, trying to calm my racing thoughts.

Sleep eludes me, my dreams a twisted maze of memories and fears. In my nightmares, I'm back in that room, the harsh lights blinding me as rough hands strip away my dignity. I didn't tell Carter about the tattoo—invisible marks on my skin—branding me as property. I wake with a start, my wrist burning as if the ink is still fresh.

When my alarm blares, it feels like I've barely closed my eyes. I drag myself out of bed, every movement an effort. My fingers automatically reach my wrist, rubbing at the invisible tattoo. No matter how hard I scratch, I can never erase what was done to me.

In the bathroom, I catch my reflection in the mirror. A stranger stares back at me. Her eyes are haunted pools in a pale face. Her hair hangs limp and lifeless as if it, too, has given up the pretense of looking good. I lean closer, searching for any trace of the woman I thought I was becoming.

"You can do this," I whisper to my reflection, the words sounding hollow even to my ears. "You have to do this." My fingers retrace the inside of my wrist, a habit I can't seem to break.

Under UV light, the mark is as clear as day, but my skin looks unblemished in the harsh bathroom lighting. If only the scars inside could be so easily hidden.

I go through my morning routine mechanically, armoring myself in layers of clothing as if they could protect me from the memories I'll have to face. Each tick of the clock is a countdown to the moment I'll have to confront my past. Pulling on my shirt, I ensure the sleeve covers my wrist completely. Even though no one can see the tattoo, I feel exposed and vulnerable.

A sudden, sharp rap on my door makes me jump. Three hard, demanding knocks—unmistakably the hand of law enforcement.

My heart leaps into my throat. Carter's punctuality is both reassuring and terrifying. My hand flies to my wrist again, rubbing frantically as if I could scrub away the memories and the invisible mark.

I take a deep breath, steeling myself, before opening the door.

SEVEN

Jenna

I OPEN THE DOOR, MAX GREETS ME FIRST, HIS TAIL WAGGING excitedly. I kneel down, grateful for the excuse to delay looking at Carter. Max's wet nose snuffles at my hands, and I flinch slightly when he nears my wrist. Even though he can't see or smell the tattoo, I feel exposed.

I bury my fingers in Max's fur, feeling the soft, warm comfort of his presence. Max nudges me, his tail wagging happily.

"Sorry, buddy," I murmur, scratching behind his ears with my other hand. "No treats today."

Finally, I force myself to stand and face Carter.

He fills the doorway, tall and confident, his rugged, handsome face framed by the early morning light. His strong jawline, the slight stubble, and those piercing eyes that seem to see right through me— they all make my heart skip a beat.

God, he's sexy.

Everything about him exudes strength and confidence. I wish he were here to sweep me off my feet and show me the kind of love I've only dreamed of. Instead, he's here to take me to a sketch artist and relive the worst moments of my life.

His eyes, warm and concerned, meet mine, and for a moment, I let myself imagine a different scenario—one where he's here to take me on a date rather than force me to relive my worst nightmares.

"Ready to go?" Carter's voice is gentle.

I nod, not trusting my voice. As I lock my door behind me, I can't shake the feeling that I'm locking away more than just my apartment—I'm locking away any hope of a normal life, of a future untainted by my past.

The invisible tattoo on my wrist feels like it's burning; a constant reminder of the horrors I'm about to relive.

As we walk to his truck, Max bounds ahead, his excitement palpable. I can't help but envy his simple joy. Carter opens the passenger door for me, his hand gently resting on my back as I climb in. His touch ignites a desire I've tried so hard to suppress.

The drive starts in silence, the air heavy with unspoken thoughts.

"How are you holding up?" Carter clears his throat, breaking the silence.

"I'm okay," I lie, my voice barely above a whisper. "Just—nervous."

"That's understandable," he replies gently. "If there's anything I can do to make this easier for you, just let me know."

"Thanks. I appreciate it." I turn and stare out the window, needing to talk about anything other than what I'm about to do but not knowing how.

Desperate for a distraction, I take a deep breath, feeling a little of the tension ease.

"Tell me about Max. How long have you had him?"

"Max has been with me for about five years." Carter's face lights up, and he glances at Max in the rearview mirror. "He's my partner in more ways than one."

Max barks softly as if acknowledging the praise, and I can't help but smile.

"He's a good dog."

"The best," Carter agrees. "He's been through a lot with me."

"It must be nice having someone like that by your side." I nod, feeling a little lighter.

"It is," Carter says, his tone softening.

He smiles, and for a moment, the weight of the day ahead feels a little more bearable. As we pull into the station, I take a deep breath. There's no way to sugarcoat this, but today is going to be hard.

We walk into the station, Carter leading the way with Max at his side. The fluorescent lights cast a harsh glow, and a little shiver runs down my spine. My heart pounds, and the walls close in as we approach a small room off the main corridor.

This is Carter's space, and that makes it special. The first thing I notice is the contrast between his desk and everything else. The linoleum is cracked, and the furniture is a bit worn, but Carter's desk is a study of brutal efficiency.

It's immaculate. Every item has its place—the stapler is perfectly aligned, there's a clean desk pad, and the pens are neatly stacked in a holder. There's no dust. No clutter. It's like a window into his mind, showing a level of care and precision that I haven't seen before.

I point to the picture of Carter and another man who looks identical to him.

"I didn't know you had a twin."

"That's my brother, Blake." Carter looks at the photo and smiles. "He enlisted in the Navy when I went to the Police Academy. Blake's a badass. Became a SEAL and now works for the same organization that Forest runs."

"Wow," I say, genuinely impressed. "That's pretty amazing."

"Yeah, he's done well for himself." He shrugs modestly. "We're close, even if our paths took us in different directions."

I nod, absorbing this new information about Carter. It makes me see him in a different light—not just as a man who comes to my café every day, but as someone with a complex and interesting life.

A sudden, sharp rap on the door makes me jump. A man in a worn tweed jacket steps in, the scent of charcoal and paper wafting in with him. His fingers are smudged black, and he clutches a drawing pad to his chest like a shield.

"Hi, I'm Joe Smith, the sketch artist," he says with a polite nod, his voice softer than I expected.

Carter's hand rests lightly on my shoulder. "Are you ready, Jenna?" His touch is warm and reassuring, but it can't quell the anxiety churning in my stomach.

I swallow hard, my mouth suddenly dry. "Not in the slightest." The words come out as a whisper. "But let's do this."

"Most people haven't done this before, but don't worry. I'll talk you through the whole thing." Joe's kind smile doesn't quite reach his eyes. He's seen too much, I realize.

Like me.

Carter guides me to his desk chair. The leather is cool against my skin, starkly contrasting with the warmth spreading from where his hand brushed mine. The chair creaks as I settle in, the sound loud in the tense silence of the room.

Joe takes a seat across from me, the scratch of his chair legs against the linoleum floor setting my teeth on edge. Max flops down at my feet with a soft whine, his warm presence comforting.

Carter wheels in another chair, the high-pitched screech making me wince. He positions it next to mine, close enough that I can smell his aftershave—an oddly calming woodsy scent.

"We're going to take it slow, okay?" Joe's voice is gentle as he flips open his sketchpad. The crisp sound of a new page turning feels like the start of something I can't take back.

"What do you want? Who do you want?" I glance at Carter, suddenly unsure.

"What about the man who recruited you?" Carter's brow furrows in thought.

"His name is Lucian Drake." A chill runs down my spine at the mention of Lucian's name. My fingers instinctively move to my wrist, rubbing at the invisible tattoo. I force myself to nod, my throat too tight for words.

"Whenever you're ready, Jenna." Joe's pencil hovers over the paper, expectant. He leans forward, his kind eyes meeting mine. "Let's start with the basic shape of his face. Was it round, oval, square?"

I close my eyes, letting the memory surface. A bustling mall fades into view, the scent of pretzels and perfume mingling in the air. I was seventeen, lost in the crowd when he appeared.

"Oval," I say, opening my eyes. "But with a strong, defined jawline."

Joe's pencil scratches against the paper, the sound unnervingly similar to a knife scraping against a plate.

"Good. Now, what about his eyes? Their shape, size, placement?"

I swallow hard, remembering how those eyes had locked onto me, making me feel seen for the first time in my life.

"Almond-shaped. Dark, almost black. They were—intense. Set deep under strong brows."

The mall around me had seemed to fade away, leaving only those piercing eyes.

"His nose?" Joe prompts gently.

"Straight. Aristocratic." My voice wavers. "It suited his high cheekbones."

Joe nods, his hand moving swiftly across the page. "Hair?"

"Dark and slicked back but with a natural wave," I remember how a single lock had fallen across his forehead as he'd smiled at me, promising a world of glamour and success.

"Any distinctive features? Scars, moles, anything unusual?"

I shake my head, my hair brushing against my cheeks. "No, he was—perfect. Almost too perfect, like a statue." The memory of his flawless face makes my skin crawl. "Well-oiled comes to mind."

"Well-oiled?" Joe's pencil pauses.

"Everything about him was smooth, polished. From his manicured nails to his tailored suit. He looked expensive, untouchable."

As Joe continues to sketch, the face on the paper becomes more and more real. It's like watching a ghost materialize before my eyes.

Max senses my distress and presses his head against my leg. I reach down to stroke his fur, grateful for the distraction.

"What about his expression?" Joe asks. "Was he smiling, serious?"

The memory hits me like a punch to the gut. His smile was charming and predatory all at once.

"He was smiling. But it didn't reach his eyes. They remained cold, calculating."

"What about his eyebrows? Were they thick, thin, arched?" Joe continues sketching, asking occasional questions about the man's features.

"Thick and slightly arched," I respond, my voice steadier now. "He had a very commanding presence."

"And his lips?" Joe asks, his pencil pausing.

"Thin, almost cruel looking." The memory becomes clearer with each detail.

Joe adds the final touches to the sketch.

"Is this him?" He turns the pad around, and the blood drains from my face.

Lucian Drake stares back at me from the paper, just as handsome and terrifying as the day he approached me in that mall, promising me the world and delivering me into hell.

"That's him," I whisper, my voice barely audible. "That's Lucian Drake."

Carter leans in, his shoulder brushing mine. The warmth of his presence anchors me to the present, reminding me that I'm safe now.

But as I stare at Lucian's face, I can't shake the feeling that he's still hunting for his next victim somewhere out there.

Suddenly, I'm seventeen again, standing before an imposing structure that looks more like a fortress than a modeling school. The summer heat beats down on me, but a chill runs through my body.

"Welcome to your new home," Lucian says, his smooth voice cutting through the hum of cicadas.

My heart pounds with excitement and apprehension all rolled into one. The facility looms before us, its high walls topped with glinting barbed wire. The knot in my stomach tightens.

"What's with the security?" I ask, trying to keep my voice steady.

"It's for your protection, of course. We want to keep you safe from the

outside world." Lucian's hand on my shoulder is meant to be reassuring, but his touch makes my skin crawl.

I nod, desperately wanting to believe him. The heavy doors close behind us with a resounding clang that echoes in my chest. The smell hits me first—antiseptic and sterile—nothing like the perfumed chaos of the world of fashion I imagined.

The interior is stark and clinical. Fluorescent lights buzz overhead, casting a harsh glow on the polished floors. Rows of identical doors line the hallways—dormitories, classrooms, training rooms. My footsteps echo in the oppressive silence.

"These are the rules. Read them carefully." Lucian hands me a booklet, the glossy pages cool against my sweaty palms.

As I flip through, my eyes widen. Curfews, restricted areas, mandatory training sessions. This isn't the glamorous life I dreamed of. It's regimented and controlled. A lump forms in my throat.

"Modeling is hard work." Lucian's dark eyes bore into mine. "You're here to work, not goof off. Do you understand?"

"Yes," I whisper, my voice small and trembling. "I understand."

The days blur together. We're isolated, cut off from our families, and subjected to relentless training and indoctrination.

The constant drone of instructors, the squeak of markers on whiteboards, the rhythmic counting during exercise routines—it all blends into a cacophony of control.

My initial excitement turns to dread, but I cling to the hope of fame and fortune.

I'm going to be a supermodel.

I repeat it like a mantra, trying to drown out the growing voice of doubt.

If only I had known. This wasn't an escape. It was a nightmare, and I walked right into it.

Shame washes over me. How could I have been so foolish? The signs were there, glaring and obvious, but I was young, desperate for a way out, blinded by promises of a better life.

The memory fades, and I blink rapidly, the office coming back into focus. My heart races, and I struggle to catch my breath. The taste of fear lingers in my mouth, metallic and bitter.

"Jenna? Are you okay?" Carter leans in, his hand gently

touching my arm. The warmth of his fingers grounds me in the present. His voice is low, concern etching his features.

I meet his gaze, finding myself momentarily lost in the depth of his eyes. There's something there—understanding, maybe even a hint of protectiveness—that makes my breath catch for an entirely different reason.

"Yeah," I manage to say, though my voice wavers. "Just—memories."

Carter's hand remains on my arm, a comforting presence. "It's okay," he murmurs, his thumb tracing small circles on my skin. "You're safe."

For a moment, the world narrows to just us—Carter's touch, his steady gaze, the subtle scent of his aftershave. It's a bubble of safety amid painful recollections.

Joe clears his throat softly, breaking the spell. "It can be triggering when recounting details of those who've hurt you," he says, his tone gentle. "Do you need a break?"

"Yes, please." I'm grateful for the suggestion.

Max nudges my leg, his warm presence a comfort. I reach down to pet him, my fingers sinking into his soft fur, anchoring me further to the present.

As I sit there, trying to steady my breathing, I can't shake the lingering smell of sterile antiseptic and lingering fear.

Shame burns hot in my chest—shame for my naivety, shame for falling for their lies, and shame for trusting too easily.

Beneath it, a tiny spark of determination flickers to life. Maybe by facing these memories, I can help others avoid the same trap.

"You have an incredibly vivid recollection of this person's face," Joe says. "That's pretty incredible."

"I've got a thing for faces." I shift uncomfortably, feeling exposed.

It's more than a *thing*.

It's a superpower.

"Are you okay?" Carter looks at me with concern.

Before I can answer, his phone buzzes. The sudden noise makes me flinch. He glances at the screen, his expression darkening.

"I have to take this," he says, stepping away.

As Carter talks in hushed tones, my gaze is drawn back to the sketch. Lucian's face stares back at me, every detail hauntingly accurate.

But it's not just his face that I remember.

In my mind's eye, I see a flood of images—the bare hallways of the facility, the faces of the other girls, the lavish parties where we were paraded like prized cattle.

I can draw them all in excruciating detail. I've drawn them many times before.

"That was the station. Another girl has gone missing." Carter returns, his jaw set in a grim line.

The air rushes out of my lungs. Joe pales, his pencil slipping from his fingers.

"How old?" I manage to ask, dreading the answer.

"Seventeen," Carter says, his voice tight. "Just like you were."

EIGHT

Carter

"WE CAN RESUME IN THE MORNING," JOE SAYS, PACKING UP HIS sketchpad. The rustle of paper breaks the silence.

Jenna's whispered "Thank you" is barely audible, but the relief in her sigh speaks volumes. As Joe's footsteps fade down the hallway, the silence settles back in, thick and palpable.

The dim light of my office casts soft shadows across Jenna's face, highlighting the delicate curve of her cheekbones and the gentle slope of her nose. My breath catches in my throat. Even exhausted and emotionally drained, she's breathtakingly beautiful.

I clear my throat, searching for words to bridge the gap between us.

"You did great today. I know it wasn't easy." The softness in my voice surprises me, laced with an admiration I can't hide.

"Thanks. I just need a moment." Jenna's tired smile doesn't reach her eyes.

"Of course." The words hang heavily between us.

My fingers itch to reach out and offer comfort, but I hold back. I want to know her, really know her—not as a witness or a barista, but as Jenna.

She shifts in her chair, and I fight the irrational fear that she'll bolt at any moment.

What makes her laugh?

What are her dreams?

What would it feel like to hold her and chase away the shadows in her eyes?

But I can't ask those questions. Not like this.

Instead, I stand, moving toward the small mini fridge in the corner.

"Can I get you some water? Or maybe some coffee?" I cringe internally at the offer of coffee to a master barista.

"Water would be great, thanks." Jenna's soft laugh eases some of the tension.

As I pour the water, I steal glances at her: the graceful curve of her long neck as she tilts her head back, the way her fingers absently trace patterns on the arm of the chair, and the soft rise and fall of her chest with each breath. Each detail sears itself into my memory.

I hand her the water, our fingers brushing for a moment. The contact sends a jolt through me, and it's an effort to resist the urge to let my hand linger.

"Thank you," Jenna murmurs, her eyes meeting mine.

"Is there anything else I can do for you?" I sink back into my chair, closer to her than before.

"I should probably get back to the shop." She shifts in her seat, fingers twisting the hem of her shirt. "Malia must be wondering where I am." Her gaze darts around the room, not quite meeting my eyes.

The sight of her looking so lost ignites something protective within me.

"How do you feel about lunch?"

"That sounds nice." Jenna's gaze flicks up to mine, a spark of interest lighting them for the first time today.

"Great." I grab my jacket, the familiar leather creaking as I shrug it on. Max's ears perk up at the jingle of his leash. "Let's get out of here."

I take Jenna to my favorite place. Big Rick's Diner comes into view. The red neon sign buzzes and flickers, casting a soft glow over the gravel parking lot. It's a place that feels like home, where I've spent countless late nights after a long shift.

We step inside, and familiar scents wash over me—sizzling bacon, fresh coffee, and the sweet aroma of apple pie just out of the oven. It's warm and welcoming. The vinyl booths squeak as patrons shift in their seats, their low murmur of conversation punctuated by the clink of silverware and the occasional burst of laughter.

Jenna's eyes widen as she takes in the view from the large windows—the vast expanse of the Pacific.

"This is beautiful," she breathes, a genuine smile tugging at her lips.

Max's tail wags as a waitress approaches, her eyes lighting up at seeing him.

"Well, hello there, handsome." She coos at Max while reaching down to scratch behind his ears. "Your usual booth, Detective?"

I nod, grateful for the familiar routine. As we slide into the booth, Max settles contentedly at our feet. Here, away from the pressures of the case and the painful memories, Jenna and I can find a way to connect.

The menu crinkles in my hands as I open it, more out of habit than necessity. I already have my order in mind. Jenna scans the options, a slight furrow appears between her brows as she concentrates. These little details, these glimpses of the real Jenna, are what I've been craving all day. I silently thank whatever impulse made me suggest lunch.

Our server, Betty, approaches our table, her seasoned eyes crinkling with recognition.

"Carter, honey, good to see you." She turns to Jenna, her smile warm and welcoming. "And who's this lovely lady?"

Before I can respond, Betty continues, her enthusiasm palpable.

"You're in for a treat tonight. Big Rick's clam chowder is fresh this morning, and his burgers are the best, but I'll give you a minute to look over the menu."

"Sounds perfect." I glance at Jenna. She nods in agreement, a small smile playing on her lips.

"Great. I'll get you both some water to start." Betty bustles off, her apron swishing with each step.

As we settle into the booth, the initial awkwardness between Jenna and me begins to fade. The panoramic view of the ocean through the large windows captivates us both. The rhythmic crash of waves against the cliffs below provides a soothing backdrop, mingling with the soft clatter of dishes and murmur of conversations around us.

I take in the familiar surroundings, seeing them anew through Jenna's eyes. Softened by years of washing, the checkered tablecloths add a homey touch. Framed photographs of the coast adorn the walls, each one a snapshot of the rugged beauty outside. The aroma of sizzling burgers and freshly baked pies fills the air, underscored by the faint, salty scent of the ocean.

The diner is sparsely populated, but we're past the lunch rush. An elderly couple shares a plate of golden fries by the window, their heads bent close in quiet conversation. A young mother sips her coffee, absently rocking a stroller with her foot as she flips through a glossy magazine. At the counter, two fishermen, their faces weathered by sun and salt, share a hearty laugh over their beers, the occasional bark of laughter punctuating the ambient noise.

"I'm glad it's not busy." I smile at Jenna. "Weekends, this place can get pretty packed. It's nice to have it quiet for a change."

"It's nice." Jenna's gaze roams the cozy space, taking in every detail. "I see why you like it here."

Betty returns with our water and pulls out a pen. "Know what you want?"

"I'll have the clam chowder, please." Jenna's smile is warm and genuine.

"Good choice." Betty nods approvingly.

"The usual for me. Burger and fries." The familiar words roll off my tongue.

Betty leaves, and I settle back into the booth.

"So, what's it like having a twin?" Jenna leans forward, her eyes bright with curiosity.

The soft glow of the overhead lamp catches the highlights in her hair, and my breath hitches.

"Like having a built-in best friend and a constant rival rolled into one." A chuckle escapes me, memories flooding back. "Blake and I were inseparable as kids. We did everything together."

Jenna's fingers trace the condensation on her water glass, her gaze never leaving mine. "Why did Blake go into the Navy, but you didn't?"

"Blake always had this sense of adventure, a need to see the world. The Navy offered that." The words flow easily, and Jenna's interest encourages me to open up. "Plus, our father was in the Navy. I think Blake wanted to follow in his footsteps."

"But you didn't?" Her head tilts slightly, a strand of hair falling across her cheek.

"I wanted to, but…" My fingers itch to tuck it back behind her ear.

"But, what?"

"I stayed because of a girl." The admission comes out softer than intended. "High school sweetheart. She got pregnant, and I stepped up. I needed a job quickly. Something to raise a family on. Found myself with a job as a cop."

Jenna's eyes widen, a flicker of something—disappointment?— crossing her face. She leans back slightly, her fingers growing still on her glass.

"I didn't realize you had a family." Her gaze darts to my left hand.

"We're not together," I quickly add, the words tumbling out. "Before we were supposed to get married, I found out she had been cheating on me. The baby wasn't mine. It was a mess. I was already on the force by the time it all fell apart. I landed here, and then it turned out I was really good at my job."

"That sounds tough." Jenna's voice is soft and sympathetic. Her hand moves across the table, not quite touching mine, but close. "What happened to her and the baby?"

"They left town. I haven't heard from them since." The old pain is there but dulled now. "By then, my life was set here. I let Blake have the adventures while I took care of things at home."

I can't help but marvel at how easy this feels. Her presence is intoxicating, drawing me in.

The soft clink of cutlery around us, the distant crash of waves, the warm aroma of cooking food—it all fades into the background.

My world narrows to Jenna's bright eyes, attentive gaze, and how her lips curve into a soft smile as she listens.

For the first time in years, I feel a spark of something new, something exciting. This isn't a witness interview or a casual chat over coffee. This is the start of something more, and I'm eager to see where it leads.

NINE

Carter

"Here you go." Betty returns, the plates steaming as she sets them down. The rich aroma of clam chowder and grilled beef fills the air.

Jenna's eyes widen as she tastes her chowder. "This is probably the best I've ever had. Want to try some?" She holds out her spoon, her eyes meeting mine with a warmth that makes my heart skip.

As I taste the chowder, I lean forward, hyper-aware of our proximity. Our fingers brush as I steady her hand, and a jolt of electricity shoots through me.

Jenna's cheeks flush slightly as she draws back, the moment charged with unspoken tension.

"You're right. That's amazing." My voice comes out huskier than intended.

Big Rick's arrival breaks the moment, his burly frame casting a shadow over our table.

"How's the food?" His deep voice rumbles, curiosity evident in his eyes as they flick between Jenna and me.

"Amazing as always." I wipe my chin.

Jenna nods enthusiastically, savoring another spoonful.

"Brought Max a treat." Big Rick sets down a paper plate with a bun-free burger.

As Max digs in, Big Rick's questioning gaze returns to me. I shake my head slightly, and he retreats, leaving us to our not-quite-a-date date.

Our conversation flows freely. Jenna's melodious laughter fills the air as she tells me about starting her coffee shop.

I lean in close, drawn in by the passion in her voice and the way her eyes light up.

"What's your favorite color?" Jenna asks suddenly, a playful glint in her eye.

"Blue," I reply, mirroring her smile. "Yours?"

"Green." She pauses, then grins. "Would you rather be able to fly or be invisible?"

Our light-hearted game continues, each question peeling back another layer. Jenna tucks her hair behind her ear when she's thinking, and her nose crinkles slightly when she laughs.

At one point, Jenna reaches out, her fingers lightly grazing the back of my hand. Without thinking, I turn my palm up, our fingers brushing. The contact sends another jolt through me, and our eyes lock.

The moment stretches, filled with possibility, before we both pull back slightly, a mix of excitement and uncertainty hanging between us. The awkward silence that follows is broken by the clatter of dishes from a nearby table, jolting us back to reality.

"I appreciate you sharing your story with me earlier." Desperate to recapture our easy conversation, I lean forward, my hand brushing against hers. "Opening up about your past like that couldn't have been easy."

"It wasn't, but… It felt good to talk about it. With you." Jenna's eyes soften, her finger tracing patterns on the tabletop. Her gaze meets mine, holding it for a beat longer than necessary.

As our lunch progresses, the space between us shrinks. Our hands rest on the table, not quite touching but close enough to feel the warmth radiating between them. The conversation flows easily now, punctuated by shared laughter and lingering looks.

"I have an admission to make." I lean forward and lower my voice to a whisper.

"You do?" Jenna's eyebrows rise, curiosity sparkling in her eyes.

"I'm not a big coffee fan." A sheepish grin spreads across my face. "I mostly go there because Max loves his treats."

"Max is the reason you come in every day?" Her laugh is melodious, sending a warm flutter through my chest.

"Partly." My grin widens. "The truth is, I go there to see you. You're the brightest part of my day."

Her cheeks flush a delightful pink, and she looks away, a small smile playing on her lips.

"What can I say? Despite how it sounds, being a detective isn't all that glamorous. There's a lot of desk work, chasing down fruitless leads, and endless paperwork. Starting my morning at your café, seeing your smile—it makes the rest of the day easier to face."

Jenna's eyes meet mine, and our connection feels stronger, more real.

"I'm glad," she says softly. "That's exactly what I hoped to create with the café."

"Why a coffee shop?" I ask, genuinely curious. "What made you choose that?"

"I always loved the idea of having a place where people could come together." Jenna's expression turns thoughtful, a mix of nostalgia and something deeper, almost melancholic. "Plus, I've always been a bit of a coffee enthusiast." She pauses, her fingers tracing patterns on the tablecloth. "But it's more than that."

I lean in, drawn by the vulnerability in her voice.

"My home life wasn't great. I never had a place that felt safe, cozy, or welcoming. A place where I could bring friends or just— be." She takes a deep breath. "So, I guess I'm trying to create what I never had. A place where people can relax, feel safe, be part of a community."

"That's—that's incredible." Her words hit me hard; admiration and fierce protectiveness well up inside me.

"What can I say? I'm trying to rebuild a past I never had and make it into something more. Something better." She shrugs, a small smile tugging at her lips.

"I'd say you've succeeded." I reach out to cover her hand with mine. "Your café is definitely a community hub. Everyone loves going there. I see the same faces every morning, people connecting, laughing. You've created something special."

"Thank you." Jenna's eyes meet mine, shining with unshed tears. "That means a lot."

We sit in comfortable silence for a moment, the weight of her revelation settling between us. As lunch draws to a close, we linger over empty plates, both hesitating to leave the cozy bubble we've created.

"How about a piece of pie to share?" I'm not ready for our time together to end. "Big Rick's pies are even better than his chowder."

"That sounds perfect." Jenna's eyes light up, banishing the last traces of sadness.

Betsy brings over a slice of warm apple pie and the aroma of cinnamon and baked apples wafts between us. Something has shifted. We're no longer just a cop and a witness or even a customer and a barista. We're two people connecting and understanding each other on a deeper level.

We dig into the pie, our forks occasionally clashing as we go for the same bite. The warm, flaky crust crumbles delicately, releasing bursts of cinnamon-spiced apple with each mouthful. Jenna's eyes sparkle with mischief as she playfully fends off my attempt to steal a slice of apple.

"Hey, that's mine." She laughs, the sound light and carefree, filling the diner with warmth.

I feign innocence, raising my eyebrows. "I have no idea what you're talking about." My fork darts out again, this time successfully snagging a piece of apple.

Our laughter mingles with the soft clink of forks against the plate.

As we finish the last crumbs, I glance out at the coast. It's a beautiful day.

"How about a walk?"

"I'd like that." Jenna's expression softens, a slight flush coloring her cheeks.

Outside, the wind carries the salty tang of the ocean, whipping through our hair. Our shoulders bump as we walk. She shivers as a gust of wind whips around us.

"Here." I shrug off my jacket.

As I drape it over her shoulders, my fingers brush against the soft skin of her neck. I gather her hair, freeing it from beneath the collar, the silky strands slipping through my fingers. Her shampoo, a subtle floral fragrance, wafts up, mingling with the salty sea air.

"Thanks," Jenna murmurs, pulling the jacket closer.

Her scent mingles with the leather, creating an intoxicating blend that makes my head spin.

We stroll along the rocky coastline, the rhythmic crash of waves a soothing backdrop to our conversation. Our steps fall into sync, and I'm acutely aware of the diminishing space between us. Occasionally, our hands brush, each accidental touch sending sparks through my body.

Max enjoys the walk, surging in front of us to check out an exciting smell. Drifting behind to investigate a rustling in the bushes. Every now and then, he looks back at us as if ensuring we're still there.

The conversation flows easily, more intimate now that we're alone. We share childhood memories, hopes for the future, and silly anecdotes that have us both laughing. The way the sunlight plays across her features captivates me. It highlights the curves of her cheeks and the sparkle in her eyes.

This feels like a first date. It's everything I imagined it would be, except it's not a date.

Jenna's soft laughter sends warmth spreading through my chest. I don't even remember what it was I might have said to make her laugh. She glances up at me, her eyes holding mine for a moment longer than necessary.

Suddenly, she stumbles on the uneven ground. I reach out, wrapping my arm her waist to steady her.

She looks up at me, our faces inches apart.

Without thinking, I pull her to me, wrapping my arms around her. Dammit, I should've gone for a kiss.

She melts against me, her head resting on my chest. Her heartbeat is quick and steady, matching my own. The soft scent of her hair fills my senses, and I wish I could freeze this moment.

"This is nice," Jenna whispers, her breath warm against my neck, sending a shiver down my spine. "I needed this."

"Me too," I reply, my voice rough with emotion. My hand moves of its own accord, gently stroking her back.

As we pull back, our faces remain close. The urge to kiss her is overwhelming.

Her lids flutter, and I lean in, our breaths mingling. I can almost taste the sweetness of the apple pie on her lips, but at the last moment, I pull back.

This isn't a date.

It's a professional encounter, no matter how it feels. Kissing her would be taking advantage of her in a vulnerable state, and honorable men don't do that.

Reluctantly, I step back, immediately missing her warmth.

"I should take you back," I say, my voice strained. "Malia must think I've kidnapped you."

Only after the words are out of my mouth do I cringe. Kidnap? Did I really say that? What a fucking idiot.

"Yeah." Jenna nods, disappointment flashing across her face. "I suppose so."

The warmth of the moment cools, replaced by a growing awkwardness. Our easy banter fades into stilted silence as we walk back to the truck, the space between us now feeling vast and empty.

Max, sensing the change, whines softly as we all climb in.

The drive back is quiet. The only sounds are the soft growl of the engine and Max's occasional shuffling. I steal glances at Jenna, who stares out the window, her expression unreadable in the passing streetlights. The jacket still drapes over her shoulders, a reminder of our brief closeness.

At her coffee shop, I cut the engine, uncertainty hanging heavy between us.

"Thanks for lunch." Her hand lingers on the door handle. "It helped me relax."

"I'm glad." I force a smile. "It was nice getting to know you better."

I walk her to the front door of her shop, hyper-aware of the space between us. There's a moment of hesitation, a pause where I consider leaning in for a kiss, but I catch myself.

I pull her into a hug, careful not to overstep. "I'll call you tomorrow."

Jenna rises on tiptoe and brushes the lightest kiss against my cheek.

And with that, she's gone.

TEN

Jenna

I WAKE WITH A START, MY HEART RACING. THE LINGERING sensations from my dream still tingle across my skin. Sunlight filters through the curtains, painting my small apartment bedroom in a soft, golden glow. As I stretch, memories of last night flood back in vivid detail.

Carter's strong hands were gentle yet firm. His touch sent electricity coursing through me, which was intoxicating. That almost kiss left me breathless, wanting more.

I close my eyes, savoring the memory of his arms around me and his body's warmth against mine. I can't help but smile.

Lunch with Carter was—unexpected.

Wonderful.

The easy conversation, the laughter, the way he looked at me—like I was the only person in the world—felt so natural, so right.

For the first time in years, I let myself imagine what it might be like to have more. More dinners, more laughter, more of Carter.

My dreams last night definitely explored 'more' in vivid, sensual detail. My cheeks flush as fragments of the dream resurface—Carter's lips on my skin, his hands exploring, the way he made me feel cherished and desired.

Shaking off the lingering tendrils of the dream, I slip into my yoga clothes. I pause at the irony as I unroll my mat in the living room. Yoga, the one thing I kept from my time at the enclave, has become my sanctuary—a way to clear my mind and find balance in the chaos of my memories.

As I move through the poses, my breath is steady and controlled. Tension slowly releases from my body, but today, unlike most mornings, my mind keeps drifting back to Carter.

To the case.

To the past.

To the memories I've tried so hard to leave behind.

After my session, drawn by an impulse I don't fully understand, I head to the back of my closet and pull out the old steamer trunk. The scent of aged leather and old memories envelop me as I rummage through items I haven't touched in years.

My fingers brush against something familiar—my old sketchbook.

I've thought about throwing it away so many times. Each spring cleaning, I held it in my hands, poised to throw it in the trash.

Something always stopped me, an inexplicable feeling that it might be important someday. I never understood why I couldn't let go of this tangible link to my darkest days.

Dusting it off, I flip through the pages. Each sketch vividly reminds me of the places I worked, the men I encountered, and the horrors I endured. Every detail is preserved with unsettling accuracy, showcasing my nearly eidetic memory. It's a gift—or perhaps a curse—I've kept hidden along with so much else.

As I stare at the drawings, guilt washes over me. These sketches, rendered with painful accuracy, could have helped Carter. I should have told him about them when he first asked for help.

But I didn't.

I kept silent, and I'm not entirely sure why.

Maybe it was the fear of dredging up the pain of my past, of reliving those horrific moments in graphic detail. Or perhaps it was the dread of seeing judgment in Carter's eyes once he knew the full extent of what I'd been through, what I'd seen.

What I'd done.

Whatever the reason, I held back, and now we're entangled with Joe, the sketch artist, working hard on recreations I could have provided effortlessly.

The weight of my silence feels heavier now, knowing a fourth girl has gone missing.

Another young life in danger, another family torn apart.

I can't help but wonder: if I had shared these sketches earlier, could we have prevented this?

Could we have saved her?

I close the sketchbook, pressing it to my chest as if I could absorb its contents and erase the guilt, but it's not that simple. I've kept this part of myself hidden for so long that it feels almost impossible to bring it into the light. Yet, it's time.

For the missing girls.

For Carter.

And maybe even for myself.

The thought of sharing these drawings and the memories that accompany them terrifies me, but the image of Carter's determined face and gentle encouragement gives me strength. The faces of those missing girls, their futures hanging in the balance, steel my resolve.

I can't change the past or my initial reluctance to share, but I can do something now. I can help with this case—really help—in a way that might make a difference.

It's time to stop running from my past and face it head-on. With Carter by my side, maybe I can find the courage to do just that.

I clutch the sketchbook so tightly that my knuckles turn white. My heart races, a mixture of fear and determination coursing through my veins.

Today will change everything—my relationship with Carter, my role in the investigation, maybe even how I see myself. What if he can't forgive me for hiding this?

The memory of his gentle touch, warm eyes, and the almost kiss that still makes my lips tingle—it all feels so precious and vulnerable.

I might lose it all.

But I have to do this.

For the missing girls.

For Carter.

For the truth I've hidden for so long.

Guilt gnaws at me as I flip through the pages. I should have told him from the beginning. I should have been brave enough to face my past.

As I stare at a particularly explicit sketch, the world around me fades, and I'm thrust back into the past.

ELEVEN

Jenna

A few years ago

THE HARSH FLUORESCENT LIGHTS OF THE ENCLAVE BEAT DOWN ON ME, their constant buzz an annoying soundtrack. The air is thick with the scent of sweat, fear, and cheap perfume—a sickening cocktail that turns my stomach even now.

"Stand up straight, Jenna." Lucian's voice cuts like a whip.

I straighten my spine, ignoring the ache in my muscles from hours of posing. The scratchy fabric of the too-small dress chafes against my skin, a constant reminder of my place here. Around me, other girls move like dolls, their eyes vacant but their movements precise.

Beautiful even.

How could I have been so blind? The signs were everywhere—the locked doors, the strict schedules, the way the handlers' eyes lingered too long. But I was naive, desperate for escape from my father's abuse.

A girl to my left stumbles, her exhaustion finally overcoming her. In an instant, Lucian is there, his face a mask of cold fury.

"Focus. Disobedience will not be tolerated." He grabs her arm. The girl—Sarah, I think her name is—whimpers as he drags her to the front of the room.

What follows is a lesson in cruelty. Sarah endures Lucian's tirade. Each word is a lash, each gesture a blow, and each moment a test of her commitment to becoming a supermodel.

That is the stated goal.

I watch, my heart pounding, as tears stream down Sarah's face.

The message is clear: comply or suffer.

That night, in the cold dormitory, I curl into myself, stifling my sobs. The sheets smell of bleach, harsh and chemical, burning my nose. In the distance, there are muffled cries—another girl breaking under the pressure.

I should leave. Being a supermodel isn't worth this price.

But where would I go? Back to my father's drunken rages? To the smell of stale beer and the sound of shattering bottles?

At least here, the pain is predictable. At least here, I know what to expect.

So I stay.

I learn to move gracefully, smile on command, and be the perfect little doll they want me to be. And in secret, late at night, I draw. Every face, every room, and every horrible detail—I capture it all, a silent witness to the nightmare around me.

OF COURSE, I LOST THOSE SKETCHES. I'VE ALWAYS WONDERED WHAT became of them. What I hold now is part of the *therapy* I underwent at the Facility. Hours and hours of rebuilding that book. The sketchbook falls from my trembling hands. The memory fades, but the fear, the shame, and the anger—it all remains, as fresh as if it happened yesterday.

Tears blur my vision as I pick up my sketches.

Carter deserves the truth, all of it. And those girls—they deserve every chance at rescue.

With shaking hands, I select the most relevant sketches. Each is a piece of my soul, a fragment of the horror I endured. But if they can help and save even one girl from suffering what I did, then it's worth the pain of remembering.

The faces of girls I once knew stare back at me—Laura, Elizabeth, Jenny, and Andrea. A wave of shame washes over me when I realize I never wondered what happened to them.

Were they deemed worthy enough to sell, or were they discarded, returned to the brutal pasts they tried to escape? My stomach churns with guilt. How could I have been so selfish, so focused on my survival?

The sky is just beginning to lighten as I step out of my apartment, the sketchbook tucked securely in my bag. A cool breeze carries the scent of the nearby ocean, mingling with the earthy smell of dew-covered grass. This is my favorite time of day—when the world wakes up, fresh and new, full of possibilities.

Our small coastal town is still sleepy, and the streets are quiet and mostly empty. The occasional jogger or early-shift worker nods a greeting as they pass. Old Victorian houses line the street, their pastel colors muted in the soft pre-dawn light. Hanging baskets overflow with colorful flowers, adding splashes of color to the tranquil scene.

Walking the few familiar blocks to my coffee shop, I savor the peacefulness of a brand-new day. The distant cry of seagulls and the gentle rustling of leaves provide a soothing soundtrack to my journey. This daily ritual, this quiet time before the bustle of the day begins, has become my meditation, my way of centering myself.

Today, though, my mind is far from peaceful. The weight of the sketchbook in my bag grows with each step. Memories and worries swirl in my head, but I try to push them aside, focusing instead on the beauty around me.

When I reach Marlowe's Café, my little slice of heaven, I'm energized and apprehensive. The familiar routine of opening the shop—unlocking the door, flipping on lights, starting the ovens and coffee machines—helps to ground me. The sweet aroma of pastries baking and the rich scent of brewing coffee soon fill the air, chasing away some of my anxiety.

As the first customers trickle in, I paste on a smile and lose myself in the rhythm of the morning rush. But beneath it all, a current of nervous energy thrums through me. It's only a matter of time before Carter arrives.

The bell above the door jingles, and I greet Frank, Doris, and Mav as they come in. Their presence is a comforting constant in my life.

"Morning, Frank. Your usual?" I ask, already reaching for the coffee pot.

Frank grins, his mustache twitching. "You know it. Extra strong today, though. Didn't get much sleep."

I chuckle and pour his coffee. "Here you go. Strong and black."

"You seem different today. Something on your mind?" Frank gives me a look as he takes his coffee.

"Just thinking about yesterday. I had lunch with a friend." I hesitate for a moment, then smile.

"A friend, huh? Anyone we know?" Doris perks up, her eyes twinkling with curiosity.

"Just a friend. It's…" I struggle to find the right words to describe Carter.

Is he a friend? Am I working for him? Helping him? Should I stay quiet about it?

"He asked me to help with something important."

"Sounds intriguing. Anything we can help with?" Mav looks up from her book, her curiosity piqued.

"Not right now, but I appreciate it. I'll keep you posted." I shake my head, grateful for their concern.

The conversation shifts to lighter topics, and I relax as I settle into the rhythm of my slice of heaven. As the regulars settle into their usual spots, the coffee shop buzzes with the comforting rhythm of daily life.

Just as the morning rush begins to taper off, the bell above the door jingles again. My heart leaps into my throat as Carter walks in. Max trots faithfully by his side.

Our eyes meet, and the softness in his gaze makes my breath catch.

After those vivid and sensual dreams I had about him, my pulse quickens and a rush of heat floods my body.

His muscular frame fills the doorway, commanding attention. Those piercing blue eyes find mine, and suddenly, I'm hyper-aware of every inch of him in a way I haven't been before.

Carter has always been attractive, but after last night—after feeling his arms around me, his breath on my skin—he's become irresistible.

I drink in the sight of him, my gaze tracing the contours of his muscular build beneath his well-fitted shirt. The way he carries himself, with that quiet confidence and strength, weakens my knees. He's ruggedly handsome, and every inch of him screams protector. From the set of his broad shoulders to the alert and caring way he scans the room, he's determined to serve and help those in need. That dedication only heightens his allure.

His jawline tenses slightly as he approaches, a sign of deep thought. A small scar above his eyebrow adds to his rugged charm. A tiny fleck of green in his left eye catches the light, visible only at certain angles. His presence is magnetic, pulling me in and making me yearn for his touch.

I subconsciously lean forward, desperate to close the distance between us. The air seems to thicken, and my breathing quickens as I take in every detail of his face. All I can see is Carter—the warmth of his gaze, the curve of his lips, and the strength in his hands as they rest on the counter.

My fingers itch to reach out and touch him, to trace the line of his jaw, to feel the stubble on his cheek.

It takes every ounce of self-control not to lean across the counter and kiss him right there, customers and propriety be damned.

"Morning, Jenna," he says, his voice low and husky, sending shivers down my spine.

"Carter," I manage, my voice barely above a whisper, thick with a mixture of desire and apprehension. "There's something I need to show you."

"What is it?" His voice is warm, with just a hint of concern.

"I have something that might help." I pull my sketchbook out from under the counter.

"That's great. Are you ready to go to the station and meet the sketch artist?" Carter's eyebrows rise in surprise and curiosity.

I take a deep breath, my heart pounding.

"I should have told you about this earlier." My voice wavers, guilt and fear tangling in my chest.

"Show me in my office." Carter's expression softens, concern replacing surprise.

"Okay." I slip the sketchbook into my bag.

As we walk out, I glance back at my regulars, giving them a reassuring smile that feels more like a grimace. The drive to the station is filled with tense silence. My thoughts race, imagining Carter's disappointment, his anger at withholding this from him.

Once inside Carter's office, the sketch artist, Joe, is already waiting. With trembling hands, I place my drawing pad on Carter's immaculate desk, flipping it open to the sketches. Carter's eyes widen in amazement as he examines the drawings.

"You're an artist?" He's clearly impressed.

"I used to draw a lot." I hesitate, the guilt overwhelming me. "I wasn't sure how important this would be, and I... I was hoping that doing the sketches with Joe would be enough. That I could answer your questions and be done."

I swallow hard, forcing myself to meet his gaze.

"But after spending time with you, learning about the case, about those girls... I realized I needed to do more, and if there was anything I could do to help find them, I should do it."

To my surprise, instead of anger or disappointment, there's only admiration in Carter's eyes.

"Jenna, these are incredible. They could really make a difference." He examines the sketches closely, his finger tracing the intricate lines. "The level of detail here is amazing. They'll be a great help in identifying the men and places involved."

Relief washes over me, and for the first time in a long time, I feel like I'm part of something meaningful, something that can bring light to the darkness of my past.

Joe leans in, his professional curiosity evident. "These are remarkably precise. The facial features and architectural details are like looking at photographs."

Carter nods in agreement. "They might be good enough to run through our databases and see if we can get any hits on the men." He pauses as he looks at the sketches of buildings and rooms. "As for the places… That might be trickier."

"What do you mean?" I ask, my heart sinking.

Carter sighs, running a hand through his hair. "My resources are limited. We're chronically underfunded, and this kind of wide-scale search… It's just not something we can execute."

My hopes deflate, but Carter quickly continues. "But that doesn't mean these aren't incredibly valuable. Even if we can't immediately locate these places, having these layouts could be crucial if we do find them."

Joe nods enthusiastically. "Absolutely. And who knows? Maybe we can find a way to get some help with the search. These sketches are too good to not use to their full potential."

As they continue to discuss the possibilities, a heavy weight lifts from my shoulders. The fear of Carter's reaction and the guilt of my initial hesitation begins to fade, replaced by a sense of purpose.

I may not be able to change my past, but I can shape a better future for those girls with these sketches.

Some good can come from the darkness I endured.

"Do you know where any of these places are?" Carter examines one of my sketches; his brow furrowed in concentration.

"I don't." I shake my head, feeling a pang of guilt. "We were always moved around, never told our location."

Carter nods thoughtfully, his attention never shifting from the sketches. "These are incredible. Even without exact locations, they're invaluable." He pauses, then adds, "I'll give these sketches to my brother, Blake. He might be able to get some of Guardian HRS's resources to perform a search."

My heart skips a beat at the mention of Guardian HRS. During my time with them, there were whispers of what the organization could do with their advanced technology and vast resources. If anyone can find these places, it will be them.

Joe wraps up his sketchpad and leaves, giving me a polite nod as he exits. Now, alone with Carter, the awkwardness returns, mingling with our simmering chemistry.

Carter clears his throat. "Would you like to grab some lunch? There's a place nearby I think you'd like."

"That sounds great." I want to spend more time with him.

We head out, and I study Carter's profile as he makes a quick call to his brother. The strong line of his jaw and how his eyes crinkle at the corners as he talks intrigue me. I'm noticing things I've never allowed myself to see before.

We arrive at a small, cozy pizza joint. The relaxed atmosphere, with its soft rock playing from an old jukebox, immediately puts me at ease. Sally, our waitress, approaches with a warm smile. Carter orders for us.

As Sally leaves, Carter leans in slightly. "I appreciate you sharing those sketches. It couldn't have been easy to do."

His words, his genuine gratitude, warm me from the inside out. For the first time in a long while, I feel like I'm doing something important.

TWELVE

Carter

As we finish our pizza, I'm reluctant to end our time together. An idea forms in my mind, and I clear my throat.

"Jenna, would you mind if we take a bit of a drive?"

"I'd love to, but what about my store?" Her eyes meet mine, curiosity sparking in their depths. "I should be getting back soon."

"It wouldn't be for too long," I assure her. "Unless... Do you need to be back right away?"

"I can call Malia in to cover." She hesitates for a moment, then smiles. "Where did you have in mind?"

"I want to check in with Blake about your sketches."

"How can Guardian HRS help?" Jenna's brow furrows slightly.

"I'm hoping I can get time on Guardian HRS's computer systems. Beg, borrow, or steal," I explain. "They might be able to locate some of the places you drew."

"My sketches aren't that good..." Jenna tilts her head, confusion evident in her expression.

"Blake mentioned Guardian HRS used photographs before to identify where hostages were being held. With the level of detail in your drawings, I'm hoping we can do something similar."

"Really? That's possible?" Her eyes widen in surprise.

"Their tech is far beyond anything we have at the station." Enthusiasm creeps into my voice. "I'm planning to convince, connive, beg, and borrow if I have to, just to get a little time with that computer system."

Jenna looks appropriately impressed and amazed. "Wow, I had no idea technology like that existed outside of movies. Do you think it could work?"

"It's worth a shot." I temper my own excitement. "If anyone can find these places, it's Guardian HRS. So, what do you say? Up for a little road trip?"

"Absolutely. Let me just make that call to cover the shop." Jenna's smile broadens, lighting up her entire face.

As she steps away to arrange coverage, my anticipation surges—not just for the potential breakthrough in the case but for the chance to spend more time with her.

I pull out my phone and dial Blake's number. He picks up on the second ring.

"Yo, bro! Howzit hanging?" Blake's voice booms through the speaker.

"A little to the left, as usual. How's it swinging on your end?" I can't help but grin.

"Can't complain, dude. What's got you calling your favorite bro?"

"You're my only brother. Need a favor, man. Got some sketches that might help with a case."

"Oh ho, the small-town cop needs the big guns, huh?" His smirk is practically audible. "Bring 'em over. I'll see what I can do."

We chat for a few more minutes, trading barbs and catching up. By the time I hang up, Jenna returns, a smile on her face.

"All set," she says. "Let's hit the road."

The California coastline stretches before us, an endless expanse of blue meeting the rugged cliffs. The sun sits high in the sky, casting a golden glow across the water. Jenna sits beside me, her hair whipping in the wind from the open window. The salty tang of the ocean fills my nostrils, mingling with her light perfume—a subtle, floral scent that embodies her essence.

Max's head pops up from the backseat as we drive along the coastal road, his nose twitching at the salty air. Jenna reaches back to scratch behind his ears, earning a contented groan from my loyal companion.

Jenna's gut-wrenching task of confronting the demons of her past and reliving the horrific memories that have haunted her for so long shows her incredible strength and resilience. The fact that she's willing to put herself through that, all in the name of helping others, is awe-inspiring.

My heart aches for her, knowing the pain she must be enduring. I wish I could take that burden from her.

The past few days have been a different whirlwind for me. The investigation has given me an excuse to spend more time with Jenna, savor her company, and get to know her. Every moment we share, every conversation we have, only intensifies the feelings growing within me.

I'm captivated by her, drawn to her strength, intelligence, and beauty, both inside and out. I'm falling for her hard and fast, and the realization thrills and terrifies me.

Even as I enjoy Jenna's company, guilt gnaws at me, a constant reminder of what I've asked her to do. I hate dredging up her painful past, forcing her to relive those horrific memories. It feels like a betrayal, a selfish act, even though it's necessary for the investigation.

Seeing her struggle, I'm overwhelmed by my desire to protect her. I want to wrap her in my arms and promise that nothing will ever harm her again. The intensity of my emotions catches me off guard, but I can't deny their truth.

Jenna shifts in her seat, drawing me out of my thoughts. Her green eyes meet mine, a silent question in their depths.

"You're awfully quiet," she murmurs, her voice almost lost in the rush of the wind. "Everything okay?"

"Yeah, just thinking."

"About the case?"

"Among other things." Mostly about her. How I want to hold

her, be more than just the guy asking her to dig up painful memories.

"I want to thank you for everything you're doing." I reach out and grasp her hand. "It's not easy facing your past like this."

"I wouldn't be doing it if I didn't believe in the cause." Jenna's fingers intertwine with mine as if we've been holding hands for years. "Those girls… They deserve justice. They deserve to be found."

Her words echo my thoughts, and a surge of admiration rushes through me. Despite everything she's been through, Jenna's strength and compassion shine through.

She's a survivor, a fighter.

The road curves ahead, hugging the cliffside as it winds toward our destination. The Guardian compound is still miles away, and my heart races with anticipation as we draw closer.

Blake's offer lingers in my mind, a tantalizing possibility. The operation's resources, technology, and sheer scale are enough to make any cop drool. Yet, even as I consider the prospect, my thoughts keep circling back to Jenna.

What would she think if I joined the Guardians? Would she see it as abandoning our small town? Or would she understand the need to do more, to make a more significant difference in the world?

Would it take me away from her?

Now, that's the real question. The thought of being separated from Jenna, of not being there to protect her, gnaws at me. We've only just begun to get to know each other, and I don't want to give that up.

"Penny for your thoughts?" As if sensing my inner turmoil, Jenna squeezes my hand.

I glance at her, surprised by the gesture but grateful for the contact. "Just wondering what you'd think if I took Blake up on his offer." A wry smile tugs at my lips.

"What offer?"

"He thinks I should become a Guardian like him."

Jenna is momentarily quiet, her gaze distant as she stares at the ocean.

"I think," she begins slowly. "That you have to do what feels right for you. If joining the Guardians is what your heart tells you to do, you should listen."

The car falls silent, a comfortable silence filled with unspoken understanding. As we continue down the winding road, the sun rises high into the sky, and a sense of peace washes over me. The tension in my shoulders eases, and my breathing slows.

"You asked *me* what I thought about you joining Blake's organization, but what do *you* think about it?" Jenna's voice breaks through my thoughts.

"Blake's always been the daredevil. Even as a kid, he was the one climbing the highest trees or jumping off the pier. He's an adventurous individual…" I pause, thinking about my brother. "He's the kind of person who doesn't think twice about the unconventional."

"Unconventional?"

"Joining a private security firm. Guardian HRS is *more* than that, but it's still kind of on the edge of things." I shake my head, knowing I'm explaining this wrong.

"What does that mean?"

"It's not part of the military. Not part of the police force. Not along any conventional *protect and serve* organizations. I *think* some of them are deputized Federal Marshals, but I could be wrong about that." I shrug this time, still not expressing myself well. "I guess I like to play things safe."

"Safe?"

"Go with the standard way of doing things." A nervous chuckle escapes my lips. "I'm more grounded. I want to make a difference in my community and help people. That meant becoming a cop or a firefighter. Blake shares that passion, but he wants more action and more suspense. Higher stakes."

"Do you ever regret not following Blake into the Navy?" Jenna nods, a thoughtful expression on her face. The question hangs in the air for a moment.

"Sometimes," I confess, the words heavy with a truth slowly growing inside me. "Especially with cases like this. I'm hitting a wall, and I can't help but wonder if I'd be more effective with the Guardians' resources."

"You're making a difference. Never doubt that." She squeezes my hand. "But just because something's comfortable isn't always a good reason not to consider changing things up."

Her touch sends a jolt of electricity through me. We've been dancing around this growing connection, the lingering glances and subtle touches, but with the case consuming my thoughts, I haven't had the chance to explore what it could mean.

After an hour or so of driving, we pull up to the gates of Guardian HRS. A familiar figure strides out to meet us.

"Welcome to the Guardians." Blake, my mirror image, grins widely as he opens the gate, waving us through. "Park your car over there. We're taking alternate transportation."

I park the car, and we climb out. Max bounds ahead to greet Blake, his tail wagging so hard his whole body shakes.

"Hey, boy." Blake ruffles Max's fur, laughing. "Well, well, Carter. You didn't tell me you were bringing such a hottie. Way to go, bro."

"Blake, this is Jenna, and Jenna, this is my incredibly tactless twin brother, Blake."

"Nice to meet you." Jenna blushes but extends her hand.

"The pleasure's all mine." Blake winks, shaking her hand. "Seriously, Carter, how do you always land the pretty ones?"

"We're working on a case together, you idiot." I roll my eyes. "Try to behave, will you?"

"Ah, you know I never behave." Blake cups his mouth in a mock whisper to Jenna. "I'm the black sheep of the family. Walk on the wild side and all that. And hey, if things don't work out with Carter, I've been told I'm a lot of fun."

"Knock it off, Blake. Jenna's with me." My jaw tightens.

"Alright, alright," he chuckles. "Message received loud and clear." Blake holds his hands up, backing away with a massive smirk.

Jenna's eyes widen at my possessive tone. A faint blush creeps up her cheeks. She glances at me, and a small, pleased smile tugs at her lips. Her hand brushes against mine, sending a reassuring warmth through me.

I cringe inwardly, pissed at myself for revealing my feelings like that.

"Relax, bro. Just having a bit of fun." Blake laughs, clapping me on the back. He throws an arm around my shoulders and gives me a squeeze before playfully shoving me away.

"Just keep your hands to yourself."

"No promises," Blake grins. "Now, let's get this show on the road. Hop in the golf cart. It's the best way to get around."

We climb into the cart, and before I can stop him, Max leaps onto the seat next to Blake like he was invited. His nose twitches wildly with curiosity.

"Looks like I've got a co-pilot," Blake laughs. "Ready for the grand tour?"

"Damn, Max." I look at my loyal dog and shake my head. "Traitor much?"

Secretly, I don't mind Max taking shotgun. It means I get to sit in the back with Jenna, and I'm all for that. The golf cart has narrow seating, which means from knee to hip to shoulder, my entire body gets to press against Jenna's soft form.

"Max seems to love your brother." Jenna nudges me with her shoulder.

"He does, but still…" Max should've waited for me to give the command, but he does love Blake.

"Keep your arms and legs inside the moving vehicle at all times." Blake pretends he's a tour guide. "And buckle up. You're in for the experience of a lifetime."

THIRTEEN

Carter

Jenna and I fumble with our seatbelts, our hands tangling, heads knocking, as we twist at the same time to buckle in. She laughs, and warmth rushes through me. We eventually figure it out, which is good.

Blake sucks as a driver, accelerating and powering around curves like he's a damn racecar driver, but it's still *just* a golf cart—with seatbelts.

Who puts seatbelts in golf carts?

The golf cart hums beneath us as Blake navigates the compound's winding paths. The air is filled with scents—the salty tang of the nearby ocean, the crisp smell of freshly cut grass, and an underlying hint of machine oil and electronics.

As we round a corner, a massive structure comes into view. Its mirrored surface reflects the blue sky and fluffy white clouds. The building hums with energy, a tangible sense of innovation.

"Over there is the tech center," Blake announces, his voice brimming with pride. "It's the heart of our operation. Mitzy, our technical lead, is a genius. She's developed some incredible AI and robotics that have revolutionized our work. Our HUDs are freakin' next level."

"HUD?" Jenna looks at me. "What's that?"

"Heads-Up Display," Blake answers swiftly. "It lets us see in different wavelengths. Night vision, infrared, visual spectrum—obviously. Our tech team feeds us intel."

As Blake continues explaining HUDs and drones, Jenna's excitement grows. Her body tenses with interest beside me, her hand squeezing mine tighter with each new revelation. The warmth of her touch sends a pleasant tingle up my arm.

"What kind of intel?" Jenna's curious, something else I love about her.

"Maps. Like if we have to hump it overground, they send us a terrain map. If we're rescuing hostages in a building, we have the schematics. Just makes life that much easier. But that's not the best of the tech we get to play with. In addition to that, we have access to a VR environment to plan missions. There's an entire town in the back quarter we use for training. And, of course, there are Mitzy's drones."

"Drones? What do you use those for?" Jenna's eyes widen with curiosity.

I love Jenna's questions. She's asking everything I want to know, which means I don't have to look like an idiot to my brother for not knowing any of this shit.

"There's *Smaug*, of course. It's a high-altitude drone that helps with mapping and other intel. Then, we have dragonflies and bumble bees. They are smaller drones that help when we need to map out where we're going, identify hostiles, find alternate routes, all the things."

"That's insane." Jenna reaches for my hand and squeezes it tight. "Must be fun to operate them."

"We have techies who do just that, but the bumblebees are autonomous."

"Autonomous? What does that mean?" Jenna's questions keep coming.

"They don't need a human at the wheel. Mitzy and her team are pioneers in AI and robotics."

"That's hard to wrap my head around." Jenna leans forward, her interest piqued.

"I keep telling Carter we've got some pretty cool toys." Blake grins and reaches out to scratch Max. "We even have robotic dogs."

Suddenly, a sleek, black, four-footed form emerges from the tech center. It moves with an eerie grace, each step precise and calculated. Max's ears perk up; his tail wags uncertainly.

"Meet Rufus, one of the Rufi."

"Rufus?" Jenna asks.

"Robotic Ultra-Functional Utility Specialist—aka RUFUS." Blake makes a sweeping gesture with his arm and pulls to a stop.

We all climb out of the cart, watching Max cautiously approach the RUFUS. The contrast between them is striking—Max's soft fur and organic movements against RUFUS's smooth metal exterior and eerily lifelike motions.

Max circles the RUFUS, sniffing curiously. The RUFUS, in turn, tilts its head, cameras whirring as it processes the living canine before it. Suddenly, the RUFUS emits a series of beeps that sound remarkably like a playful bark. Max's tail begins to wag more enthusiastically.

To our amazement, the RUFUS drops on its front legs while its rear remains raised. It's rear end even wiggles.

Max, recognizing the universal dog language, responds in kind. Before we know it, the two are engaged in a game of chase, circling the cart and darting between our legs.

The sound of Max's excited barks mingles with RUFUS's electronic yips, creating a weird blend of man's best friend meeting machine's best approximation.

"Well, I'll be damned," I mutter, watching the unlikely pair play.

Jenna laughs, the sound light and carefree. "It's like watching the past and future of canine companionship collide."

"The Rufi are invaluable in the field," Blake says. "When there's more than one of them, we call them Rufi. Mitzy hates that. We're supposed to say *Rufuses*, but that's a mouthful. We've recently begun integrating the Rufi into the team, partnering each two-man pair with a Rufi."

"They seem to be getting along." Jenna laughs, the sound warm and rich.

"Like two peas in a pod. Come on, Max. Time to go." Blake pats the seat next to him. Max leaves the Rufus, and Blake steers the cart onward. "Over there is the medical facility, run by Skye Summers, a brilliant doc and co-founder of Guardian HRS with her brother, Forest."

"Impressive," I murmur, taking in the state-of-the-art building.

As we continue the tour, Blake points out the various training facilities—the gym complex with its towering rock wall, the shooting ranges designed for every scenario imaginable, and the mock town used for urban combat simulations.

"You've really thought of everything," Jenna says, her voice filled with admiration.

"We have to be prepared for anything." Blake shrugs, but pride fills his expression. "Our missions have high stakes, and we can't afford to be caught off guard."

"There's a lot more to see and other cool stuff I want to show you, but..." We stop at a cafeteria, the smell of food wafting through the air. "I thought you might be hungry." Blake hops out of the cart. "Or, at least, I am. The food here is top notch. Our chefs are world class."

As we enter the cafeteria, I'm struck by the variety of options— everything from classic comfort foods to exotic, international dishes. Despite our recent meal, Jenna and I load up our plates and find a table. Max curls up at our feet.

"So, what do you think?" Blake asks, his eyes flicking between Jenna and me.

"I had no idea the scale of what you were doing here." I shake my head in wonder.

"We're making a real difference," Blake says, his voice serious. "The work we do... It matters. We're saving lives, bringing people home to their families. Right now, my team is involved in tracking down a major organization involved in some bad shit."

"It's amazing what you've built here." Jenna nods, her expression thoughtful. "The resources, the technology… It's like something out of a science fiction movie."

Blake beams with pride. "Just wait until you see what else we've got. This is only the beginning, and we're always looking for talent to join the team." He shoots me a pointed look.

"Blake…" I start, but he waves me off.

"I know, I know. You're happy being a detective, but we could use someone like you."

My mind whirls with possibilities. The thought of working alongside Blake and accessing these incredible resources is tempting, but I have a duty to my community and the missing girls I've sworn to find.

As if sensing my inner turmoil, Jenna squeezes my hand. I meet her gaze, seeing the warmth and understanding in her eyes.

Sitting in the cafeteria, the conversation shifts to Blake's recent missions. He leans back in his chair, a glint in his eye as he regales us with tales of high-stake rescues and narrow escapes.

"You should have seen it," Blake says, his voice filled with excitement. "At Citadel, we were outnumbered, outgunned, but we managed to get the hostages out safely. It was a thing of beauty."

I chuckle, shaking my head. "You always did have a flair for the dramatic."

"What can I say? It's a gift." Blake grins, but then his expression turns serious. "But it's not all fun and games. We've been tracking an organization that's proved to be a real thorn in our side."

I glance over at Jenna, trying to gauge how overwhelmed she might feel. It's been a big day, and I've yet to tell Blake why we're here. I'm hoping he might be able to get one of the tech geeks to take on a side project for my case.

Blake continues, his voice low and intense. "This is the only thing we have on them. It's a symbol, really—Chinese." He pulls out a pen, scribbling something on a napkin—哨兵. "Isn't that weird?"

Jenna goes rigid beside me as he slides the napkin across the table. Her face drains of color, and her breathing turns shallow and rapid.

"*Shàobīng*," Jenna whispers, her voice trembling. "It means Sentinel."

The cafeteria seems to disappear, the background noise fading as I turn to Jenna. "Have you seen this symbol before?" I ask softly, dread creeping into my voice.

Jenna nods, her eyes filling with tears. "Yes. When I was… When I was taken, the man who bought me had a tattoo on his wrist. It was that symbol. And he…" She trails off, absently rubbing her wrist as if trying to erase an invisible mark.

I notice her action, my eyes drawn to her wrist. In the cafeteria's harsh fluorescent light, I can make out faint, barely perceptible markings on her skin. Before I can ask about it, Jenna reaches for her bag. Her hands shake as she pulls out her sketchbook, urgently flipping through pages. The rustling paper fills the tense silence. Finally, she stops, laying the pad flat on the table.

A Chinese symbol is there, rendered in harsh, angry strokes of black. It dominates the center of the page, surrounded by jagged lines that pulse with danger and fear. The drawing is raw and visceral, a visual representation of the trauma Jenna endured.

"Holy fuck." Blake leans in, his face a mask of shock and dawning realization. "Do you know what this means?"

I meet my brother's eyes over Jenna's bowed head, a silent understanding passing between us. The missing girls, Jenna's past, and the organization Guardian HRS has been hunting are all connected.

"We're working the same case." The realization hits me like a physical blow.

"This is… It's huge." Blake nods slowly, his eyes never leaving the sketch.

"Jenna is a phenomenal artist. She's got pictures of some of the men involved and some of the facilities she was taken to." I pause, the weight of what I'm about to ask settling on my shoulders. "I was hoping that Guardian HRS could help me find some of these facilities or help with facial recognition to track down these men and start drawing some connections."

"This is… It's fucking gold." Blake's eyes widen as he flips through the sketchbook taking in the detailed sketches." It's precisely the kind of stuff we've been looking for. With these sketches and our resources…" His expression shifts from shock to determination.

"If it can help prevent what happened to me from happening to anyone else, then it's worth it." Jenna nods, her eyes still glistening with unshed tears, but her gaze now has a steely resolve.

"So, what's our next move?" I slip my arm around Jenna's shoulder, pulling her close.

"We need to get these to our tech team right away." Blake stands, a new energy radiating from him. "Mitzy's going to have a field day with this."

Blake's words sink in. We're standing on something much bigger than my small-town investigation. This case has just become so much more than finding missing girls. We're about to take on a criminal empire, and the stakes couldn't be higher.

Just then, two figures enter the cafeteria. Max, who had been dozing under the table, perks up, his tail wagging as he recognizes Jeb. The man I know as one of Blake's former team members is accompanied by a petite woman with long, raven-black hair and dark eyes, exuding a distinct goth vibe.

"Jeb, it's good to see you again," I say, standing and shaking his hand. Max trots over, nudging Jeb's leg for attention.

"You too, Carter," Jeb replies, returning a crushing handshake before giving Max a quick pat. His eyes shift to Jenna, curiosity evident.

Blake jumps in with introductions. "Jenna, this is Jeb. He used to be on Charlie team but jumped ship to work with the techies. And this is Stitch." He gestures to the woman. "Our resident criminal hacker turned model citizen."

"Hey!" Stitch playfully punches Blake's arm. "You make it sound bad."

"Am I wrong? You were arrested for hacking into the NSA." Blake grins. "Mitzy got her sentence commuted if she agreed to work here. Now, she's a vital part of our tech team. Helped bring down Citadel and everything."

"Nice to meet you." Stitch rolls her eyes but extends her hand to Jenna and me. "What brings you to Guardian HRS?"

The innocent question hangs in the air, suddenly loaded with implications.

"Funny you should ask." Blake clears his throat. "Jenna might have just given us a new lead on Sentinel. The man who—bought her had their symbol tattooed on his wrist."

Stitch's eyes widen. "Bought? I'm sorry, I didn't realize…"

"It's okay," Jenna says softly, shrinking back in her seat. Max, sensing her discomfort, moves to lay his head on her lap. "I don't know if what happened to me is connected. It was years ago, and that tattoo could have been unrelated."

Jeb and Stitch exchange a look.

"It's one hell of a coincidence," Jeb says, his brow furrowed.

"Let's not jump to conclusions." As a detective, the worst thing we can do is jump to conclusions before understanding the data. "We're here because Jenna made detailed sketches of the places she was taken. I hoped to use your resources to identify the buildings, trace ownership, and follow the money trail."

"We can do a lot better than that," Blake says, his eyes shining excitedly. "It's time to bring in the big guns—Mitzy, CJ, Sam, and Forest. We need to investigate this from all angles."

"I'll set up a meeting," Stitch says, pulling out her phone.

We're on the brink of something huge. Max whines softly, pressed against Jenna's leg, as if he senses the weight of what's to come.

Jenna and I find ourselves momentarily alone as the others disperse to set up the meeting. She rubs at her wrist again, a gesture I've seen her repeat several times today. She seems to withdraw into herself, her eyes becoming distant.

"Hey, are you okay? I know this is a lot." I lean in close, my voice low.

"I just… I never thought I'd have to face this again. I thought I left it all behind." She takes a shaky breath, her eyes meeting mine. "I don't think I'm okay with it." Her eyes pinch in pain.

"I'm sorry. I can make excuses. Take you home… I know this isn't easy, but…"

"You don't have to do that." A flicker of determination flashes in her eyes. "I want to help. If Sentinel is behind your missing girls and behind what happened to me… I want to stop them. It's just overwhelming."

Pride swells in my chest at her words. Despite everything she's been through, Jenna's strength and courage never cease to amaze me. I pull her into a hug, holding her close. Her body trembles slightly, but she doesn't pull away. Instead, she melts into my embrace, finding comfort in our shared warmth.

"You keep rubbing your wrist. I can't help but notice there are faint lines there."

Jenna hesitates, her eyes meeting mine with a mix of fear and trust. Slowly, she turns her wrist over, exposing the delicate skin on the inside. At first glance, I see nothing, but as she traces her finger over the area, I make out the faintest of lines.

"It's a UV tattoo," she whispers, her voice barely audible. "The man who… Well, after he stripped me and before he…Well, he had that tattoo put on my wrist. It's the same Chinese character; next to it, he placed a number. The number nine."

I lean in closer, my heart racing at this revelation. "Nine? Do you know what it means?"

"Not really." Jenna shakes her head, her eyes glistening with unshed tears. "I assumed it meant I was his ninth acquisition." The pain in her voice breaks something inside me.

"You're not a number," I murmur into her hair. "You're so much more than what they did to you. You're strong, brave, and resilient."

Her breath hitches, but she nods against my chest, the warmth of our connection providing a small but much-needed comfort. Her shoulders shake as she lets out a quiet sob. My arms tighten around her, wishing I could shield her from the pain of her past.

"I'm scared," she admits, her voice muffled against my shirt. "I thought I'd left all this behind, but now…" Suddenly, Jenna's body trembles more violently, and her grip on me tightens.

"We're going to figure this out together, okay? I won't let anything happen to you." I run a soothing hand down her back. I pull back slightly to look into her eyes, seeing the raw terror there. "What is it? Tell me."

She pulls back slightly, her tear-stained face looking up at me. The vulnerability in her eyes makes my heart ache, but there's also a flicker of something else—trust, maybe even hope.

"It's all happening so fast," she says, her words tumbling out in a rush. "If this organization, Sentinel, is the same one that took me all those years ago… It's bigger than I ever imagined. And if they're connected to what Guardian HRS is hunting down…" She shakes her head, unable to finish the thought. "How are we ever going to find your missing girls?"

"I don't know, but I'm not giving up on them."

"The man who bought me," she continues, her voice dropping to a whisper. "If he finds out where I am…" Her eyes fill with fresh tears. "He'll come after me. He'll find me, and he'll…"

I cup her face in my hands, forcing her to meet my gaze. "Listen to me. I won't let that happen."

"But what if word gets out?" she asks, the fear palpable in her voice. "It's all moving so fast, and I feel like I'm losing control. I'm terrified of being found, of being taken again."

"Your fear is completely understandable, but you're not alone. You have me, and now you have Guardian HRS's resources behind you. We're going to figure this out, and we're going to keep you safe."

"Thank you," she whispers, a small smile tugging at her lips.

I'm struck by how right this feels as we stand there, wrapped in each other's arms. Jenna isn't just a witness or someone I'm trying to protect. She's become something more, someone I care deeply about.

The sound of approaching footsteps reminds us that we're not truly alone. We reluctantly separate, but I keep hold of her hand, giving it a reassuring squeeze.

"Ready?" I ask, searching her eyes.

"As I'll ever be." Jenna takes a deep breath, squaring her shoulders.

While we had a moment to ourselves, Stitch was busy. She finishes a call and then approaches us.

"Meeting's set," she says, joining us as we bus our dishes and head outside.

The missing girls are still my priority, but now I have another reason to see this through—to help Jenna find closure and justice for what was done to her. As we climb back into the golf cart, Jenna's hand finds mine again. Her grip is tight, terrified, and clingy, yet she remains resolute.

FOURTEEN

Jenna

THE DRIVE TO THE BRIEFING ROOM IS A BLUR. THE SCENERY OUTSIDE the golf cart melts into a kaleidoscope of colors as Blake races through the compound. Just minutes ago, I was enjoying the tour, marveling at the advanced technology and the sense of purpose that seemed to permeate every corner of the facility.

But now, everything has changed.

A palpable sense of urgency fills the air, a crackle of energy that seems to emanate from Blake, Stitch, and Jeb. Their faces are set in grim determination. Their eyes narrow with a focus that sends a chill down my spine.

I can't shake the feeling Sentinel is more than *just* a criminal organization—it's a force to be reckoned with, a shadow that looms over everything and everyone.

How could what happened to me all those years ago be connected to the missing girls Carter is searching for now?

It seems impossible, a cruel twist that threatens to drag me back into the darkness I've fought so hard to escape.

The golf cart screeches to a halt, and we pile out, our feet hitting the pavement with a sense of purpose. Max stays by my side as if sensing I need to ground myself in the gentle reassurance of a canine friend. I run my fingers through the scruff at the back of his neck, staying in contact with him using my right hand while Carter takes my left. His grip is firm.

Confident.

The building looms before us, all glass, steel, and sharp angles, a monument to Guardian HRS's cutting-edge technology and unwavering determination.

We approach the front door, and I hesitate. Carter squeezes my hand, then places his hand on the small of my back as if to urge me forward. That lasts for the briefest moment before he suddenly tugs me to his side and wraps an arm around my waist.

"I'm with you," he whispers into my ear, saying exactly what I need him to say.

We enter together, me leaning against Carter while Max checks me with his soulful brown eyes and leans against my thigh.

I'm bracketed by strength, compassion, and maybe something more.

It's too early to use the word *love*. Carter and I are still relative strangers—casual acquaintances who are quickly becoming more.

But I don't care. It already *feels* like more.

As we step inside, I'm struck by the energy that crackles through the air. Everywhere I look, people move with purpose, their eyes fixed on screens, and their fingers fly over keyboards. It's as if they're bound together by a single mission, a shared commitment to bringing justice to those who have been wronged.

But as we approach a briefing room, my heart pounds, and my palms slick with sweat.

I know what awaits me on the other side of that door—a barrage of questions and a demand to relive the most traumatic moments of my life in front of a room full of strangers. It was hard enough to share my story with Carter, a man I've grown to trust and care for deeply.

But this…

This feels like a violation, a stripping away of the carefully constructed walls I've built around my past.

The briefing room door looms before me, a portal to a world I thought I'd left behind. Each painful beat of my heart is a reminder of the trauma I've tried so hard to forget.

"Ready?" Carter's voice is soft, his eyes searching mine for any sign of hesitation.

I take a deep breath. The scent of his cologne fills my lungs—a warm, woody aroma with hints of leather and spice. I've come to associate his unique aroma with comfort, safety, and the promise of something more.

"As I'll ever be," I whisper, my voice barely audible over my pounding heart.

The door swings open, and I'm greeted by a sea of unfamiliar faces. The room is abuzz with activity, voices overlapping as people speak in hushed tones and tap on keyboards.

I fight the urge to shrink back, to disappear into the shadows, and escape the scrutiny of these strangers, but then Blake steps forward, his smile warm and welcoming.

"Everyone, this is Jenna. She's working with Carter on a case involving four missing girls. It appears there might be a connection between her past and Sentinel. Of course, you all know Carter."

The weight of their gazes presses down on me, making my skin prickle and my mouth go dry.

"Umm… Hi." A feeble finger wave accompanies my greeting, feeling stupid even as I do it. The urge to tuck tail and run grows stronger by the second.

Carter pulls me a tiny bit closer, his presence a shield against the strangers' scrutiny.

"Jenna, this is Charlie team." Blake gestures to a group of men, their faces a blend of rugged and refined. "Ethan, our leader. That's Gabe, Walt, Hank, and Rigel, our newest member." He points to each man in turn.

It's a lot of testosterone to process, but their expressions are kind. I try to commit their names to memory, but my mind is a whirlwind of emotions. Their names are here and gone between one breath and the next.

"And this is Mitzy, our technical lead, and Skye, our medical expert." Blake points to two women, one with hair that defies description—vibrant purple, pink, green, and blue display of psychedelic swirls with highlights of orange, yellow, and—glitter?

How does her hair—sparkle?

There's a mischievous glint in Mitzy's eye but also an undercurrent of intense compassion. The contrast is jarring yet oddly comforting.

"Welcome to Guardian HRS." Skye's voice is as serene as her smile. A wave of calm washes over me, easing some of the tension from my shoulders.

"And this is CJ and Sam," Blake continues. "CJ is in charge of the Guardian teams. Mitzy leads our technical teams. Sam is their boss, and of course, you already know Forest."

The room suddenly feels too small, the air too thin. My gaze lands on a familiar face, and time seems to stand still. Forest Summers, the man who saved my life, stands at the back of the room, his expression unreadable.

A tidal wave of memories crashes over me: the cold bite of pavement against my bare skin, the acrid stench of gasoline and burnt rubber filling my nostrils, and the distant baying of dogs growing closer with each passing second. My heart pounds in my chest, echoing the terror of that night.

"Forest." His name escapes my lips, barely a whisper, yet carrying the weight of years of unspoken gratitude.

He steps forward, his eyes softening as they meet mine. "It's good to see you again, Jenna. I wish it were under better circumstances."

My throat constricts, a lump of emotion threatening to choke me. The room spins slightly, and I sway unsteadily on my feet. Carter's hand finds mine, his fingers intertwining with my own. The warmth of his touch anchors me to the present, a silent reminder that I'm not alone.

"I—I never thought I'd see you again," I manage to say, my voice trembling. The scent of his cologne—the same as that night—brings the memories into sharper focus. "You saved my life."

"You saved yourself. I just gave you a ride." Forest's eyes crinkle at the corners, a mix of sadness and warmth in his gaze.

The room falls silent, the weight of our shared history palpable in the air. For a moment, it's just Forest and me, connected by a night that changed my life forever. Then, slowly, the present reasserts itself. The hum of computers, the shuffle of feet, the quiet murmur of voices—all serve to remind me why I'm here.

I straighten my spine, drawing strength from Carter beside me and the memory of what I've overcome.

"I'm ready to help in any way I can. If there's a connection between what happened to me and these missing girls, I want to find it."

"Then let's get started. We have a lot to discuss." A glimmer of pride shines in Forest's eyes.

FIFTEEN

Jenna

———

"Jenna, we've been partially briefed." Ethan keeps his tone brisk yet empathetic. "If you don't mind, could you tell us everything you know about Sentinel?"

"I…" My mouth goes dry, memories threatening to overwhelm me. Carter's hand tightens around mine, anchoring me. "I never said they were Sentinel. I only recognized a tattoo."

"Of course. Anything you can tell us could be invaluable." Ethan nods, apologetic.

"It's just when Blake drew the character for *shàobǐng*, I recognized it as the one on—on that man's wrist." I absently stroke the inside of my wrist, where my tattoo resides.

The words come slowly at first, each one a struggle, but as I delve deeper, the floodgates open. I recount the training facility—a clinical place with endless corridors and locked doors—the grueling hours spent learning to walk in impossibly high heels, how to laugh at the right moment, to be seen and not heard, and how they taught us to be the perfect companion, molding us into living dolls for the wealthy and powerful.

I describe the opulent parties; my voice catching as I recall the crystal chandeliers, the champagne flowing like water, and the leering faces of men who saw us as nothing more than exquisite toys, and how the air hung thick with cigar smoke and expensive cologne, masking the stench of corruption and greed.

Then, I reach the night of the auction. My voice wavers as I describe the cold metal stage beneath my feet, the blinding lights that left me feeling exposed and vulnerable, and the cruel curl of the buyer's lip as he raised his paddle, his eyes raking over me like I was a prized mare at a horse auction.

"He had a tattoo on his wrist," I say, my voice barely above a whisper. "Harsh lines and angles. Chinese characters. It caught my eye when he… When he touched me."

Mitzy leans forward, her vibrant hair catching the light. "Was he the only man you saw with a tattoo like that?"

I pause, thinking back. "I-I'm not sure. They all wore suits to these events, with long sleeves and cufflinks. I didn't pay attention to their wrists. It's possible others had them, but I can't say for certain."

I pause, steeling myself for what comes next. "After he bought me, they—they held me down. Tattooed me with invisible ink." I turn my wrist over, tracing the spot where the mark lies. "It's the same symbol as his tattoo, but there's also a number—the number nine."

The room is silent, the weight of my words palpable. Carter's grip on my hand tightens, his eyes blazing with a mix of anger and determination.

"Why do you think they used invisible ink on you when the man who purchased you had a visible tattoo?" Mitzy taps her fingers on the table. "That doesn't make sense."

I shake my head, feeling lost. "I don't know. Maybe—maybe they didn't want us visibly marked? Or perhaps it was a way to track us without others knowing. I'm sorry, I don't understand their reasoning."

The room falls silent as everyone processes this information. Minds turn, trying to piece together the puzzle of Sentinel and its operations.

I look up, meeting the pensive expressions of those around me.

"I don't know if nine meant I was the ninth girl he bought or if it was some serial number. I just… I never understood what it meant."

The silence stretches, broken only by the soft hum of computers and my ragged breathing. I've laid bare my darkest memories, and now I wait, hoping that somehow, this painful recollection might bring justice to others who have suffered.

When I describe the man's wrist tattoo and the intricate lines that have haunted my dreams, Forest's face flashes with a flicker of recognition. He and Skye exchange a look. The interaction between them is gone in an instant, but it's enough to make me wonder what they know.

The room falls silent as I finish recounting my story. Carter squeezes my hand gently, then turns to address the group.

"Jenna has something else that might help us," he says, his voice steady. "Jenna, would you mind showing them your sketchbook?"

I hesitate for a moment, my grip tightening on my bag. These sketches are deeply personal, a visual record of my trauma, but they could be crucial to the investigation. Slowly, I pull out the sketchbook and place it on the table.

"These are drawings of the men, the facilities, the auction house." I open the book, my hands trembling slightly.

As I flip through the pages, the charcoal line sketches come to life—haunting images of my past. The team gathers around, their faces reflecting both curiosity and concern.

"This is the training facility." I point to a detailed drawing of a building with high walls. "And here's the auction house."

Mitzy leans in, her eyes widening. "The level of detail here is incredible. Stitch, are you seeing this?"

Stitch nods, already snapping pictures with her phone. "We might be able to run these through our image recognition software and see if we can find any matches."

Mitzy looks up, her vibrant hair catching the light. "Jenna, do you know where these places were located?"

I shake my head, a familiar sense of frustration washing over me. "No, I'm sorry. We were never allowed to see outside when we were traveling. The windows were always blacked out."

"How long were you in the vehicles when you traveled between locations?" Stitch leans in, her dark eyes intense.

"It varied." I try to recall, my brow furrowing. "Sometimes, it was as short as an hour. Other times, it could be five or six hours, but we were never flown anywhere, always driven."

Mitzy's eyes light up at this information. "That's very helpful. If you were always driven, it narrows our search parameters significantly. It seems like everything might be located within California."

As they flip through the pages, Ethan points to a sketch of a stern-faced man. "Is this Lucian? The one you mentioned earlier?"

"Yes," I confirm, a chill running down my spine at the sight of his face. "He was the main trainer, the one who—who prepared us for the auctions. He was—cruel. Efficient."

"Were there other trainers?" Skye asks gently.

I nod, flipping to another page. "This is Marcus. He was in charge of our physical training." The sketch shows a muscular man with a cruel twist to his mouth. "And this," I turn another page, "is Vivian. She taught us etiquette and how to—please the clients."

As I speak, Carter's hand tightens on mine, a silent show of support.

Suddenly, Stitch leans in, her eyes fixed on a detail in the background of one of my sketches. "Wait, what's that?" She points to a small brooch pinned to a man's lapel.

I squint, trying to remember. "I… I'm not sure. I saw it a few times on some of the higher-ranking men. I didn't think it was important at the time."

"Do you have any sketches with a more detailed view of the brooch?" Stitch asks, her brow furrowed in concentration.

I shake my head. "Sorry, no. It was just a small detail I noticed in passing."

Stitch taps her head, looking frustrated. "I've seen it before, I'm sure of it. But I can't place where." Stitch studies the sketch intently, her brow furrowed in concentration. "There's something about this brooch… I can't quite make out the details, but it seems significant."

Mitzy leans in, examining the drawing. "Jenna, your sketch is incredibly detailed. Is there any chance you might remember more about the brooch?"

I close my eyes, trying to focus on the memory. "I—I'm not sure. I have a good memory for visual details, but I didn't pay much attention to the brooch then. It was just something I noticed in passing."

"We might be able to use some advanced AI to extrapolate from what you've drawn and find similar designs or symbols." Mitzy taps her chin, then looks to Stitch. "What do you think?"

"Definitely worth looking into." Stitch interlaces her fingers and cracks her knuckles.

"We'll run all this through our image recognition AI, cross-referencing with known symbols, corporate logos, and mythological imagery." Mitzy pours over the sketches. "It'll take some time and serious computing power, but it might give us a starting point."

The room falls silent as Mitzy and Stitch get to work. The only sound is the soft hum of powerful computers processing the data. After what feels like an eternity, Mitzy's screen lights up.

"Can you tell me a little bit more about Sentinel?" Carter clears his throat. "How does it tie into all of this?"

"Sentinel is a global criminal organization we've been tracking for some time." Ethan steps forward, his expression grave. "We first encountered them when we took down a subsidiary of theirs called Citadel."

Blake nods, picking up the thread. "More recently, we helped a biochemical engineer obtain asylum in the United States. She worked for a company called Red Phoenix Pharmaceuticals in Shanghai and discovered they were diverting heavy water for use in nuclear weapons. That's when we first became aware of the Chinese character '哨兵' being connected to Sentinel."

"We've seen evidence of them all over the world. Involved in varying criminal activities. Montana, Shanghai, and now here in California. They're incredibly well-organized and deeply embedded in various industries," Mitzy chimes in, her fingers flying over her tablet while she talks.

"So, you think there's a connection between what happened to me and this—this global organization?" I'm in awe of the scope of what we're dealing with.

"We never like to jump to conclusions," Skye says, "but with the tattoo on not just your wrist but the man who bought you, it's looking more and more likely."

Jeb leans in, studying the sketch of the auction house. He's been quiet up until now. Gently, he clears his throat to speak.

"Jenna, you mentioned a bidding system. Paddles, you said, but did they use anything else?"

"Like what?"

"Electronics?"

I close my eyes, trying to recall. "The bidders all had these small devices, like tablets. I remember the glow of the screens in the darkened room. A large display at the front showed the current bid."

"Interesting," Mitzy murmurs, already tapping away at her tablet. "That kind of tech leaves traces. We might be able to track purchases or shipments."

As they discuss possibilities, I feel a surge of hope. My painful memories might help bring down this organization.

"Jenna," Blake says, his voice gentle. "I know this is difficult, but is there anything else you can remember? Any details about the people involved, the operations, anything at all?"

I take a deep breath, searching my memory. "There was… There was a man who visited often. He didn't participate in the auctions, but the others deferred to him. I only saw him a few times, but he had this presence—like he was in charge of everything. Which was interesting considering how short he was."

I flip to a sketch of a distinguished-looking man with piercing eyes. The room falls silent as they take in the image.

"This could be big," Forest says, his voice low. "If we can identify this man, we might be able to unravel the whole operation."

Ethan leans forward, his eyes intense. "Did he only appear at the auctions, or did you see him elsewhere?"

"He visited the training facility quite a few times." A shudder runs through me at the memory. "It was a very uncomfortable feeling whenever his eyes landed on me."

Gabe speaks up. "Did anything change after his visits?"

I nod slowly, a chill running down my spine. "Sometimes, after one of his visits, one of the girls would disappear. We never knew what happened to them. They didn't seem to be taken to auction like the rest of us. They just—vanished."

The room falls silent, the weight of this information settling heavily on everyone.

"Do you have any idea why certain girls were chosen?" Carter asks gently, his hand finding mine under the table.

I shake my head, frustration and fear mingling in my voice.

"No, I could never figure out a pattern. Some were the most beautiful, some the most obedient, others… It seemed random. But his presence always meant change, and rarely for the better."

Forest exchanges a glance with Blake. "This man could be a key figure in Sentinel's hierarchy. If we can identify him, it might lead us to the core of their operations."

"Jenna," Skye says softly, "can you tell us anything else about him? Any distinguishing features, the way he spoke, anything at all?"

I study the sketch I've drawn, trying to recall every detail. "He was short, dressed in expensive suits, but always looked a bit disheveled. His voice was—cultured, with a slight accent I couldn't place. And he always wore one of those brooches we were discussing earlier."

As I speak, Mitzy is typing, likely running my description through their databases. The room is tense with anticipation, everyone aware we might be on the verge of a significant break-through.

"One more thing," I add, the memory surfacing suddenly. "I overheard some of the handlers talking once. They referred to him as 'The Curator'. I don't know if that was a title or a codename, but that's what they called him."

"The Curator," Ethan repeats, his brow furrowed. "That's something we can work with."

SIXTEEN

Jenna

As the team buzzes with this latest information, I can't help but feel a twinge of disappointment. I came here with my sketchbook hoping to provide clear answers, to be the key that unlocked this mystery. Instead, it feels like I've only opened a Pandora's box of more questions.

Each revelation leads us further down a rabbit hole of uncertainty. The mysterious Curator and the disappearing girls—they're all pieces of a puzzle that's growing larger and more complex by the minute. I can't shake the feeling that instead of moving forward, we're spinning our wheels, getting further away from answers than we were before.

The memories I've dredged up are painful, each one a reopened wound. And for what? Vague images and half-remembered details that only seem to muddy the waters further?

Am I helping? Or am I leading everyone on a wild goose chase through the darkest part of my past?

And underneath it all, there's a growing sense of unease. With each piece of information we uncover, each layer we peel back, I can't shake the feeling that we're poking a very dangerous bear.

What if I'm drawing attention to myself?

What if Sentinel realizes where I am?

I glance around the room at the determined faces of the Guardian team. They seem energized by these new leads, but I feel more lost than ever. I came here hoping for clarity, for a straight path to justice. Instead, I find myself at the center of a web of intrigue that's growing more tangled by the moment.

"You're doing great." Carter squeezes my hand reassuringly as if sensing my turmoil. "Every piece of information helps, even if we can't see how it all fits together."

I draw strength from his words, but as the team continues their animated discussion, doubt creeps in. Are we really getting closer to the truth, or did I lead them down the wrong road?

Gabe grabs my sketchbook and draws it close to him. He flips to the beginning and then questions me again.

"What about this building here?" Gabe inquires, tapping a sketch of an opulent mansion.

"That's where some of the parties were held," I explain, my voice tight.

Jeb leans forward, his brow furrowed. "Jenna, in this sketch of the auction room, do you remember if there were any security cameras? Any tech we should be aware of?"

"I… I think there were cameras in the corners. And some kind of electronic bidding system." I close my eyes, trying to recall.

The questions continue, each team member focusing on different aspects of the sketches. Forest and Skye exchange glances as they study a drawing of a man with a distinctive scar.

Finally, Carter speaks up. "Is there anything we can do with this information? Can we identify these men or locate these buildings?"

Mitzy nods enthusiastically. "Absolutely. We can run facial recognition on the sketches of the men and cross-reference the buildings with satellite imagery. It'll take some time, but this is golden. It's more information than we had before."

"You okay?" Carter leans in close, his voice low.

"Yeah. It's—it's a lot, but if it helps, it's worth it." I manage a small smile.

The room devolves into several conversations at once. Mitzy and Stitch huddle over a computer, their fingers flying across the keys as they input the information from my sketches. The men of Charlie team confer in hushed tones, their expressions grim and determined. Forest gravitates over to his sister, Skye. They lean toward each other, heads pressed close, talking in hushed whispers. Sam and CJ sit beside each other, arms crossed, expressions brooding as they observe the others.

Thankfully, I have Carter. His presence keeps me grounded. When he rests his hand on my knee, his touch soothes my frayed nerves. Max whines beside me and places his chin on my knee. Soulful doggy eyes stare up at me. He doesn't know what's wrong, only that I'm upset.

I wish I had a treat for him. Instead, I pat his head and tell him everything's going to be alright.

"You did great," Carter murmurs, his breath warm against my ear. "I'm so proud of you."

I manage another small smile, but the moment is short-lived as Mitzy's voice cuts through the chatter.

"We've got something." Her tone is flat and devoid of the excitement such a statement should bring. "Or rather—nothing."

The room falls silent, confusion etched on every face.

"What does that mean?" Forest's deep rumble fills the room, shaking the air like thunder.

"The men in Jenna's sketches don't exist." Mitzy's eyes flicker with irritation.

My heart stops. The world around me blurs and the voices become distant—muffled.

"How do they not exist?" Carter's voice cuts through my haze, tight with tension.

"There's no record of them anywhere," Stitch explains, her voice gentle but firm. "No birth certificates, no driver's licenses, no social security numbers. It's like they've been erased from every system we can access."

"But—they existed. They're real." My voice comes out barely above a whisper.

When I close my eyes, I can still feel their hands on me, see their leering faces, and hear their cruel laughter.

They were real.

They had to be.

The room falls silent, with all eyes on me. I feel their doubt, and it's suffocating. My hands shake, and I clench them into fists to stop the trembling.

"Jenna, we absolutely believe you." Forest steps forward, his expression serious. "The fact that we can't find any records doesn't mean these men don't exist. It means someone has gone to great lengths to erase their digital footprint."

Ethan nods in agreement. "This level of information scrubbing lends credence to your story. Only an organization with immense resources and reach could pull this off."

Relief washes over me, but a new kind of fear quickly replaces it. "But how? How can someone erase people from existence like that?"

"That's what we need to figure out," Mitzy says, her fingers already flying over her keyboard. "This isn't about hiding identities. It's about rewriting reality."

"This proves how big and dangerous Sentinel really is." Carter's hand finds mine, squeezing gently.

I bite my lower lip, trying to process it all. The men who hurt me were real; I know that with every fiber of my being. Now they're ghosts, erased from every system. It's terrifying but also—validating.

Only an organization as powerful and sinister as I remember would go to such lengths.

"We *have* encountered this before." Stitch leans forward, her fingers splaying across the table.

"You have?" I look at her, more confused than ever.

"With Citadel." Stitch leans back and looks toward Mitzy.

"I was thinking the same thing." Forest nods, his expression grim. "Jenna, what we're seeing here… It's not unprecedented. It's time we filled you in on what we discovered during the Citadel raid."

"What do you mean?" I search for answers.

"Not too long ago, we became aware of an organization called the Citadel," Ethan takes over, his voice steady and professional. "They kidnapped women and auctioned them to the highest bidder, like what happened to you. The only difference is that those women weren't trained like you were. It took us months of investigation, but we finally located their base of operations."

Blake continues, "When we raided Citadel, we freed dozens of women, but what we found inside was disturbing, to say the least."

"What did you find?" My stomach clenches because whatever the answer is, I won't like it.

"We discovered surgical suites," Skye adds, her medical expertise evident in her tone. "State-of-the-art facilities where they were altering the women's facial features. It went beyond simple cosmetic changes—they fundamentally changed these women's appearances."

Stitch nods, her eyes intense. "But it wasn't just physical changes. We found evidence of extensive digital erasure. Birth certificates, driver's licenses, social media accounts—all wiped clean. It was as if those women never existed. Which means they're nearly impossible to find."

"We always suspected," Forest says, "this was done to evade facial recognition and make it nearly impossible to identify or rescue these women in the future."

"Unfortunately, during our extraction, Citadel collapsed," Mitzy jumps in. "We lost a significant amount of evidence in the process."

"Including most of the files detailing their identity erasure methods," Stitch adds, frustration evident in her voice.

"So you think what's happening with Jenna's sketches is related to what you saw at Citadel?" Carter leans forward, his brow furrowed.

"It's a similar pattern, but on a much larger scale." Forest nods grimly. "If they are capable of erasing victims' identities, there's no reason to think they wouldn't also do that for the perpetrators."

I sit there, trying to process all this information. It's terrifying to think of the scale of what we're dealing with, but at the same time, it's oddly comforting to know I'm not alone, that what happened to me isn't isolated.

"Jenna," Ethan says, "your account aligns with patterns we've seen in Sentinel's operations. The fact we can't find any digital trace of these men doesn't mean they don't exist. It means Sentinel has gone to extraordinary lengths to hide them."

Mitzy nods, her fingers flying over her keyboard. "This level of information scrubbing is unprecedented in scale but not in concept. It fits with what we know about Sentinel's capabilities and methods."

"But why?" I ask, struggling to understand. "Why go to such lengths?"

"Protection," Forest says grimly. "By erasing these men from every database, Sentinel ensures they can operate with impunity. No records mean no trail to follow."

"So what do we do now?" I ask, looking around at the determined faces of the Guardian team.

Forest's expression is grim but resolute. "We dig deeper. If Sentinel can erase people from existence, we must find out why and, more importantly, how to undo it. Your sketches, your memories—they're more valuable than ever now. They might be the only record left of these men."

But they don't need me to do that. I breathe out, long and slow. My part in this is done. That should bring relief, but I'm still a ball of nerves.

"I need… I need a moment," I manage to choke out my words as I stagger to my feet.

Carter jumps up beside me and glances at his watch. "Wow, I didn't realize how late it was getting. We can wrap up and head out."

I wave him off with a small smile, my heart clenching at the worry etched on his face. He's torn between his desire to comfort me and his duty to see this through. The conflict plays out on his face in the way his jaw clenches and how his fingers twitch at his side. He's reluctant to step away from the table.

"I'm okay." I pat his shoulder, trying to reassure him. "You stay. I need a moment to clear my head—and process all of this."

I make a vague gesture, trying to encapsulate what's happening in the room. All of this is beyond me.

"Are you sure?" he asks, his voice low and gentle. "I can come with… If you need me."

"You stay. This is *your* case."

A flicker of guilt crosses his face, but determination quickly replaces it. He nods, sinking back into his chair, his attention already turning back to the files and screens in front of him.

Carter won't rest until he brings those missing girls home.

He can't.

He's the kind of man, much like the others in that room, who was born a hero and became a protector by choice.

I excuse myself, my legs shaky and my head pounding. I need a moment to process the whirlwind of emotions within me. As I step into the hallway, I collide with a solid wall of muscle.

When did…

How did Forest leave the room and I didn't notice?

Strong hands grip my arms, steadying me, and I look up and up to see Forest's ruggedly handsome face, his expression a blend of concern and understanding.

"Jenna, I'm so sorry." His voice is low and sincere. "I never meant for you to be dragged into this."

"How did you know?" The question bursts from my lips, the words trembling with a mixture of anger and confusion. "How did you know what happened to me could be connected to those missing girls?"

Forest sighs, his shoulders slumping under the weight of his guilt. "I didn't, but things never added up after I found you. It felt too organized, too methodical to be a one-time thing. If there's one thing I've learned, these people operate in small circles. It may seem as if they're all isolated with no connections, but I find rats like to live in the same cesspool of human depravity."

"I still don't know why you put Carter in contact with me."

"I have a sense about these things. When Blake talked to his team about Carter's frustration with his case, it brought up that night I ran into you."

"The night you rescued me."

"No, you pretty much rescued yourself. I just happened to be in the right place at the right time." How he says it as if what he did means nothing makes me wonder about the enigmatic giant of a man standing before me.

This man is complex. On so many levels.

"So you kept digging?"

"Not digging. I filed that night away and packed it into a nice, tidy box, but my Spidey-senses lit up when I overheard Blake talking about his brother. It just *felt* connected."

"You're an incredible human being. Has anyone told you that?"

"I don't know about that." His lip twists, and a low, rumbly chuckle emanates from his chest.

It's not a question but a statement of fact. Because, of course, he knows. Forest Summers is something out of this world.

"We've run across Sentinel twice now. Their tentacles reach far and wide, and they're not limited to human trafficking. They've stumped us for too long, and we've recently discovered they're also into the black-market trade of nuclear weapons. We need to bring them down, and you might be the key we need to do it."

"I don't know about that." His words hit me like a punch to the gut. The air rushes from my lungs in a painful gasp. "I remember so little about that night, and now my sketches are of no help."

"Little?" His left brow arches in question. "I have an eidetic memory and recognize when someone else does too."

"I don't. I have good recall, but that's about it."

"Your sketches are next level. Don't downplay how important those will be in helping us on this case."

"All this time, I thought I was a random victim of a cruel twist of fate, but you're saying I was just a pawn in a game I never even knew I was playing. It's terrifying to know what could have happened to me."

"And yet it didn't. I'm sorry, Jenna." Forest's words are soft, his eyes filled with a deep sadness. "I'm sorry I couldn't protect you then, and I'm sorry I have to ask for your help now, but we need you. Those missing girls need you."

Tears prick at the corners of my eyes, hot and stinging, but I blink them back, my jaw clenching with a newfound determination.

"I think my part in this is done. You have the sketches, for whatever they're worth, and I want to return to my very simple and safe life." My voice bleeds with emotion.

Forest nods, his expression full of pride tempered with gratitude. He pulls me into a brief hug, his strong arms enveloping me in a cocoon of safety and comfort.

"You're braver than you know."

As we part, I glimpse Carter through the doorway. His face is a mask of concentration as he pores over a stack of documents. Tension girds his entire frame. It tightens his shoulders and firms his jawline.

He's thinking about the missing girls, about the weight of responsibility that rests on his shoulders. I'm reminded of why I fell in love with him in the first place.

And yes, I have fallen head over heels in love.

Irrevocably and absolutely.

Because Carter Jackson is a man who will stop at nothing to protect the innocent and bring justice to those who have been wronged. I love watching him work. His dedication and passion shine through everything he does.

SEVENTEEN

Carter

THE BRIEFING ROOM IS A MESS OF TENSION AND EXHAUSTION. WE huddle around the table, poring over Jenna's sketches. The weight of the case hangs heavy in the air, punctuated by faces etched with grim determination.

Mitzy carefully removes each sketch from Jenna's book, handling them like precious things. Her psychedelic hair sparkles under the lights as she spreads Jenna's sketches out on the table, arranging and rearranging them like puzzle pieces.

"Look at this." She points to a detail in one of the sketches. "This building, it has unique architectural features. We might be able to use that to narrow down the location."

"How do we narrow down the location based on the architecture?" Stitch, Mitzy's complete opposite with her long, raven-black hair and goth persona, leans in closer.

Mitzy taps her chin thoughtfully. "We can cross-reference it with known buildings in the area. We might land a hit on the architect who designed it. Use that to work back to this place."

The door to the briefing room suddenly swings open, and a staff member enters, carrying a stack of pizza boxes. The aroma of melted cheese and garlic wafts through the air, mixing with the scent of freshly brewed coffee.

"It's gonna be a long night, folks. Thought we could use some fuel." Sam stands, his voice cutting through the chatter.

The team cheers, grateful for the sustenance. They dig in, grab slices, and refocus on the task at hand, but I hesitate. Jenna's not in the room, and eating without her doesn't feel right.

Ethan speaks up after taking a bite of pizza. "Hey, Mitzy, what about what we did when we rescued Eve? Call in your cyber geeks that do that geolocate thing."

"I'm one step ahead of you." Mitzy's eyes light up. "Already sent a request."

"What does that mean?" My brow furrows.

Ethan, the team strategist, chimes in. "When we rescued Eve Deverough, all we had to go on was a photo. Mitzy worked her magic, and we located the compound. We're hoping they can do the same with Jenna's sketches."

"Yeah, they're the best of the best," Mitzy says. "Give them a blurry photo and a half-eaten bagel, and they'll find its location faster than you can say 'enhance.'"

I lean back in my chair, rubbing my temples. The fluorescent lights flicker overhead, casting harsh shadows across the room. My gaze drifts to the open door, catching a glimpse of Jenna in the hallway. She's talking to Forest, her shoulders hunched, her body language screaming discomfort.

A pang of guilt twists in my gut. I did this to her, dragged her back into the nightmare she's tried so hard to escape.

Max, my loyal German Shepherd, sits at my feet. He senses my unease. His ears perk up, and his eyes fix on me. I reach down, scratching behind his ears.

"Hey, buddy. Go take care of our girl, will you?"

Max tilts his head, his tail thumping against the floor. He stands, shaking out his fur, and trots out of the room. He approaches Jenna, nuzzling her hand, and the tension in her shoulders eases. A small smile tugs at her lips, the first smile since this briefing began.

I turn back to the briefing. Jenna's sketches, the ones she poured her heart and soul into, are spread out on the table. The faces may have changed, erased by Sentinel, but the landscapes and the buildings have not—those are the key.

Jeb points to a sketch. "This looks like a warehouse district. Lots of places to hide, lots of room for illegal activities."

Rigel nods in agreement. "Just gotta locate it, but we should start there, see if anything stands out. It's not much, but it's a start."

The room falls silent, the gravity of the situation sinking in. We're nowhere close to cracking this case. I fear another girl will be taken before we make any headway.

It's a heavy weight on my shoulders.

I glance back at the hallway, catching sight of Jenna and Forest. They're still talking, but Jenna's posture has changed. She's standing taller, her shoulders squared. Whatever Forest is saying, it's giving her strength.

Jenna is the strongest person I know, a survivor in every sense of the word. She's facing her demons head-on, and that takes a kind of courage most people can only dream of.

I turn back to the table, my resolve hardening. With the might of Guardian Hostage Rescue Specialists, I might find who took my four missing girls. Hopefully, before Sentinel adds a fifth and a sixth to the list.

"Jeb, can you snap pictures of all the buildings Jenna drew? Got a response from my dark web contacts, and they're eager to begin." Mitzy is a flurry of activity. Her fingers fly across her keyboard, her eyes glued to the screen. The monitor's glow illuminates her face, casting an eerie blue light across her features.

I push back from the table, my chair scraping against the floor. The sound is harsh, grating against my nerves. I need to check on Jenna and make sure she's holding up under the weight of all this.

She looks up as I approach, her eyes shimmering with unshed tears. Max stands diligently at her side, enjoying a little neck scratch courtesy of Jenna. The urge to pull her into my arms is overwhelming.

"Hey," I say, my voice soft. "How are you holding up?"

"I'm okay. Just... It's a lot, you know?" Jenna takes a shaky breath, her fingers curling into Max's fur.

"I wish I could make this easier for you." The lump in my throat makes it hard to speak.

"Don't be sorry. I want to help. I need to help." She shakes her head, and a stray lock of hair falls across her face. "If my sketches can bring those girls home, it's worth it."

"You're amazing, you know that?" The words slip out before I can stop them, my heart laid bare in the space between us.

"I'm just doing what anyone would do." A blush stains Jenna's cheeks, and her gaze drops to the floor.

"No, you're not. You're facing your demons head-on, and that takes a kind of courage most people can only dream of."

Jenna looks at me, her eyes searching mine. For a moment, the rest of the world falls away, and it's just us, suspended in this fragile bubble of understanding.

The team's chatter inside the briefing room breaks our moment. Reality comes crashing back in, and the weight of the case settles heavily on my shoulders once more.

"I should get back in there. There's pizza if you want it?" I clear my throat, stepping back.

"Honestly, I'm not hungry."

"Will you be okay here with Max for a bit?"

"Yeah, we'll be fine. Go do what you need to do." Jenna's fingers tighten in Max's fur.

I hesitate; the urge to stay with her wars with my duty, but the case calls, and I can't ignore it. With a final nod, I turn and head back to the team, my heart heavy with the knowledge of what we're up against.

Back in the briefing room, ideas bounce off the walls as Blake and his teammates dig deeper into Jenna's sketches. Each revelation sparks another lead to chase down.

Mitzy's dark web contacts are already working their magic, and I am overwhelmed with gratitude for the resources and expertise that Guardian HRS is bringing to my case.

But as much as I want to dive in and lose myself in the hunt,

Jenna needs me more. She's been through hell today, reliving her worst nightmares for the sake of this case. The least I can do is make sure she gets home safely.

I catch Ethan's eye across the table and give him a nod. He understands immediately, waving me off with a silent "go."

I find Jenna and Max in the hallway, her hand buried in his fur as she leans against the wall. She looks up as I approach, exhaustion etched into every line of her face.

"Hey, you ready to get out of here?" I ask softly.

Jenna nods, pushing off the wall. "More than ready. Do you mind if we swing by a drive-thru on the way? I'm starving all of a sudden."

"There's still some pizza left, if you want it."

"Not really in the mood for pizza."

"Of course. Anything you want."

Max woofs softly, his tail wagging at the prospect of a car ride and a potential treat.

We pile into my truck, the silence comfortable as we navigate the quiet streets. The fluorescent glow of a 24-hour burger joint beckons, and I pull into the drive-thru without a second thought.

"Two burgers and a plain hotdog, please," I order for us both, not realizing I never asked Jenna what she wanted. She sits in silence, absorbed in her thoughts.

I watch Jenna out of the corner of my eye, mesmerized by the delicate way she holds her burger and savors each bite. Meanwhile, Max wolfs down the pieces of hotdog I feed him.

"What?" She catches me staring and quirks an eyebrow.

"Nothing. Just… It's nice to see you relaxed. Even if it's just for a moment."

"It feels good. Normal, even. Like maybe the world isn't ending after all." Jenna smiles, a real smile that reaches her eyes.

"We're going to get through this. I promise." I reach across the console and take her hand, gently squeezing it as if I can pour my emotions into the touch.

"I trust you. More than I've ever trusted anyone." She squeezes back, her fingers warm against mine.

We finish our burgers in comfortable silence, the tension slowly easing from our shoulders. I dump our trash in a nearby trashcan, and we're back on the road.

The drive to Jenna's place is a blur of streetlights and shadows. The silence between us is thick, the weight of the day hanging heavy in the air. Jenna's exhaustion radiates off her in waves, the toll this is taking on her evident in every line of her body.

Miles pile up behind us as I drive her home, the silence broken only by the soft hum of the engine and Max's occasional yawn from the backseat. Today's events replay in my mind. Jenna's strength and vulnerability intertwine in a way that makes my heart ache.

As I pull up to her apartment building, Jenna turns to me, her bottom lip caught between her teeth. The war behind her eyes is clear: the fear of being alone clashes with the fear of asking for help.

"I hate to ask, but I don't want to be alone tonight." Her voice is small and delicate, almost lost in the space between us. "Do you think… Would it be too much if I asked you to stay with me?"

It's a big step, crossing that line from professional to personal, but the thought of leaving her alone after everything she's been through is unthinkable.

"Of course. Whatever you need, I'm here." I reach across the console, taking her hand in mine. Her fingers tremble slightly, and I give them a gentle squeeze.

"Thank you." Relief washes over her features, and she blinks back tears. "I just… I don't think I can face the night alone. Not after today."

"You don't have to explain. I get it." And I do.

EIGHTEEN

Carter

The thought of Jenna waking up in a cold sweat, haunted by the nightmares of her past, with no one there to comfort her… It's enough to make my blood boil. My heart breaks in equal measure.

We climb out of the vehicle. Max trots ahead, making a quick stop at a tree as we make our way up to her apartment. The air between us is charged with something new, fragile, and precious.

As we step into her apartment, Jenna flicks on the light. It is small but cozy, with worn furniture and soft lighting, creating an inviting atmosphere. The walls are adorned with framed photos and artwork, adding a personal touch that speaks of warmth and creativity. Bookshelves line one wall, filled with an eclectic mix of novels and knickknacks. A faint scent of vanilla lingers in the air, making the space feel even more comforting.

Jenna moves through the space like a ghost, her footsteps barely making a sound on the hardwood floors.

"I'll take the couch." I set my keys on the counter. "You should get some rest."

"Actually, I was hoping…" Jenna hesitates, her fingers twisting together in front of her. She takes a deep breath as if steeling herself for rejection. "Could you maybe stay with me? Just until I fall asleep?"

The request hangs between us, a fragile thread of trust and need. I swallow hard, my heart pounding against my ribs. The thought of holding her, of being the one to chase away her demons —feels right.

I hesitate, the war within me raging fiercely. My need to protect and hold her battles against my body's natural responses, the raw attraction I feel for her. The last thing I want is to make her uncomfortable or to cross any boundaries.

"Of course," I manage, my voice rough with emotion. I step closer, every muscle in my body tensed with the effort to stay composed. "I'll stay with you."

I hesitate momentarily, unsure how to navigate this new intimacy between us. She turns to me, her eyes searching mine. A soft smile curves her lips as if she's reading the conflict written all over my face.

"Make yourself at home. I have a spare toothbrush in the bathroom if you need it."

"Thanks. I appreciate it."

She leads me into the kitchen, the soft glow of the overhead light casting warm shadows across her face.

"Can I get you anything to drink? Water? Tea?"

"I'm good, thanks." I shake my head, my throat suddenly dry.

Max trots over to Jenna, his tail wagging expectantly. She laughs, reaching down to ruffle his fur.

"Okay, okay. I guess it's treat time for you, huh buddy?"

The sound of her laughter and the easy way she interacts with Max put me at ease. For a moment, the weight of the case fades into the background.

"I'm going to go change in the bathroom really quick. You can use it after me." Jenna turns to me with a hint of shyness in her voice.

I nod, not trusting my voice. She disappears down the hallway, leaving me alone with my thoughts and the steady thump of my heart.

I take a deep breath, trying to calm my racing pulse, and wander into the bedroom, taking in the simple but cozy decor. The bed looks inviting, piled high with pillows and a soft, worn quilt. I hesitate for a moment before sitting on the edge, wondering what I'm going to sleep in.

My go-bag is back at the station, leaving me with limited options. I finally settle on stripping down to my undershirt and boxers, folding my slacks and button-down neatly on the chair in the corner.

The sound of the bathroom door opening pulls me from my thoughts. Jenna stands in the doorway, dressed in loose-fitting pajamas that still highlight her gorgeous figure.

She's always hiding away under baggy clothes and messy buns, but now, with her hair falling softly around her face and the silk of her pajamas skimming her curves, I'm struck by just how beautiful she really is.

I swallow hard, trying to keep my eyes from lingering too long.

"All yours," she says softly, gesturing to the bathroom. Suddenly, Jenna lets out a huge, jaw-cracking yawn. Her hand flies up to cover her mouth. "Oh my God, I'm so sorry." Her cheeks flush pink.

I can't help but chuckle, the tension between us easing slightly. "No worries. It's been a long day."

"The longest."

I'm about to respond when Max, not one to be left out, lets out a massive yawn, his pink tongue curling as he stretches. A soft whine escapes his throat, and Jenna and I both burst out laughing.

"Looks like we're not the only ones ready for bed." I shake my head at Max's timing.

"I think that's our cue, buddy." Jenna giggles, reaching down to scratch Max behind the ears.

Her easy affection with Max strikes me, and I'm caught by how normal this all feels. For a moment, I forget about the case. It's just me, Jenna, and Max getting ready for bed like any other night.

The thought sends warmth spreading through my chest, a sense of rightness that I can't quite explain.

I clear my throat, reluctantly pulling myself back to the present. "I'll be right out." I gesture to the bathroom.

"Take your time. We'll be here." The corners of her lips curl into a soft, sleepy smile.

As I close the bathroom door, I glimpse my reflection in the mirror. For the first time in days, I feel relaxed, the lines of tension around my eyes and mouth smoothed away.

Jenna's presence affects me in more ways than one. The sight of her in those soft, silky pajamas, the domesticity of getting ready for bed together—it's left me with a rather insistent problem straining against my briefs.

"Damn it, Carter, get it together." The last thing I want is to make Jenna uncomfortable, especially when she's vulnerable.

I take a few deep breaths, trying to will my body into submission, but the more I try not to think about the gentle curves of Jenna's body, the way the silk clung to her in all the right places, the worse it gets.

With a groan of frustration, I turn the shower tap to cold, twisting it as far as it will go. I strip off my clothes and step under the icy spray, gritting my teeth as the frigid water hits my overheated skin.

Wincing at the shock of the chilly water, I grip the shower wall for support and let out a shuddering breath. The intense chill seems to help momentarily, but my arousal doesn't abate. As I wash my hair, I try to focus on anything but Jenna—the feel of her body against mine, her familiar scent, her soft whispers in the darkness.

But it's no use; my mind keeps drifting back to her.

I close my eyes tightly and try to picture something else, anything else—a waterfall cascading down a rockface, a babbling brook in a lush forest—but all it does is remind me that I'm about to spend the night in her bed.

My cock twitches and throbs in response. Damn this stubborn hard-on.

With a growl of exasperation, I give in and reach down. Needy and insistent, my cock twitches, eager for release even as I struggle against it. Gritting my teeth, I stroke myself, determined not to rush this. The water drips onto my skin, tickling and cooling the sensitive skin beneath my fingers as they glide over my shaft.

I lean against the tiled wall of the shower, trying to find some semblance of pleasure amidst the swirling chaos of desire and discomfort. Moaning softly under my breath, I stroke myself harder, imagining Jenna's fingers wrapped around me instead of my own.

Suddenly, it's as if she's with me, whispering dirty secrets in my ear that drive me wild with need.

The icy water streams down my body, sending tingles up and down my spine that only heighten the sensations coursing through me. Each slide of my hand along my shaft feels like her velvety tongue caressing every inch.

Despite myself, I groan low in my throat at the intensity of feelings flooding into me.

My movements become more urgent. With each stroke upward pushing into my palm, parts of me that hadn't hardened before now begin to throb in time with each downward pull back down again—like she's pulling me deeper inside her than ever before…

Even though she isn't here.

I close my eyes and let myself get lost in the fantasy, feeling her lips on mine, her hot breath against my skin as she whispers my name.

The pleasure builds within me until I can no longer hold back. With a low growl, I come undone, my release spilling over my hand and mingling with the cold water cascading down my body.

Panting heavily, I lean against the shower wall, trying to catch my breath and steady myself as the last waves of pleasure wash over me. But even as my heartbeat slows and the fog of lust clears from my mind, I can't help but feel a deep sense of emptiness.

It's because Jenna isn't with me.

With the edge taken off, I turn off the water and get out of the shower. I brush my teeth quickly, splashing some cold water on my face for good measure. I catch my reflection in the mirror, giving myself a stern look.

"She needs you to be her friend tonight, Carter. Nothing more. Get your head on straight."

Quickly drying off, I return to Jenna, where she's already waiting for me in bed. She looks up at me, her eyes heavy with exhaustion and something else, something tender and trusting that makes my heart clench.

Max is curled up at the foot of the bed in doggy heaven. Jenna took all the pillows from her bed and made him a decadent doggy bed. As always, his presence is a comfort.

I slip into bed beside her, careful to leave a respectful distance between us.

Jenna rolls onto her side, facing me. In the dim light, her features are soft and vulnerable, the mask of strength she wears during the day stripped away.

"Thank you." Her hand finds mine under the covers. "Thank you for staying." Her fingers thread through mine, and my heart stutters at the contact. "I don't think I could face the night alone."

"I'll always be here when you need me." I squeeze her fingers, my thumb brushing over her knuckles.

She smiles, a real smile that reaches her eyes, and my heart stumbles in my chest. I want to kiss her, to taste that smile and make it mine. Unfortunately, tonight is about comfort and safety. It's about being the rock she can cling to in the storm.

And that's enough for me.

We settle into bed. To my delight, Jenna curls against my side, her head on my chest. I wrap my arms around her, holding her close, marveling at how perfectly she fits against me. The scent of her shampoo, something floral and sweet, fills my senses, making my head spin.

We lie there in the darkness, the silence broken only by the sound of our breathing. Jenna's body slowly relaxes, the tension draining out of her as sleep claims her. I press a soft kiss to the top of her head, my heart aching with the need to protect her, to keep her safe from the horrors of the world.

I marvel at the peace that settles over her features. She looks younger and softer, the weight of the world temporarily lifted from her shoulders.

Then, with a whispered goodnight, I close my eyes, letting her steady breathing lull me into slumber. It's going to be a long night, but there's nowhere else I'd rather be.

NINETEEN

Carter

Morning comes too soon. The first rays of sunlight filter through the curtains, and dust motes dance in the air as I slowly wake from a fitful sleep. Jenna's nightmares seem nonstop. Other than holding her through the worst of them, I'm at a loss.

I feel guilty.

If not for me, her traumatic past would've remained in the past, right where she locked it up and shoved it in the deepest recesses of her mind.

I'm the asshole who asked her to unpack all that darkness to help me solve a case.

Guilty is the operative word.

Fortunately, I know exactly what I can do to help out.

I slip out of bed, careful not to wake Jenna, and make my way to the kitchen. Max, my traitorous four-footed companion, stays right by Jenna's side.

The two of them are quickly developing a tight bond, and if he can't be bothered to get out of bed, I can't be bothered to take him outside.

Normally, he's my priority in the morning, but Max doesn't

seem interested in heading outside. He groans, stretches, and opens one sleepy eye as I pad out of the bedroom and head to the kitchen.

My small gesture of comfort is to make breakfast.

It doesn't take long to familiarize myself with her kitchen, and she has everything I need to whip up a killer breakfast. Before long, the decadent aroma of coffee percolates through the air, and the sizzling goodness of bacon provides a soothing backdrop to my racing thoughts.

I'm lost in my head, trying to piece together the fragments of the case, when a prickle of awareness runs down my spine. My muscles tense, and instinct kicks in. Spinning around, my gaze locks on Jenna, standing in the hallway in her thin pajamas.

Her hair, tousled from sleep, tumbles over her shoulders, drawing my eyes to the way her chest rises and falls with each breath. Her wide eyes, soft and vulnerable, register shock at my abrupt turn, but then the brightest smile fills her face.

My lord, the woman is stunning. My heart trips and stumbles, finally picking up the beat after a moment of madness.

I take her in, drinking in her beauty. Most notably, and devasting for me, her thin pajamas fail to hide any of her curves. She's model-thin but has curves in all the right places. Simply stunning doesn't begin to scratch the surface of my attraction for her.

"Morning." I point to the skillet with the bacon. "I hope you're hungry."

"Starving. It smells amazing." Her smile, a small, tentative curve of her lips, sends a jolt of electricity straight through my chest, where it hijacks my heart and settles in with an odd buzzing sensation.

She moves closer, her bare feet padding softly on the tiled floor. I turn back to the stove, flipping the bacon, trying to ignore the heat of her body so close to mine.

"Thank you." Her hand comes to rest on my arm. "For staying last night. For being here."

"You don't have to…"

Her delicate arms wrap around my waist, and she gently rests her chin on the middle of my back. The fabric of her pajamas is soft, but the warmth of her body seeps through, capturing my senses and sending them on a perilous journey I may not be able to stop.

To make matters worse, her silken hair sweeps against my skin, sending tiny bursts of electricity racing down my spine. I curl my lower lip and suppress a moan.

When her hands move down to my waist, I lose the battle to remain unaffected. My body wakes with vicious hunger, eager to take, claim, and slake my thirst.

A hit of her perfume mingles with the aromas of bacon and the coffee percolating in the background, sending my senses on an adrenaline-fueled ride into dangerous territory. Her soft breaths are nothing like my ragged inhales. I'm quickly losing the ability to control my body's responses to a beautiful woman.

I turn to face her, my breath catching in my throat. She's so close, her eyes shimmering with something I can't quite name.

"You don't have to thank me." I place my hands on her hips. "It's the least I can do."

We're close.

Close like lovers.

Yet, we've yet to have our first kiss.

The words hang in the air between us: a promise and a plea all in one. Jenna's gaze lifts to my lips, her tongue darting out to wet her own. The air crackles with tension, the pull between us magnetic and undeniable. My mind screams at me to be professional, growing louder and more insistent as blood rushes to engorge my cock.

Be professional.

Be professional.

Goddammit, be professional!

Jenna's hands move up to my chest, her touch tentative and yet full of desire. She leans in close, lifting on tiptoe, her lips hovering inches from mine. I do the most natural thing and lose the battle for control over my own body.

Damn the consequences.

My hand rises to cup her head, and my fingers tangle in her hair. Jenna lets out a soft sigh, her body relaxing into mine. And then, as if we've done this a thousand times, our lips crash together, setting off fireworks.

The energy crackling between us ignites into a blazing firestorm that consumes any remaining doubt or reasons why I shouldn't pursue my desires.

Her response is immediate, and while her lips are soft and pliant, fire and passion simmer below the surface. I deepen the kiss, my tongue teasing against hers as our bodies press together.

She lets out a soft moan, her fingers digging into my skin as if it's an anchor keeping her in place. The kiss grows more urgent, becoming something unstoppable.

I pull her as close as I can, obliterating any space between us. The hard length of my erection presses against her belly, letting her know my intentions.

The kiss deepens.

It becomes wild and unhinged.

Desire courses through me like wildfire, consuming any rational thoughts or doubts. I want her; want to taste every inch of her skin and feel her body writhing under mine.

My hands roam freely over her body, exploring every curve and dip. Jenna responds eagerly to my touch, sending electrifying shocks coursing through my veins.

We break the kiss momentarily to catch our breaths, but our eyes remain locked in an intense gaze. Desire, uncertainty, but most of all, trust fill the intense green of her eyes.

"We can stop." Stopping is the last thing I want, but I'm a gentleman first and foremost. I won't proceed without her consent.

"Don't stop," Jenna whispers breathlessly against my lips. "I've wanted this for so long."

She's wanted this?

For how long?

"Me too." I gently brush a strand of hair behind her ear and cup her cheek.

What can I say? It's the truth.

Before I can say anything else, she pulls me down for another kiss. Our bodies move together with an urgency that is almost animalistic in nature, and it's not long before the kiss turns fierce and hungry.

I lift Jenna onto the counter without breaking the kiss. Her legs wrap around my hips, drawing me close. The heat of her core presses against the raging hardness of my dick.

The kiss intensifies.

The kitchen fades away into background noise as we lose ourselves in each other completely. Nothing else matters except this moment—the taste of her lips, the feel of her body against mine, and the sweet smell of her arousal.

"Is this really happening?" A soft laugh escapes her. "I'm not dreaming?"

"Not a dream." The air around us crackles and sparks as I press my body firmly against hers.

She pulls back from the kiss just enough to catch her breath, her chest heaving in rhythm with my own labored breathing. Our eyes lock in a silent exchange, speaking volumes without uttering a single word.

Confident this is what she wants, I trace the hem of her pajama top, fingers dancing underneath the buttery-smooth fabric to encounter the warm, silken texture of her bare skin.

I may have found heaven.

She shivers at the contact, goosebumps blossoming across her flesh in the wake of my exploring hands. With a deftness born of urgency and desire, I slip her top over her head to reveal her intoxicating and very bare breasts.

Her skin is warm and inviting, and I take full advantage to tease the swell of her generous breasts with my hands and then my mouth. She arches against me, thrusting her tits against my face.

Flicking my tongue over a stiffening nipple, I relish the way she begs for more.

I acquiesce, lavishing attention on her full breasts, sucking gently at one pert nipple before lathing the other with the same attention.

Sensations rocket through her body, causing her hips to undulate beneath me. As I switch back and forth between her hardened peaks, I slip a hand down her stomach, trailing my fingertips along the feminine curve of her waist and around her hip.

From there, I skim my hand along her creamy skin from her hip, along her outer thigh, and all the way to her knee, loving the feel of her skin against the roughness of my hand. Then, I move back up, along the inside of her knee, to her inner thigh, and all the way to her very core.

Her scent is intoxicating as I inch my way down her quivering form, drawing me in like a bee to honey. My lips leave a trail of open-mouthed kisses from her delicate collarbone to the dip of her navel.

Jenna's breath becomes ragged as I tease the sensitive skin at her hip.

With a devilish grin, I swirl my fingers around the apex of her thigh, sweeping closer and closer to her core without actually touching her there.

She gasps as I lift her hips and relieve her of the constraints of her pajama bottoms. Cool air greets her damp folds, making her gasp. But that gasp is short-lived as my mouth finally finds its way to her core.

Tentatively, I graze my tongue along her swollen labia, eliciting a low moan from deep within her chest. Encouraged by her response, I delve deeper, lapping up every drop of her sweet nectar.

Her taste is exquisite, a blend of arousal and the unique essence that is purely Jenna. My hands roam her body, fingertips dancing across the softness of her skin like a maestro conducting a symphony of want and need. The crescendo builds within her as I focus my attention on her clit.

Her thighs tremble, and her moans turn to needy cries. With gentle determination, I suck on her clit, grazing it with my teeth and then soothing it with my tongue in an intoxicating rhythm that has Jenna writhing beneath me.

She's close; I can tell by the way her breath hitches and by the way she grasps at my hair, pulling me closer.

I replace one hand at her breast, thumb circling a taut nipple while the other hand delves into her folds, slipping two fingers inside to stroke the velvety walls that clench around me. Her moans morph into a symphony of passion as she arches against me, seeking an even deeper connection.

I pick up the pace, flicking my tongue fervently while my fingers curl within her, finding that tender spot that turns her moans into cries of ecstasy. Her legs lock around me as her body tenses like a bowstring drawn tight.

Then she shatters, a wave of sensations tumbling through her as her orgasm rips through her body. Jenna's cries of pleasure fill the room with their primal melody while she convulses around my fingers and against my mouth, riding out the intense pleasure that consumes her entirely.

I continue to worship her until the final tremors fade away. Her grip on my hair loosens. Her chest heaves as she attempts to catch her breath. A fine sheen of perspiration glistens across her skin.

Her eyes flutter open after a moment of silent recovery, finding mine filled with adoration and an undeniable hunger for more.

My heart pounds like a tribal drum because her hands are not idle. They weave into my hair, tugging with impatience and need. I stand between her legs, our bodies speaking their own language— one composed of breaths, movements, and whispers that could be words or just expressions of pleasure.

Her hands shift lower, fingers scrabbling for the waistband of my briefs. Between one moment and the next, she frees me, and all I can feel is the heat of her hands holding my very erect and very eager cock.

Her fingers trace down my turgid length, tracing the ridges of engorged veins. Her touch sends ripples of pleasure through me that pool in places yearning for her touch. Every sensation is magnified —the smooth texture of the countertop, the scent of mingled perfumes and raw passion, and most overwhelming of all, the warmth of Jenna's hand as she strokes me toward pleasure.

Her touch is tender yet determined. Her grasp tightens, then releases, in a rhythm that echoes in my heart. Her hand moves up and down my cock, her thumb exploring the sensitive underside before curling around to circle the tip. My toes curl, and a low groan escapes me.

She's good—very good—every stroke is a deliberate act meant to tantalize, tease, and draw out every shiver and moan from my lips.

My gaze locks on her beautiful eyes, where a mischievous glint tells me she knows exactly what she's doing.

Her lips part, and her tongue darts out as if she's savoring the heat between us. The only sound filling the room is my ragged breathing as her talented touch turns the steady beat of my heart into a frenzied drumbeat of desire, need, and want.

Pressure builds within me. Incrementally, yet inevitable. A crescendo of delicious agony rises within me as her fingers dance along my cock. The slow drag across my flesh, the slight twisting of her hand, and her palm pressing against my length make me acutely aware of every point where our bodies connect.

The press of her thighs around my waist, the softness of her other hand as it rests against my hip, and the drag of her fingernails drive me wild.

She guides me toward an edge I'm more than willing to fall over. With each pass of her hand, pleasure ignites until it turns into something blinding and unstoppable.

Her grip becomes more urgent as if she knows how close I am to breaking beneath her touch. I'd stop her and fuck her, except for one important thing. I find myself shamefully lacking in the tiny foil pouch department.

The first thing on the list after this is to purchase a box of condoms because I plan on being buried balls deep within her before day's end.

But—for right now, there is nothing beyond the hitch in her breath and the magic of her hand.

I groan out her name like a prayer. I'm close. Close to unraveling and coming apart in her more than capable hands. Another moan escapes me, along with a prickling sensation at the base of my spine.

My balls draw up with the pleasure she bestows upon me. My

arms fly around her, steadying myself as my orgasm breaks and barrels down inside of me.

I crest into oblivion, a tidal wave of ecstasy crashing over and through me. White-hot cum spurts between us as my balls clench and release.

Once spent, Jenna wraps her arms around me, enveloping me in the warmth of her body. In the dizzying aftermath of my release, I float in a state of utter peace.

This moment redefines everything, ushering in the beginnings of intimacy savored without restraint. We break apart, breathing hard, our foreheads resting together.

Then, Jenna laughs.

"What's wrong?"

"I think you're burning the bacon."

The acrid scent of bacon burned beyond repair hits my senses.

"Shit."

TWENTY

Jenna

THE SCENT OF BURNING BACON JOLTS ME BACK TO REALITY. I PULL
away from Carter's embrace, my lips still tingling from the intensity
of our kiss.

His eyes snap open and the expression on his face turns into
alarm.

"Oh no." He turns toward the stove, where thick, black smoke
billows from the pan. "Shit! Shit! Shit!"

Carter springs into action, grabbing the handle and moving the
pan off the heat. But it's too late—the bacon is charred beyond
recognition, a blackened mess fused to the bottom of the pan.

The eggs fare no better, the edges brown and crispy, the yolks
cooked solid through.

"I owe you a pan. This one's ruined." Carter looks at the crispy,
charred mess. "Sorry about that. In my defense, I was distracted."

For a moment, we just stare at the ruined breakfast, and then, as
if on cue, we burst out laughing.

"I can't believe we got so carried away we forgot about the
food." My laughter has me leaning against the counter for support.

"I guess you could say things got a little—heated." Carter's eyes sparkle with mirth, and something deeper, something naughty and delicious, sends a shiver down my spine.

"That was awful." I groan at the terrible pun, swatting him playfully on the arm.

"Yeah, well, so is this bacon." He pokes at the blackened mess with a spatula, sending another puff of bitter smoke into the air. "Officially ruined."

"I should open some windows."

The fan over the stove struggles to clear the billowing black smoke. Already, it fills the room. I wave my hand in front of my face, trying to clear the air.

"I think it's safe to say breakfast is a bust."

"I wanted to make you something nice, and instead, I nearly set your kitchen on fire." Carter turns to me, his expression softening. "But, I have to say it was worth it."

"Definitely worth it." My hand lifts to rest on his cheek. "The thought was sweet, but the kiss... That kiss was..."

I trail off, heat rushing to my cheeks as I remember the warmth of his lips pressing against mine, the way his hands tangled in my hair, sending shivers down my spine, and the delicious thrill that coursed through me.

Best damned orgasm ever.

"Just the kiss?" Carter's eyes darken, his gaze dropping to my mouth and then further down.

"Well, the kiss and the..." *Do I tell him?*

"What's wrong? Cat got your tongue? Or is this my woman pretending she's shy about what we just did."

His woman? I like the sound of that.

Shy? Not shy exactly, but he just had his head buried between my legs and his mouth... His mouth and that decadent tongue were phenomenal. It's not shyness. I'm simply not used to talking openly about sex.

His heated gaze makes me tremble. For a second, I think he's going to kiss me again, and my heart kicks into overdrive, but then he clears his throat, stepping back slightly.

"How about I take you out for breakfast instead?" He brushes a strand of hair behind my ear, his touch lingering. "There's a great little diner down the street."

As tempting as the offer is, the thought of abandoning my café for even longer sends a pang of guilt through me.

"Actually, I need to get to the café. I've been neglecting it, and I don't want to leave Malia in a lurch again."

Carter's shoulders relax, but a flicker of disappointment flashes in his eyes. An idea strikes me, and I reach out to take his hand.

"But why don't you and Max come with me? I'll make you a coffee. We can have scones, and we can sit and talk before the morning rush hits."

"That sounds perfect." His face lights up, a genuine smile spreading across his handsome features.

Warmth spreads through my chest. The significance of his willingness to join me at the café fills me with a sense of contentment.

"Great. Just let me get changed, and we can head out."

Taking a look around, I see the mess we've made—the burnt food, dirty dishes, and the general chaos of my usually tidy kitchen—and I don't mind it one bit.

The air remains charged with the palpable chemistry sparking between us. A glimmer of something new, something precious and fragile, is blooming between us.

I have a pep to my step and a new vitality surges through my body. It's strange how Carter has this effect on me. He turned an ordinary morning into something extraordinary.

This thing between us—feels real, like the beginning of something more than a fling. My heart flutters at the thought, and excitement bubbles up inside me.

However, the urgency of getting back to reality and back to work helps me focus. I slip into the bedroom, pulling on my usual attire—a pair of comfortable jeans and a soft, loose-fitting cotton shirt that somehow always smells faintly of cinnamon and vanilla, the signature scents of my café.

As I brush my hair, I take a moment to look at myself in the mirror. I can't help but smile.

The reflection shows a woman transformed, her eyes sparkling with a newfound excitement. My face has a radiance, a glow that wasn't there before.

I head back to the living room to find Carter dressed and casually leaning against the wall, looking every bit the man who unraveled me less than an hour ago.

Max sits beside him, ever attentive, but when I walk into the room, Max's tail thumps wildly, making his butt wiggle with excitement.

The walk to my shop is quiet, filled with comfortable silence and stolen glances. The crisp air nips at our skin, an invigorating reminder of the start of a fresh, new day. Carter walks close beside me, his presence a magnetic force I naturally gravitate toward. Max trots a few feet ahead, enjoying sniffing all the wonderful smells that fill a dog's world.

Every now and then, our hands brush against each other's, and the brief contact sends a jolt of electricity surging through me.

I feel like a kid again. Like a girl on her first date.

Of course, I never had one of those.

This is all new and thrilling; it's awakening a part of me I thought was long buried. The butterflies in my stomach flutter wildly, making me feel both nervous and exhilarated. It's a sensation I never imagined I'd experience, and it fills me with a giddy, almost youthful excitement.

By the time we round the corner and the café comes into view, I'm a bundle of nerves. My home away from home, the café's windows are frosted from the warmth inside, meeting the cool embrace of morning air outside.

The quaint charm of my small establishment always fills me with pride—the hanging baskets outside, still blooming with vibrant fall flowers, and the hand-painted sign I created myself, which sways in the wind over the door.

When we arrive, the bell jingles. My shop is quiet, the peaceful ambiance contrasting with the passion we shared a short while ago.

Malia is already here. She looks up from behind the counter, her eyes widening when she sees Carter and Max walking in with me. Her apron is dusted with flour, giving evidence of the early baking we do every day to ensure our customers have only the freshest baked goods.

Immediately upon entering, the rich aroma of freshly ground coffee envelops us, a comforting embrace that feels like home. The familiar sounds of clinking dishes and soft music fill the air, creating a soothing background noise that blends seamlessly with the hum of conversation.

The warm, earthy tones of the rustic wooden tables and the soft cushioned chairs invite patrons to sit and stay a while.

To get comfortable… As if they were at home.

The sunlight streaming through the large windows casts a golden glow, adding to the cozy ambiance. This place is more than just a coffee shop; it's a haven, a sanctuary where the outside world fades away, and people can relax and be themselves.

It's the heart of our little community, where every brewed cup and smiling face reminds me why I love what I do. This is where connections are made, laughter echoes, and I find peace.

The morning rush is nearly over, but soon, it will fill back up with regulars craving caffeine, conversation, and light lunch fare.

"Have a seat." I squeeze Carter's arm. "I'll whip us up something special. Something not burned."

"Ah, but the burning was worth it." Carter wraps an arm around my waist and tugs me close.

In full view of the café, he plants a kiss on my mouth and releases me. Carter and Max settle into a corner booth while I head behind the counter to whip up some coffee and scones to replace the charred mess we dumped in the trash.

When I brush past Malia, she whispers low in my ear. "It looks like someone had an interesting morning." Her knowing smirk causes me to sweat. "About time Detective Carter stepped up to the plate. I take it you had a good night?"

"Is it that obvious?"

"Please," Malia scoffs, tying her hair back into a ponytail. "The sexual tension between you two could power the whole block. I'm just glad you finally did something about it."

"I'll fill you in later." Although, the blush creeping up my cheeks will make that conversation unnecessary.

"Abandoning your shop for a man and his dog? I'm guessing a *good* night and an even *better* morning? Is that why you're late?" Malia's smart and can easily put two and two together. "I must say I approve. We've all been taking bets on when the two of you would finally give in to the sexual chemistry swirling in the air whenever the two of you are together."

"Give in?" My brows tug tight with a question. "You've been taking bets?"

How can that be? Carter's basically ignored me until this case forced his hand.

"It's about damn time the two of you figured things out." Her eyes twinkle with amusement.

I start the espresso machine—it sputters to life, ready to craft a masterpiece.

Ever since Carter mentioned he's not really into coffee, I've been thinking up different concoctions, hoping to find one he'll love.

I get to work on my creation, steaming milk until it reaches a satiny perfection, extracting shots that drip with molten goodness into pre-warmed cups. Each gets topped with a latte, and I add an artful flourish imbued with care and attention.

As I prep Carter's coffee, I steal glances at him sitting in the booth. He's chatting on the phone with someone. Max sits at his feet, ears perked as if he understands every word.

It strikes me how effortlessly Carter has woven himself into the fabric of my life. Just days ago, we were virtual strangers.

He came in every day like clockwork, and I had his order hot and waiting for him. We were casual strangers.

Today, however… Well today, we crossed an invisible border into becoming something else.

I assemble a variety of scones prepared earlier by Malia—some plump with berries, others fragrant with a bit of zest, and, of course, one with chocolate chips nestled inside. I plate them along-side a drizzle of honey and a dollop of clotted cream. A sprig of mint adds the final touch.

Perfection.

Minutes later, I carry a tray laden with steaming cups and freshly baked scones. Max glances up at me, eyebrows twitching and nose going a mile a minute.

"Breakfast is served." I present the entire thing with a dramatic flourish. "And not a crumb is burnt."

"Smells amazing." Carter takes a deep inhale and closes his eyes, taking a moment to enjoy the rich aroma of the espresso before diving in.

"One coffee for you." I pass Carter his drink. When our eyes meet, a flash of heat burns within me. "And one doggy treat made with extra love for you." I grab one of the scones I make for all four-footed friends who enter my shop and hold it out to Max.

Max takes the treat eagerly, but there's no teeth and no bite. I don't know how a dog like him accomplishes such a feat, considering he's all tooth and fang, but he's got the softest mouth when it comes to me.

Carter takes a sip of his coffee and closes his eyes as the savory flavors hit his tongue. When his eyes open, they fill with barely restrained heat.

"This is incredible." His words are simple, but they're exactly what I need. "It actually tastes good."

"Good? Just good?"

"Absolutely delicious. You may convert me yet to this foul-tasting brew."

"Well, if you'd told me you weren't a coffee fan, I could've converted you before now."

"Ah, it was worth the wait." He takes another sip. "This is really good."

I slide into the booth opposite him and take a sip of my drink. Soon enough, we're settled into our own world.

Malia is a good employee. I should make her a partner. She takes care of the shop while Carter and I finish our breakfast. His steamy gaze never leaves me, and those molten eyes of his hold mine with unspoken promises and lecherous thoughts that go beyond breakfast. It's hard not to squirm in my seat when he looks at me with a knowing smile.

We talk about small things—music we like, books we've read—allowing ourselves this pocket of time to be a normal couple sharing coffee and scones.

It's a bubble of normal, only slightly adjacent to the small part I may or may not play in bringing his missing girls home.

He asks how the shop is doing. How it is that I make the best scones in the world. I answer those animatedly.

We don't discuss heavy things, like his case or what happened between us. As we slip into comfortable conversation, I wonder if this isn't how life could be—filled with simple moments like these.

I like that more than I'm willing to admit.

Max rests his head on Carter's knee while my foot finds its way to Carter's under the table. We play a dangerous game of footsie as if testing whether what happened this morning was a one-and-done kind of thing or the start of something new.

Something exciting.

My heart says the latter.

I don't get a sense Carter's the kind of man who does one-night stands, but if I've read things wrong, I'm willing to make that mistake. I do so because life's too short, too fleeting, not to take a chance.

When his hand reaches across the table to take mine in his, his strong, warm, and reassuring grip puts any fears to rest.

"I should've asked you out a hundred times before this."

"Why didn't you?"

"Because you're gorgeous, and I'm…"

"Only the hottest bachelor in town." *Does he not know?* "I wish you had as well, but that's water under the bridge. We're here now." I lean toward him and lower my voice to a whisper. "For the record, I would've said yes, and Malia tells me there's a bet going around on when the two of us would finally figure things out."

"Really?"

"Yeah." I lean back, drawing my hands back toward me, but

Carter grabs my hands, interlaces our fingers, and pulls my hands back to the center of the table.

When he squeezes my hands, my heart flutters, and I squeeze back. Here in my café with Carter sitting across from me and Max at our feet, breakfast becomes less about the meal and more about whatever this is between us.

After we've devoured all the scones and finished our coffees, I place our dishes on a tray to bus back to the kitchen. When I stand, Carter rises with me.

"Let me help you with those." He reaches for the tray, his hand brushing against mine.

"You don't have to—"

"And yet, it's exactly what I want." He insists, despite my protests, and I don't have the heart to tell him no.

A few minutes later, he's behind the counter with me, back in the kitchen, moving around my space as if it's exactly where he belongs.

There's a certain rightness to it all, and I love how his laughter mingles with the clink of dishes.

It's enough to make me believe in a future of countless mornings exactly like this—the two of us together.

Carter glances at his watch, a slight frown tugging at his lips.

"I should probably get going." Reluctance fills his voice. "I need to get to work."

"Of course." My heart sinks a little, but I understand. I try to keep my disappointment from showing. "I know how important it is."

"Not as important as you." Carter reaches across the table, taking my hand in his. His thumb brushes over my knuckles. "Can I see you tonight?"

"I'd like that." A smile blooms on my face, warmth spreading through my chest. "Who else is going to walk me home?"

"Exactly." He grins, bringing my hand to his lips for a quick kiss. "I'll be here at closing time."

With a final squeeze of my hand and a whistle for Max, Carter heads out, the bell above the door jingling in their wake.

TWENTY-ONE

Jenna

THE REST OF THE DAY PASSES IN A BLUR OF COFFEE ORDERS AND pastry sales, but my mind keeps drifting to Carter, to the promise of seeing him again tonight. Closing can't come soon enough.

As the sun sets and the last customers trickle out, I begin my closing routine. I wipe down tables, restock supplies, and count out the register, the familiar tasks soothing in their repetition.

I'm just locking the front door when Carter and Max approach, silhouetted against the fading light. My heart skips a beat, a smile already tugging at my lips.

"Hey, you," I greet him, stepping onto the sidewalk.

"Hey, yourself." He pulls me in for a hug.

I sink into his embrace, breathing in the scent of him, all coffee and spice and something uniquely Carter.

Max whines, nudging our legs, and we break apart with a laugh.

"Okay, buddy." Carter ruffles the dog's fur. "I think he's jealous."

"I didn't forget about you." I crouch down to pet Max and pull out a treat I grabbed just for him.

With the scent of his treat, Max suffers through my hug, barely restraining himself for his treat.

We set off toward my apartment, Max trotting happily beside us. Carter's hand finds mine, our fingers intertwining like it's the most natural thing in the world.

"How was the rest of your day?" Carter glances down at me.

"Busy, but good. Better now that you're here." I shrug, leaning into his side.

"I know the feeling." He smiles, pressing a kiss to the top of my head.

We walk in comfortable silence for a bit, enjoying each other's presence. It's easy being with Carter. Like I can finally breathe after holding my breath for so long.

When we reach my apartment, I unlock the door. Max bounds inside ahead of us, like he owns the place. Carter follows me in, his hand resting on the small of my back.

"Are you hungry?" I turn to face him. "I could make us something."

"I'm not hungry for food." He shakes his head, his eyes never leaving mine.

"What are you hungry for?" My breath catches when his heated gaze simmers. As his meaning sinks in, my pulse quickens and a blush creeps up my neck. "Oh."

In answer, he cups my face and kisses me, deep and slow and thorough. I melt into him, my hands fisting in his shirt, pulling him closer.

We stumble toward the bedroom, shedding clothes as we go. There's no hesitation, no uncertainty. Just the two of us, lost in each other, in the fire burning between us.

As we reach the bedroom, he gently pushes me back onto the bed, his body hovering over mine. His weight is grounding, cocooning me in safety and arousal. His hands map my curves reverently, igniting sparks of pleasure beneath my skin. His lips never leave mine, the kiss growing more intense with every passing moment. He's all virile masculinity, radiating heat, passion, and desire.

I grip his arms, loving his strength as he holds himself above me. But I want more. I arch into his caress.

"Carter," I breathe, his name a benediction on my lips. I need to feel his skin against mine, to be one with him.

His heated gaze rakes over my bare flesh. Admiration and desire burn in his eyes, making me feel cherished and beautiful. He drinks in the sight of me.

"You're exquisite," he murmurs, voice heavy with need and want.

He trails his fingers down my side, sending shivers of pleasure coursing through me. His touch is gentle yet insistent, exploring every curve and contour of my body. I arch into him, craving more, and he answers my silent plea, his lips moving to my neck, then lower, painting a trail of kisses down to my collarbone.

The ache between my legs grows, throbbing with insistence. I reach for him, desperate to feel his bare skin against mine. To taste him, to be claimed by him.

His hands slide up my thighs, his touch igniting a fire within me. I gasp as he teases me, his fingers skimming the edges of my most sensitive areas. The anticipation is almost unbearable, and I squirm beneath him, desperate for more.

Carter smiles against my skin, knowing exactly what he's doing to me. He takes his time, drawing out every sensation, every feeling. His mouth finds its way to my breasts, lavishing them with attention, drawing out a moan from deep within me.

I reach for him, my hands gripping his shoulders, pulling him closer. I want to feel him, all of him. He obliges, positioning himself between my legs, the heat of his body pressing against mine. Our breaths mingle, our hearts beating in sync as we become one.

Then, with a smirk, he kisses a hot trail of kisses from my breasts to my core. He settles between my thighs, hot breath ghosting over my slick folds. He hesitates a moment before making contact, his tongue a searing swipe through my soaked heat.

The sensation is electric, a live wire of pleasure shooting through my veins. I cry out, fingers twisting in his hair, anchoring him to me. Demanding more. He licks me deeply, savoring my taste and my responsiveness. Building me higher with each swirl of his tongue, each nip of his teeth.

"Yes, exactly like that," I gasp, hips undulating, seeking the exquisite pressure of his mouth. Pressure coils low in my belly, coiling tighter and tighter. I'm spiraling ever higher, climbing towards the pinnacle.

He works me expertly, intimately, until I'm shuddering around him, my release crashing over me in intense, white-hot waves. Pleasure courses through me, radiating from my core to the tips of my tingling fingers and toes. I moan his name, a rapturous chant.

With a deep groan, he abandons my throbbing sex, kissing his way back up my quivering body, lingering at my breasts, sucking and biting, stoking the embers once more.

With a quick rip of foil, the thick head of his cock nudges my slick entrance. His muscles are coiled, taut with restraint as he braces himself above me, his forearms caging me in his strong embrace.

He enters me slowly, his eyes locked on mine. I gasp at the fullness, the stretching, the perfect fit. He's overwhelming me, completing me. My body was made for his.

"You are mine now," he growls, voice rough with lust and possessiveness. And then he starts to move, driving into me with deep, powerful strokes.

We move together, our bodies in perfect harmony, each thrust building the fire within us.

I cling to him, nails raking down his back, hips rising to meet his thrusts. The pleasure builds again, cresting higher each time his pelvis grinds against mine.

"Yes, yes, yes," I chant, lost in the exquisite friction, in the moment of abandon, of letting go. "Don't stop! I'm so close..."

He takes me hard and fast, giving me everything I need and more. Angling his hips to hit that magic spot deep inside, pushing me over the precipice.

Ecstasy explodes through me, more intense than before. I convulse around him, crying out, my pleasure consuming me. I'm drowning in sensation, in emotion, in love.

Seconds later, he joins me, his body tensing before he collapses on top of me, his breath ragged. His choked shout of my name is rapture personified. We collapse together, a tangle of writhing limbs. Skin slick with sweat. Hearts pounding. Basking in the afterglow.

Pressing tender kisses to my face, my eyelids, my nose, he whispers in my ear. "Now, that was worth the wait."

I burst into laughter, the sound bubbling up from my chest. "You have no idea," I murmur against his lips, shaking my head in amused disbelief. "I've imagined it so many times but never thought it would be so—incredible."

"You doubted my skills?" He brushes an errant strand of hair off my face.

"Never."

"Good, because that's just the beginning, my love." His eyes twinkle with wicked intent. "We've got a lifetime of nights like this ahead of us."

"You're impossible." I can't help but laugh, feeling a wave of warmth and happiness wash over me. I smile up at him, my fingers tracing the lines of his face.

In his arms, I find home. Safe, cherished, secure. And loved, wholly and completely. Here, I can escape my nightmares. Here, I can heal.

In his arms…

The world outside fades away, leaving only Carter and me. We're lost in each other, in the heat and passion of our connection.

We cling to each other, our bodies tangled together, our breaths slowly returning to normal. The room is filled with the lingering scent of passion, and I can't help but smile, feeling a sense of completeness I've never known.

Exhausted but sated, we lie tangled together, Carter's heartbeat steady beneath my cheek. A profound sense of peace washes over me. I feel like I'm exactly where I'm meant to be. We're two halves of a whole, inextricably linked. With his arm wrapped around me, I drift off to sleep, safe and content in his arms, unaware of the nightmares lurking in my dreams.

TWENTY-TWO

Carter

I barely drift off to sleep before Jenna's sudden thrashing and whimpers jolt me awake. In the darkness of her bedroom, the only light comes from the faint moonlight filtering through the curtains, casting eerie shadows on the walls.

Jenna's forehead glistens with sweat, her body tangled in the sheets as she battles her nightmares.

"Jenna, wake up. It's just a dream," I whisper, my voice steady and soothing.

"No… Please… I'm sorry…" Her mumbled words are punctuated by unintelligible pleas. "Don't… Please, don't put me in there…"

I reach out, gently smoothing her damp hair away from her face, but my touch triggers a violent response.

Jenna's eyes snap open, wild and unfocused, and before I can react, her fist connects with my jaw. Pain explodes in my face, the sharp taste of blood on my tongue.

Despite the throbbing ache, I can't help but chuckle at her mean right hook.

"Jenna, wake up." I try to keep my voice calm, but urgency bleeds through. "You're having a nightmare."

Alerted by the commotion, Max jumps up on the bed, his soft whines joining my efforts to wake her. He nuzzles Jenna's hand, offering his own brand of comfort, then licks her face. Though I don't usually allow him on the bed, I let it slide, seeing how Jenna responds to his presence.

Jenna finally wakes. She scrambles away from me, pressing herself against the headboard. Her chest heaves with panicked breaths; her fear a palpable presence in the air.

Max cocks his head, a low whine escaping as he moves in to cuddle with her. Not wanting to add further insult to injury, I hold up my hands in a placating gesture.

"Hey, it's okay. It's me, Carter. You're safe. You're in your apartment. In your bed. Max is here too. Everything's alright."

Recognition slowly seeps into her eyes, her body sagging with relief as she whispers my name.

"Carter?"

"Yes, love. It's me. And Max is here too. He's worried about you."

Gathering her into my arms, she shakes against me, her skin clammy and her nightgown damp with sweat. The sour scent of fear clings to her, mixing with the lavender of her shampoo and the fragrance of her sheets.

"I've got you. You're safe. It was just a bad dream." I rub slow circles on her back, trying to calm her down.

She clings to me, her fingers digging into my shoulders almost painfully. Max offers his own brand of comfort as he senses her distress. Which means he nuzzles and licks her until she lifts an arm and pulls him close to her side.

The three of us stay like that for a long moment, holding each other in the darkness as Jenna's breathing gradually evens out. Tension slowly drains from her body. I brush a strand of hair from her damp forehead, tucking it behind her ear.

"Want to talk about it?"

"It was Lucian. He was punishing me…" Shuddering, she presses her face into my chest, her voice muffled against my skin. "He was making us run laps in the freezing rain. I collapsed… And then—and then he put me in the hole."

Anger and protectiveness surge through me. My arms tighten around her. The thought of what she endured and the cruelty she faced makes me want to find Lucian and make him pay.

"He can't hurt you anymore. I won't let anyone hurt you ever again." My voice is rough with emotion, my jaw clenched tight.

She nods against my chest, trembling with the aftereffects of her dream. Her heart races beneath my palm, and her breaths come out staggered and raw.

"I'm sorry I woke you." Her fingers brush over my jaw, feeling the tenderness there. "Oh God, did I hit you?"

"It's nothing. I've had worse from Max's tail when he's excited." I catch her hand and press a kiss on her palm.

That earns me a watery chuckle and a small smile curving her lips. We settle back down. Jenna curls into my side, her head on my chest. Not to be left out, Max snuggles with us. His warmth and weight are a comfort to her, so I don't order him off the bed.

He can have this.

I stroke Jenna's hair, trying to soothe her back to sleep, and smile at how she and Max are bonding. It means a lot to me because as much as I love Jenna, I could never get rid of him.

"Max, you're such a good boy." She scratches his ears as we all settle back down.

I have a feeling my No-Dogs-In-Bed-Rule is about to be broken.

He's a good dog, and he makes her happy. When it comes down to it, that's all that matters. Although, I'm not sure how I feel about sharing my bed with a dog.

I press a kiss to the top of her head and breathe in her scent, cherishing this moment, but even as her breathing deepens and evens out, I remain awake, staring into the darkness.

My mind churns with worry, with the need to protect her and find the bastards who hurt her, ensuring they never touch her again.

Her anxiety and fear are getting worse by the day.

This isn't lost on me. It breaks my heart to see her like this, to know that even in sleep, she can't escape the horrors of her past.

With those thoughts swirling in my head, I finally drift into an uneasy sleep.

I wake to the soft sound of Jenna's breathing, her body warm and pliant against mine. The first rays of morning light filter through the curtains, casting a gentle glow across her peaceful face.

Careful not to disturb her, I press a soft kiss on her forehead and slip out of bed. Max lifts his head, his tail thumping against the mattress as he watches me with sleepy eyes. I give him a quick scratch behind the ears before heading to the kitchen to start the coffee.

It doesn't take long before the rich aroma fills the apartment, mingles with the crisp morning air that seeps in through the cracks in the windows. It's cold, hinting at the coming winter, but the warmth of the coffee and the promise of a hot shower chase away the chill.

I'm just pouring two steaming mugs when Jenna surprises me by wrapping her arms around my waist. I was so intent on making breakfast that I didn't hear her enter.

"Morning. Smells good." She molds her body against my back. Her voice is still husky with sleep.

"Coffee or me?" I turn in her arms, handing her a mug with a smile.

"Both." She takes a sip, her eyes sparkling over the rim of the mug.

She sets the mug down and grabs the waistband of my briefs, pulling me out of the kitchen with a seductive smile. I stumble slightly, torn between my desire for her and the sizzling bacon on the stove.

"Wait." I chuckle and gently stop her. "As much as I want to follow you right now, I'm not burning breakfast twice. I learned my lesson last time."

"Well, we can't have that, can we?" Jenna's eyes sparkle with mirth and mischief.

She releases me with a wink, letting me hurry back to the stove to save our meal. I quickly flip the bacon and scramble the eggs, the tantalizing aroma filling the kitchen.

"Okay," I announce, putting the food in the oven to keep it warm and safe from Max. "Breakfast is officially saved. Now, where were we?"

Jenna saunters over, a playful grin on her face. "I believe I was about to lure you back to the bedroom."

"Ah, yes." I pull her into my arms. "Lure away, my temptress."

Laughing, she takes my hand and guides me down the hallway. We make our way back to the bedroom, the promise of sex hanging thick in the air.

Her fingers trail along my skin as we move, leaving goosebumps in their wake. I can't resist pulling her close, capturing her lips in a deep, lingering kiss. She tastes like coffee and something uniquely Jenna, a flavor I'm quickly becoming addicted to.

We shed our clothes slowly, savoring each brush of skin against skin. Jenna's hands explore my body, her touch both tender and electrifying. I return the favor, mapping out her curves and planes, committing every inch to memory.

Our kisses grow more heated, more urgent, as our desire builds. Jenna's fingers tangle in my hair, tugging gently as she pulls me closer. I groan into her mouth, my hands sliding down to grip her hips, pressing her against me.

We stumble toward the bathroom, reluctant to break contact for even a moment. Jenna reaches into the shower and turns on the water, adjusting the temperature until steam fills the room.

She steps back into my arms, her skin flushed and her eyes dark with want. "I need you," she whispers, her lips brushing against mine. "Now."

Words fail me in the face of her raw honesty. I guide her into the shower, following close behind.

The shower beckons, steam already fogging up the glass. We step in together, the hot water cascading over us. Jenna tilts her head back, letting the spray wet her hair, and I can't resist pressing kisses along the column of her throat.

She sighs, her hands sliding over my slick skin, pulling me closer. Our bodies align, fitting together as if we were designed solely to please each other. The heat between us builds to a slow, delicious burn that consumes every thought and every breath.

We take our time exploring and discovering, losing ourselves in sensation. Jenna's sighs and soft moans mingle with the pounding of the water, a symphony of pleasure that echoes off the tiled walls.

As we make love to each other under the spray, the outside world fades away. There's nothing but this moment, this connection, the overwhelming rightness of being together.

Afterward, we towel off languidly, stealing kisses and soft touches. Jenna's skin glows, her eyes bright and sated. I pull her close, breathing in the scent of her damp hair, a mix of her shampoo and something intrinsically her.

"I could get used to mornings like this." I nuzzle her neck, wishing we never had to leave her apartment.

She hums in agreement, her fingers playing idly with the hair at the nape of my neck. "Me too. Waking up with you, it feels…"

"Right," I finish for her, pulling back to meet her gaze. "It feels right."

She smiles, soft and radiant, and leans in to kiss me once more. It's a promise, a seal on this moment, on everything we've shared.

As we eventually make our way back to the kitchen, drawn by the enticing aroma of coffee and the promise of breakfast, I can't wipe the grin off my face.

This, right here, is everything I never knew I needed. Now that I've found it, I'm never letting go.

I turn the stove back on and finish cooking the eggs and bacon. Today, the wonderfully delicious aroma of crisp bacon and eggs fills the apartment, rather than the charred stink of burnt eggs.

Jenna laughs as she watches me man the stove, spatula in hand. Her eyes are bright with glee, and she can't resist a little teasing.

"At least this time, we didn't ruin breakfast because we got distracted."

"I'm a fast learner." I flip a perfectly crispy strip of bacon.

We eat at the counter, Jenna's hand resting on my thigh as we talk about the day ahead. It's a simple moment, but one that fills me with warmth. These small pockets of time feel precious and fragile in the face of all we're up against.

Max and I walk with her to the café. The streets are quiet. The town's just starting to wake up around us.

Max trots at our heels, his nose to the ground as he takes in all the fascinating smells. At the door to the café, I pause, an idea forming in my mind. I scratch Max behind the ears.

"What would you think if I left Max with you for the day? He can look over you while I'm gone."

"That would be great. Max is always welcome here." Jenna's face lights up, her hand automatically reaching out to pet Max's head.

Max senses a change in plans. His tail wags with excitement as he leans into Jenna's touch. As I head off toward Guardian HRS headquarters, there's a strange emptiness at my side, a space that's usually filled by Max's comforting presence.

TWENTY-THREE

Carter

While I miss Max at my side, he's in good hands with Jenna. If I had to be jealous of anyone stealing my dog's affection, I'm glad it's her.

I make the hour-long drive to Guardian HQ in record time. It's early, and traffic is light. As I pull up to the entrance of the tech center, Blake waits for me, his tall frame leaning against the sleek glass doors.

"Well, well, well, look who decided to show up," Blake calls out as I exit my vehicle, a smirk playing on his lips.

"I wasn't expecting a welcoming committee." I grab my bag from the passenger seat. "And what do you mean by 'decided to show up'?" I glance at my watch. "I'm right on time."

Blake chuckles, shaking his head as I approach him. "In the world of Guardian HRS, on time is late. Early is on time."

I roll my eyes. "I'll keep that in mind for next time."

"You do that." Blake grins, pulling me into a quick hug. "It's good to see you."

"You too. Even if you are busting my chops first thing in the morning."

"First thing? Dude, I've been up for hours. It's practically mid-day for me."

We head inside, and I can't help but be impressed by the sleek, modern interior. The Guardian HRS building is all clean lines and reinforced steel, designed to withstand any threat. It's an imposing structure, and walking through its doors fills me with a sense of awe.

"Impressive, isn't it?" Blake watches my reaction with a smirk on his face and a mischievous glint in his eyes.

"It's certainly something," I admit. "I'm extraordinarily lucky to have Guardian HRS helping me with this case—although I hate that you are."

"Why's that?" Blake's expression turns serious.

"The only reason you're involved is because my case ties in with an organization you've been struggling to bring down. It's fortuitous, but I hate that it means there are other victims in need." My jaw clenches, and my gut churns.

"Unfortunately, it's true, but look at us, Blake and Carter Jackson, the super twins working together again. Vile assholes aside, I'm stoked we finally get to work together. It's been too long since we've been a team."

We continue into the main part of the facility, and I'm struck by the level of activity. Computers hum, their screens casting a bluish glow across the faces of the analysts hunched over their keyboards. Monitors line the walls, displaying real-time feeds from around the world. The air crackles with tension and purpose.

Everyone here is focused on a singular goal—protecting the innocent and bringing the guilty to justice.

"It's a bit mind-boggling, if I'm being honest." I run a hand through my hair, feeling a pang of defeat. "I wish I had access to similar resources at my job."

"Well, that's what happens when you work for the underfunded good guys instead of the super-secret, high-tech organization with all the dough in the world."

I elbow him in the ribs. "Watch it, or I'll tell everyone about the time you cried during 'The Notebook.'"

"You wouldn't dare." Blake narrows his eyes at me.

"Try me." I grin.

Blake shakes his head, a smile tugging at his lips. "Come on, let's go see what miracles we can work with that evidence of yours."

I follow him deeper into the facility, ready to see what Guardian HRS can bring to the table. With their resources and my determination, it's only a matter of time before we find a way to bring down the monsters behind this case and save the lives hanging in the balance.

I have to say, it puts my dingy office to shame. As we walk to a briefing room where we'll work on my case, I make a conscious effort not to leave my jaw gaping.

This place is—*intense.*

I can't help but reflect on the path not taken. As twins, Blake and I are close—closer than most siblings. Nearly inseparable comes to mind.

But our lives took very different turns.

He joined the Navy, became a SEAL, and now works with this incredible team. I was lied to; told I'd knocked a girl up. I did the honorable thing. Then I found out I got played. By then, it was too late to change course.

Sometimes, I wonder what my life would look like if I had followed Blake into the Navy. But then I think of my work as a detective, of the people I've helped and the difference I've made.

It's not as flashy as what he does here, but it matters.

I'm good at what I do—exceptional even—and I wouldn't trade it for anything.

My thoughts are interrupted by Mitzy, who enters with flair and a bustle of energy. She moves to the front of the room, a grim look on her face, and says nothing. Immediately, her fingers fly over her keyboard as images flash across the screen behind her. She starts speaking without lifting her eyes from the screen in front of her.

"I've been working on identifying the men in Jenna's sketches. We found nothing on facial reconstruction, but I thought I could tweak the parameters to adjust for any reconstructive work done. Unfortunately, I've hit a wall. These men—they've undergone extensive surgery, making facial recognition impossible, even for my algorithms."

Everyone in the room deflates a little at the news of the facial reconstructions. It's a dead end, a roadblock in our investigation. A murmur goes through the room. The frustration and disappointment of the others is palpable. I feel it too, a sinking feeling in my gut.

Blake has mentioned Mitzy's incredible skills more times than I can count. Mitzy Magic, he calls it, and I expect miracles.

"If Mitzy can't work her magic, where does that leave us?" I nudge Blake and lean in close, keeping my voice low.

"Just wait." Blake leans back with a shit-eating grin on his face. "You've yet to see it."

"It?"

I look around the room at the stony expressions of Blake's teammates and the pensive expressions on Stitch and Jeb's faces. They're locked into whatever they're doing with their computers, but if there's any magic going on, I fail to see it.

"Mitzy isn't one to give up easily." He gives a cheekish grin.

Suddenly, Mitzy's eyes light up, a spark of excitement animating her features.

"The architecture." Her voice rises with anticipation.

"What?" Once again, I lean toward Blake, hoping for an explanation.

"Just wait…" Blake places his hands behind his head, lacing his fingers together. Asshole is having fun with this.

But I still don't see any Mitzy Magic.

"Stitch…" Mitzy points to the goth chick, another female hacker with impressive skills—or so I'm told. "That building has a distinct style. Have you run it to see if we can identify the architect? That might give us what we need."

"On it, boss." Stitch leans close to Jeb.

Stitch and Jeb put their heads together. Then they turn as one to face their screens. The interaction is a bit creepy as if they're thinking with one brain.

The room erupts into a flurry of activity, everyone energized by this new lead. Meanwhile, Mitzy leans forward, resting her elbows on the table. She looks directly at me, a glint of determination in her eye.

"I've already sent the sketches to my geo-locating friends. Jenna's drawings aren't as good as actual photographs, but it's something."

"How does that matter?" I don't pretend to understand a tenth of what this woman can do.

"Photographs capture the height of the sun, cloud cover, shadows, and other visual clues, but Jenna's sketches are better than nothing. They're working on pinpointing the location of the facility as we speak. I'm just waiting for word back from them."

Maybe this is Mitzy Magic?

Hard to say. This seems to be an everyday thing for these people, but my mind is blown. I'm an excellent detective and can close cases with basically nothing but the barest thread to stitch together a case.

Now, if I had access to their resources?

Fuck, that would be epic.

As if on cue, Mitzy's computer pings, a new message flashing across the screen. Her brow furrows in concentration. The room holds its collective breath, waiting.

Then, a grin spreads across Mitzy's face. "They found it. The compound where Jenna was trained. It's about a three-to-four-hour drive from here." She looks up at me, her expression softening. "About two hours north from you."

The entire vibe of the room suddenly shifts. Everyone, including me, sits up straighter, and the air crackles with renewed energy.

Blake leans in. "Told ya. Now that's a bit of Mitzy Magic."

"Great." Sam, the leader of both the technical and Guardian teams, leans back in his chair, crossing his arms over his chest. "So we know where it is. But who owns it?"

Mitzy's fingers fly over the keys, pulling up new windows and documents. "I'm tapping into the local government's records now. Building plans, construction permits, everything they have on this place."

We watch as blueprints and schematics fill the screens. The

estate takes shape before our eyes. It's a sprawling compound with high walls and fortified gates, just like Jenna described.

Jeb lets out a low whistle. "That's some serious security. Whoever built this place didn't want anyone getting in—"

"Or out." Stitch completes his sentence. "Looks like a prison."

My phone buzzes in my pocket. It's Jenna. I step into the hallway to take the call, concerned something's wrong.

"What's up, love?"

"How's it going over there?" Her voice is warm and comforting in my ear. There's no sign of stress, which means I can relax.

"We're making progress." I lean against the wall, feeling some of the tension drain from my shoulders at the sound of her voice. "How are you holding up?"

"Max has been keeping me company. He's quite the charmer with the customers." Her voice carries a smile, making it easy to imagine the warmth in her eyes. "I think he's interviewing for Marlowe Café Mascot."

"I'm glad you two are getting along. I might start getting jealous."

"Don't worry, Detective." She laughs, and the sound warms me from the inside out. "You're still my favorite."

"Better be after this morning's shower."

We talk for a few more minutes about everything and nothing. Just hearing her voice, knowing she's safe and surrounded by the comforting bustle of the café, eases something in me.

When I step back into the briefing room, the energy is palpable. Mitzy is already deep into planning mode, her fingers flying across the keyboard.

"It's isolated, way off the grid." She pulls up satellite images of a dense forest surrounding the compound. "But it matches Jenna's descriptions perfectly."

"We need eyes on this place. See what we can learn." CJ steps forward, his arms crossed over his broad chest.

"Drones or a recon mission?" Ethan, the leader of Charlie team, speaks up.

"Both." CJ stops his pacing and glances at the schematics of the building displayed on all the monitors in the room. "Mitzy's drones are the best to see if anyone is still there and to get a basic lay of the land, but we need boots on the ground. Drones first to see who's there. Then Charlie team. We'll go in at night and gather what intel we can."

Murmurs of agreement fill the room as they start to plan.

"Mitzy, Stitch, and Jeb," CJ says, "the three of you work on mapping out the compound and identifying potential entry points. Ethan, you take care of logistics—gear, transportation, contingencies."

"Copy that."

"Isn't it risky—showing our hand like this?" I can't help but step up and insert a voice of caution into the mix. "I'm worried us poking around is going to raise questions we don't want them asking."

"We'll be discreet. They won't know we're on to them," CJ's gruff voice fills the room. "It's a risk we have to take. The drones can give us a lot of intel, but boots on the ground is always superior."

They're the experts, but I feel as though this is our first mistake.

TWENTY-FOUR

Jenna

THE NIGHTMARES CONTINUE, AS THEY HAVE EVERY NIGHT THIS WEEK. I'm back in that cold, sterile room, the harsh fluorescent lights buzzing overhead, with the sickly-sweet scent of antiseptic burning my nostrils. Lucian stands before me, his face a mask of cruel indifference.

"Your performance has been unsatisfactory." His voice drips with disdain. "How do you expect to be a successful model if you refuse to follow the simplest commands?"

I try to defend myself, but my tongue feels like lead in my mouth. Lucian's iron will and unyielding gaze rob me of my voice.

"You leave me no choice." He shakes his head in mock disappointment. "You must learn the consequences of disobedience."

Two of his burly guards appear from the shadows, their faces devoid of emotion. They grab me roughly by the arms, their fingers digging into my flesh hard enough to bruise. They drag me down a long, narrow hallway, where the air grows colder with each step, and the walls press in on me.

I can't breathe.

I know where they're taking me.

The solitary detention cell.

I've managed to avoid it since my arrival, but the whispers of the other girls who've spent time down here echo in my mind. Tales of darkness, isolation, and a silence so deep it threatens to swallow you whole. It's the thing nightmares are made of.

They toss me into a small, dark room, the door slamming shut behind me with a sickening thud. I pound on the unyielding metal, my screams echoing in the suffocating darkness.

"Lucian, please!" I beg and scream and beg some more. "I'll do better. I promise."

No one comes.

No one cares.

The dream shifts, and I'm on a cold metal table, my body exposed.

The lingerie savagely ripped from my body. Thick leather straps bind my wrists and ankles. The man who bought me looms over me, his face hidden in shadow.

"This is to mark you as mine." He takes out a small tattoo gun and a bottle of ink. A guard holds my arm steady as the man who bought me begins to tattoo a small, intricate design onto the inside of my wrist. The sharp sting of a needle pierces my skin, a searing pain etching indelible marks into my flesh, but I don't make a sound. I won't give him the satisfaction.

"There," he says, stepping back to admire his handiwork. "Now, you belong to me."

I jolt awake, my heart pounding and my breath coming in short, panicked gasps. The nightmare clings to the edges of my consciousness, but the warmth of Carter's body beside me pulls me back to reality.

I curl into him, his arm draped protectively over my waist, and try to steady my breathing.

"Another nightmare?" His voice is thick with sleep, his fingers combing through my tangled hair.

I nod against his chest, not trusting myself to speak. He pulls me closer, and I bury my face in the crook of his neck, letting his familiar scent and the steady beat of his heart soothe my frayed nerves.

"Do you want to talk about it?" His words are gentle, a lifeline in the darkness. His fingers comb through my tangled hair, soothing me—erasing my fears.

I take a shuddering breath and recount the dream, my voice trembling as I describe the suffocating darkness of the isolation room, the cruel indifference in Lucian's eyes, and the terror of being strapped to that table. Carter listens patiently, his jaw clenching with barely contained anger.

"You're safe now." He presses a soft kiss to my forehead, his promise fierce.

I want to believe him, but the nightmares feel like a warning, a reminder that my past is never far behind.

As dawn breaks, Carter and I begin our morning routine. He's stayed at my place every night since we met with the Guardians, and he's not alone. Max, his loyal German Shepherd, is here too, following us around the apartment, his tail wagging with quiet contentment.

Carter has Max guarding me during the day, a silent protector who brings a sense of security to my battered soul.

What I love best are our mornings.

The domesticity of it all—brewing coffee, sharing a quick breakfast, stealing kisses between bites—feels good.

Carter and Max's presence transforms these simple moments into something precious, making me feel safe and cherished.

"Are you sure you're okay with going to the café today?" Carter asks, concern etching his features as he buttons his shirt. "After last night… I don't want you to push yourself too hard."

I give him a reassuring smile, even as the remnants of the nightmare linger in the shadows of my mind.

"I'll be alright. They're just dreams. With everything that's happened recently, with opening up about my past—it's not surprising they've resurfaced." I rub absently at the hidden tattoo on the inside of my wrist.

In the years since it was placed, I blocked out the memory, completely forgetting about the table, the straps, and the sting of the needle.

Sentinel Nine.

It's hard to believe I was that man's ninth acquisition.

Carter pulls me close, his strong arms wrapping me in the security of his embrace. His gaze conveys incredible compassion and understanding.

"If you change your mind, if you need me, I'm just a phone call away."

"I know." I lean in, pressing a soft kiss to his lips. "But you have important work to do with the Guardians. I've given you all the images and sketches I have. My part in this case is done, which means I can forget about it and focus on what matters."

In other words, I spend my days trying to bury that part of my past. If my nightmares are any indication of how successful that is, then I'm doing a piss poor job of it.

"I don't like being separated from you." Carter's gaze softens.

"Malia's been holding down the fort at the café for too long. It's time for me to return to some semblance of normalcy."

With a final embrace and a promise to check in throughout the day, Carter heads out to continue his collaboration with the Guardian Hostage Rescue Specialists. Max whines softly as the door closes behind Carter, and I give the dog a comforting pat.

"Looks like it's just you and me, buddy." Max's tail thumps against the floor in response. "Let's get this day started."

We walk the few blocks to the café. Max stays by my side, following Carter's orders to protect me. The moment I step through the doorway to my domain, the rich aroma of freshly brewed coffee and the warmth of the ovens chase away any lingering fear from my nightmares.

The familiar routine of brewing coffee and baking scones helps to ground me, and soon, I'm lost in the comforting bustle of the morning rush.

Around mid-morning, a man walks into the café. He's tall and broad-shouldered, with a neatly trimmed beard and dark piercing eyes. His well-tailored suit and polished shoes speak of refinement and wealth. When he approaches the counter, his deep, cultured voice sends an involuntary shiver down my spine.

"Two large coffees, please."

Something in his voice is vaguely familiar, but I can't quite place it.

I ring up his order and set about preparing his coffee. As I work, he watches me, his gaze assessing and intense—intrusive even.

It's not unusual—I'm used to men staring, a byproduct of my appearance—but it still makes me uncomfortable. I focus on the task at hand, trying to ignore the prickle of unease on the back of my neck.

When I hand him the coffee, our fingers brush briefly. A feeling I can't quite name passes through me, gone as quickly as it came. He takes the drinks with a polite nod, leaves a massive tip, and exits my shop, climbing into a nondescript sedan parked across the street.

As the day wears on, I glance out that window more times than I care to admit. Something about that man makes me edgy and jumpy.

My thoughts drift to Carter. I wish he were here. His solid presence is reassuring when my thoughts get muddied. I'm ashamed to admit it, but the stranger's visit unsettles me more than it should.

I shrug it off, however, attributing it to my nightmares, and if I'm being honest, all he did was order two coffees and leave.

I feel out of sorts.

Hyperaware.

Letting my imagination run wild.

As much as I wish Carter was here with me, his work is important. The missing girls need him more than I do. I know this, but the longing persists, a dull ache in my chest that won't go away.

The next few days pass in a blur of caffeine and growing paranoia. The same man returns every day, always cordial and polite, but something about him puts me on edge.

His car is parked outside the café at odd hours, sometimes in the early morning when I arrive to open up, other times late at night as I'm locking the doors. Sometimes, he comes alone, ordering a single coffee, but other times, he orders two. When he does, I peek out the window and see another figure in the sedan, not in the passenger seat, but in the back.

It makes me think the man works for whoever is sitting in the car, an odd arrangement that sets off alarm bells in my head.

But I'm being foolish.

My nerves are frayed, and tension twists through me as my overactive imagination creates shadows in every corner. I remind myself it's just the lingering effects of my nightmares and that I'm overreacting.

But the unease continues to build.

Every now and then, a prickling sensation of being watched comes over me. It never quite goes away and turns into a constant companion that sets my nerves on edge.

I rationalize my unease, chalking it up to my recent nightmares, but the feeling of being watched persists.

I wish for Carter's presence more and more, longing for the safety and comfort of his arms. But I don't want to burden him, not when he's so close to cracking the case of the missing girls. So, I keep my fears to myself, trying to push through the growing sense of dread that follows me like a shadow.

As I walk home from the café with Max by my side, the unease that's been building over the past few days reaches a crescendo. The streetlights flicker to life, casting eerie shadows on the pavement. Max presses close to my leg, a comforting presence in the growing darkness, but I still feel uneasy.

I can't explain it better than that.

Inside my apartment, I make dinner. The routine of chopping vegetables and stirring pots helps soothe my frayed nerves, but it's a temporary distraction.

Max settles at my feet, his warm weight a reminder that I'm not alone. He makes me feel safe, and if anything bad happens, he'll alert and protect me.

No sooner does that thought cross my mind than Max's head jerks up. His ears thrust forward, and a low, menacing growl reverberates deep within his chest.

The hairs on my arms stand up.

A sharp and insistent knock rattles the door, setting Max off. He erupts in a frenzy of snarling and barking, all teeth and fangs. His hackles raise as he lunges toward the door, snapping with his teeth at a threat beyond the door.

TWENTY-FIVE

Jenna

Max is all teeth and fur, terrifying yet comforting. His presence reassures me, a fierce protector in the face of unknown threats. I'm profoundly relieved he's on my side.

Yet, my heart catches in my throat. Hands trembling, I creep toward the door and press my eye to the peephole.

My breath hitches.

But there's no one there.

The silence is deafening, broken only by Max's growls and the erratic thump of my heartbeat. I swallow hard, forcing myself to stay calm, but the unease refuses to dissipate.

Who knocked on my door?

Why did they disappear?

Or are they still out there?

Waiting for me to open the door and look?

"There's nobody there, buddy." I glance down at Max, but my reassurance is more for me than it is for him.

I'm about to turn away when the sound of a key in the lock sends me stumbling back. The door swings open, and there's Carter. The moment he sees me, his expression turns from casual to concerned.

"What's wrong?" He takes in my pale face and Max's agitated state. "I heard Max barking from down the hall."

"Someone knocked." My voice is thin and reedy, my hands trembling as I wrap my arms around myself. "But when I looked, no one was there. And then you showed up…"

"I didn't see anyone in the hall." Carter's brow furrows, concern etched in the lines of his face. "Tell me what happened. No detail is too small."

I hesitate, biting my lip. "I'm just being silly. It's probably nothing, but…" I trail off, unsure how to put the nagging unease into words.

"But, what?" Carter's hand rests reassuringly on my arm, his touch gentle and encouraging.

"It's just… There's been this new customer. An out-of-towner, probably here on business. I get this weird vibe from him." The words tumble out in a rush, my heart hammering in my chest. "I'm just jumpy."

"A weird vibe?" Carter's eyes sharpen, his body tensing. "What do you mean?"

"I don't know, exactly. It's like—there's just something that feels off about him. He's never there at the same time each day, and I feel like I'm being watched when he's around." A shudder runs through me, goosebumps rising on my skin.

"I'm calling Blake. We need to get you better protection, not that Max isn't good." Carter clenches his jaw. He reaches for his phone, his movements swift and purposeful.

I open my mouth to protest, but the words die on my lips as Carter holds up a hand, his phone already pressed to his ear.

"Listen, we've got a situation." He quickly recaps what I told him, his voice tight with barely contained urgency. "I'm with her at night, but is there something we can do?"

There's a pause as he listens to whoever's on the other end of the line. His free hand clenches and unclenches at his side. Then he nods and his shoulders relax a fraction.

"Okay, good. Thanks, Blake. You're a godsend. Have whoever it is meet me at Marlowe's Café in the morning. I'm not taking any chances with her safety."

He ends the call, turning back to me with fierce determination in his eyes. "Starting tomorrow, Blake says one of his teammates will be at the café during the day. They'll provide protection."

"I don't know that I need protection." I reach down and dig my fingers into the scruff of Max's neck. "Max is plenty of protection."

"Max is a phenomenal dog, but I want more."

"I'm scared." A lump forms in my throat. "Do you think, maybe, that I'm overreacting? Maybe my imagination is out of control. I could just be making things up. Hell, I don't know if I can trust my reactions."

"I find gut instinct is rarely wrong, and if this stranger is some perfectly normal dude, then no harm, no foul. But if it turns out to be something, I'd feel better knowing you have someone close. I'd stay, but—"

"You have a case to solve. I don't want you taking time from that to watch over me. I'll be fine."

But I'm not fine.

My entire body trembles and my hands shake. There's an unsettled feeling in my gut; my ears ring, and it feels as if the world spins beneath my feet.

Is this what a panic attack feels like?

I don't know, and I don't like feeling this way. I'm not some helpless damsel in distress.

When I was building a new life for myself at the Facility, they told us we weren't victims—we weren't allowed to use that word—we were victors, and I've always liked that way of looking at things.

I'm not a victim of my past, but victorious over it.

But…

The reality of the situation crashes over me, and the fear I've been trying to suppress rises to the surface.

Am I really as strong as I believe?

Doubt creeps in, whispering that maybe, just maybe, I'm not as victorious as I've tried to convince myself.

In an instant, Carter's there, pulling me tight against his chest, his embrace tight and fierce.

"I know, baby. I know. I won't let anything happen to you. I swear it."

I cling to him, drawing strength from the solid warmth of his body and the steady beat of his heart against my cheek. For a moment, the world falls away, and it's just us, two people holding onto each other in the face of the unknown.

The safety I feel in his arms is profound.

After a brief and tasteless dinner—the evening's events robbed me of my appetite—Carter and I retire to bed. He holds me through the night, his presence reassuring.

His arms around me—a shield.

His breath against my hair—a reminder I'm not alone.

But closeness stirs our desire.

What begins as a comforting embrace deepens into something more. Cuddling turns to kissing, kissing turns to touching, and touching turns into an exploration of the bond we share. His lips are soft yet insistent against mine, a silent promise of protection and love.

Desperate hands and fervent kisses become physical affirmations of the love that binds us. My fingers trace the contours of his face, memorizing every line and curve, while his hands roam my back, pulling me closer. Each kiss is an expression of need and reassurance, our breaths mingling in the space between us.

"I need you," I whisper against his lips, the vulnerability in my voice echoing the longing in my heart.

"I'm here," he murmurs, his voice thick with emotion. "Always."

Our movements are slow and deliberate. The outside world fades, leaving only the warmth of our bodies and the intensity of our emotions. In the darkness, we find refuge in each other.

The physical becomes a bridge to the emotional. Our bond deepens, not just in passion but in the silent promises we make with every touch.

His hands are gentle yet firm, guiding me, holding me, and cherishing me. In his arms, I find peace I didn't know was possible.

When we finally lie still, our breaths heavy and intertwined, Carter's presence banishes the darkness. I rest my head on his chest, the steady rhythm of his heartbeat lulling me into a peaceful slumber, safe in the knowledge that, together, we can face anything.

That night, there are no dreams.

No nightmares.

Nothing to disturb my slumber.

Morning comes, and with it, a renewed sense of determination. Carter walks me to the café, Max trotting along happily beside us, sniffing at everything in his path. Carter stays with me as I go through the familiar motions of opening up. His eyes constantly scan the street outside.

There is no sedan. No sign of that man.

About an hour later, a massively muscled man enters the café. I remember him from the meeting at Guardian HRS, but his name escapes me. He and Carter shake hands, a silent communication passing between them. Carter turns to me, his hand resting reassuringly on the small of my back.

"Jenna, you remember Walt?"

Ah, yes, Walt.

"Yes, of course." I shove out my hand to shake, only to have Walt's massive hand engulf mine. Despite the differences in our sizes, his handshake is surprisingly gentle. "Thanks for coming. I feel kind of silly, but I appreciate it."

"Not a problem. Happy to help, and I hear you make the best scones on the planet."

"I don't know about the planet, but they're pretty tasty."

"Nice." Walt glances at the counter, where Malia is taking orders. He pauses for a moment, then heads over with a confident stride. "Hey there, gorgeous." He flashes a charming smile. "What's a guy gotta do to get a cup of the best coffee in town?"

Malia looks up, slightly taken aback but intrigued. "Haven't seen you here before, big guy."

"Well, that is a mistake I intend to rectify. Name's Walt. Friend of Carter's." He introduces himself, leaning casually on the counter. "I've heard a lot about your coffee and scones. Thought I'd see if the hype is real."

"Well, you're in for a treat." Malia smiles, a faint blush coloring her cheeks.

"Only if I have company while I enjoy them. You think your boss will mind?" Walt shamelessly flirts, leaving Malia speechless.

I shake my head at his antics and give Malia the 'Okay' sign. With as much time as I've been taking off, she's due a little bit of fun, and it looks like Walt's willing to give it to her.

Malia laughs softly. "I'll get your order started. You can tell me if it lives up to your expectations."

Walt grins, a playful glint in his eye. "If the coffee is half as sweet as your smile, I'm sure it will."

Malia blushes, her smile widening. "Well, I'll do my best not to disappoint. One coffee and a scone coming right up."

"Thanks." Walt leans on the counter and flashes a roguish grin. "I'm looking forward to it."

Malia's smile lingers as she turns to prep his order.

Oblivious to Walt and Malia's interaction, Carter leans close and gives me a final kiss with a promise to return as soon as possible. I take a deep breath, squaring my shoulders, and turn to face the day ahead.

Walt and Malia hit it off immediately. He hangs by the counter all day, shamelessly flirting with Malia. A big man, his presence is reassuring. I hate to say it because I still think Carter's being overly protective, but I'm glad to have Walt with us for the day.

I try to lose myself in the work, in the familiar rhythm of brewing coffee and greeting customers. The strange man with the dark eyes doesn't come. Not that day or the next.

His absence is more unnerving than his presence. I glance at the street more times than I'm willing to admit, looking for his car. Now, I know I'm being paranoid, and I'm definitely jumpy.

My heart pounds with every shadow that passes by.

As the days go by, each morning brings another of the Guardians to babysit me. Blake, Gabe, Hank, Rigel, and Walt all take turns, but soon, it becomes apparent Walt is here more often than not.

I can't shake the feeling I'm being watched.

That doesn't make sense.

It's been days since the stranger stopped by, which suggests he was in town for business and has since moved on.

My imagination needs to dial it back a notch or two.

One night, after a particularly frantic day, I'm wound tighter than a spring, my nerves frayed to the breaking point, by the time Carter arrives to walk me home.

He steps into the café, his eyes immediately scanning the room until they land on me. The moment he sees my face, his expression shifts from casual to concerned.

"What's wrong?" He strides over, not bothering with greetings. "Did the man show up?"

"No." I shake my head, feeling like a fool. "It's just been a busy day, which is good for business, but I gave Malia the day off. I've been non-stop all day, and I'm just overreacting. It's silly, and I'm a little embarrassed, to be honest."

Carter pulls back slightly, his hands resting on my shoulders, eyes searching mine. "Your instincts are good. If something feels off, it probably is. Let's get you home."

As we leave the café, his protective presence by my side, I feel safe, but a bit of lingering anxiety stays with me. That night, the nightmares return in full force, each one more vivid and terrifying than the last.

I'm back at the compound, forced to run laps around the outer courtyard with the other girls in the pouring rain as punishment for some perceived slight. My lungs burn, and my legs ache, but I don't dare stop, not with Lucian's cruel gaze fixed upon me.

Sophia is there—in my dream—defying Lucian. She stopped running with the rest of us and went up to Lucian, screaming that what he was doing was wrong. She told him she wasn't going to spend one more minute inside his prison.

All Lucian did was snap his fingers.

Before I could blink, those two guards appeared. They dragged

Sophia away. A week later, she returned, bruised and beaten, her fiery spirit extinguished.

In another nightmare, I'm at that final party, the one where I thought I was serving drinks. Sophia warns me to leave. She tells me we are being sold.

I didn't believe her until I stood in front of a stranger who ripped the skimpy lingerie off my body and proclaimed that I belonged to him now.

That night, I was lucky.

I escaped.

But I never saw Sophia again.

The horror of my dreams wakes me each night. I scream and thrash in Carter's arms. He holds me through the worst of it until his soothing words and gentle touch ease me back into a restless sleep.

Each morning, the weight of those nightmares clings to me, a lingering shadow that drains my strength and leaves me feeling hollow inside.

The memory of Sophia's beaten body and the terror of that final party haunt my thoughts, making it hard to focus and hard to breathe.

During the day, I go through the motions, operating on autopilot. At night, the nightmares find me. They sap my strength, making every task feel monumental, every interaction a strain. I flinch at sudden noises, my heart racing as if I'm still trapped in those horrific memories.

And every night, they return in full force, relentless and unforgiving. The darkness brings no relief, only the resurgence of my deepest fears. Carter is always there, his presence calming, but even his strong arms can't shield me from the horrors that replay in my mind. They're a cruel reminder that my past is never truly behind me.

But I refuse to be ruled by fear.

TWENTY-SIX

Carter

IT'S BEEN A WHILE SINCE I WAS A BEAT COP, BUT THE FAMILIAR weight of the gear and the cold steel of a rifle in my hands bring back memories. The skills are forever etched into my muscle memory.

As we gear up, I reflect on the invitation to join Charlie team to check out the compound. I'm grateful for the opportunity but determined not to let the Guardians overshadow my case.

They may want to bring Sentinel down, but I have four young women to save.

The days leading up to the reconnaissance operation are a blur of intense training and meticulous preparation. Blake guides me through the intricacies of Guardian's tactical gear and drills me on coordinated movement until it becomes second nature. I push myself, knowing I need to prove my worth to Blake and his team.

I will not be a liability.

What I'm not used to are the R.U. F. U. S.'s. Robotic Ultra Functional Utility Specialists, affectionately called Rufi, the mechanical dogs move with an uncanny, predatory grace that sets my teeth on edge. I miss Max's presence at my side, but glad he's with Jenna, protecting her when I can't.

The night before the mission, sleep eludes me. I lie awake, staring at the ceiling, my mind churning with dark thoughts and darker possibilities. This may be a recon mission, but the thought of setting foot in the place that haunts Jenna's nightmares fills me with grim, cold anger.

I need to see it, to understand even a fraction of what she went through, to make sense of the horrors she's shared with me. And I believe every word, every painful memory she's trusted me with.

Dawn comes too soon, cold and gray. We muster in the early hours, the base a hive of activity despite the ungodly hour. There's tension in the air, a coiled anticipation that sets my nerves on edge.

We go over the plan one last time, each checking and double-checking our gear. Weapons are cleaned and oiled. Equipment is tested and retested. There's no room for error, not on a mission like this.

Blake catches my eye across the room, giving me a nod of reassurance. I return it, grateful for his steady presence and the unspoken support of his team.

The morning passes in a blur of final preparations and last-minute intel. We pour over the satellite imagery again, committing every detail of the compound's layout to memory.

Mitzy updates us on the latest drone reconnaissance, confirming that the place appears abandoned.

We all know how quickly that can change.

As the hour of our departure draws near, my thoughts turn to Jenna. She survived unimaginable horrors yet built a new life for herself.

That takes grit.

I draw on that now, letting it steel my resolve and sharpen my focus.

We leave after a tense, silent lunch. The weight of what we're about to do hangs heavy in the air. The journey to the target is long, and the silence in the transport is broken only by the occasional crackle of the comm and the low thrum of the engine.

I stare out the window, watching the landscape blur past, my mind racing with possibilities and contingencies. Every mile brings us closer to the place that haunts Jenna's nightmares.

As we travel northward on PCH-1, the rugged coastline and endless ocean to our left, the sun dips toward the horizon, painting the sky in shades of molten gold and crimson fire.

We near our destination, and the fiery colors reflect off the waves, casting a warm, ethereal glow over the landscape. Then comes an hour or so of waiting for darkness to envelop the land.

We park some distance away and navigate with the aid of night vision goggles. The compound rises like a malevolent specter, its high walls and barbed wire looming in the shadows, a foreboding presence against the starless sky.

"Drones show no signs of activity. It looks abandoned." Mitzy's voice crackles over the earpiece.

The Rufi fan out silently around us, their sensors probing the darkness. Through the eerie green of our night vision, the world takes on a ghostly quality. Shadows writhe, and every sound cuts through the silence like a knife, each one sharp enough to quicken the pulse.

"Comms check." Ethan's voice is a low rumble in my ear.

The team checks in one by one: Blake, Walt, Gabe, Hank, Rigel, and finally, me.

Blake sticks close to me, keeping me in formation with the team. Ahead, Gabe and Walt take point, their movements fluid and ghost-like in the faint light.

Shadows stretch and twist, every rustle of leaves or snap of a twig setting my nerves on edge.

We pause at the edge of the compound, where a hulking, malevolent presence lurks behind high walls and rusted gates. It's like something out of a nightmare, with harsh angles and oppressive architecture.

"No heat signatures detected," Mitzy reports. "You're clear to proceed."

It's eerily still, with no signs of life or movement. Just the whisper of the wind through the long grass and stunted trees. Gravel crunches softly beneath our boots.

Ethan gives the signal, and we move in, melting into the darkness. The gates creak open, the sound unnaturally loud in the stillness of the night.

"Two on the door." Ethan's command is sharp and focused.

Gabe and Walt stack up on the door, their movements fluid and precise. The door swings open with a rusty creak, revealing a long, dark hallway.

We move forward, our steps echoing in the emptiness. The air is stale and thick with the smell of dust and decay. It tastes like abandonment, like forgotten things left to rot.

The first room we come to looks like a classroom, with desks and chairs arranged in neat rows. A whiteboard stands at the front, faded lessons still scrawled across its surface.

"Clear." Walt's voice is a tense whisper.

Dust coats every surface, muffling our footsteps as we move through the abandoned halls.

We clear the rooms methodically, the Rufi sweeping ahead. Their sensors probe every corner and crevice. We press on, moving from room to room. A dormitory, beds stripped bare. A cafeteria, tables, and benches coated in a layer of grime. It's like a ghost town, a snapshot of a life interrupted.

But it's when we descend to the lower levels that the true horror of this place reveals itself. The air grows colder, damper. The walls are narrow and oppressive. Then we see them.

The cells.

"Jesus Christ." Hank's voice is rough, echoing my own thoughts.

They're small, barely big enough to stand in. The walls are scored with desperate, clawing marks. The floors are stained with things I don't want to think about. In one corner, a pile of shattered fingernails lies crusted with old blood.

Nausea rises in my throat, mingling with a white-hot rage that threatens to choke me. The thought of Jenna trapped in this hellhole, alone and terrified, is almost more than I can bear.

What about the four missing girls?

Are they also trapped in an unspeakable hell like this?

"I've got something." Rigel's call pulls me from my thoughts.

We crowd into another room, and my stomach turns at the sight. It's a torture chamber, complete with a rack and shackles hanging from the walls. The floor is stained a rusty brown, and I don't need to be a detective to know it's blood.

"She never mentioned this." My voice is hoarse, barely recognizable to my own ears.

Blake's hand lands on my shoulder, a solid weight. "She might not remember. Trauma—it does things to the mind."

I nod, swallowing hard against the bile rising in my throat. This is worse, so much worse than I could have imagined.

We search the rest of the compound, but there's nothing else. No clues. No evidence. It's been wiped clean and sanitized.

A professional job.

Whoever was here knew what they were doing.

"Charlie team, moving out." Ethan's voice is quiet, somber.

We retreat the way we came, shadows disappearing into the night, and we return empty-handed.

Time is running out for the girls I'm desperate to save.

TWENTY-SEVEN

Carter

Back at Guardian HRS headquarters, the disappointment of what we've seen hangs heavy in the air. The team is quiet as we file into the briefing room, each of us lost in our thoughts.

"We need to go over everything, piece by piece." Blake is the first to break the silence. "There has to be something we missed."

"That place was wiped clean. Sanitized. Lots of money behind that cleanup job." I scratch at the back of my neck, feeling stumped.

"I agree with you there." Ethan leans back, frustration evident in his tone.

"From utility records, it looks like that place has been abandoned for at least two years." Mitzy leans toward her screen.

"Where does this leave us?" Gabe pushes back from the table with a groan.

"We lean on old-fashioned detective work." I hate to come across yet another dead end, but it's part of the process.

"Such as?" Blake's eyes narrow, the hint of superiority clear. He doesn't think my old detective methods will find anything Guardian HRS can't.

"We trace the funds used to build the place. The funds used to maintain it." I scratch my chin, thinking. "They had to have maids and gardeners. Security was probably handled internally. In my experience, the little things will lead us to whoever's behind this."

Blake's skeptical expression doesn't waver, but I press on.

"We look at utility bills, deliveries, maintenance records. Who delivered their food? What about waste disposal? Someone had to pay for electricity, water, and internet."

I pace a bit, the gears in my mind turning. "We dig through property records and zoning permits. No matter how well they think they've covered their tracks, there's always a paper trail. We can check for any nearby businesses or residents who might have noticed unusual activity."

I stop and meet Blake's gaze, making sure he understands. "And don't forget surveillance footage from traffic cameras or neighboring properties. We chase the money and look for patterns in everything surrounding the building. Someone, somewhere, saw something."

With years of detective work behind me, I know what to look for. It's going to be a slog, but I don't mind hard work.

"Carter's right." Mitzy is already typing furiously on her laptop, furrowing her brow in concentration. "I'm on it."

"It's more than maids and gardeners." I pull at my chin, feeling the scruff of a beard poking through. "It's the carpenters and repairmen. Windows need replacement. Doors need new seals. Tiles get cracked. A florist, if they bothered with flowers. Security cameras and others. If we can get the serial numbers…"

"Already on it. Sending the bumblebee drones in to pull that data," Mitzy interjects without missing a beat.

"That's great." Yet again, Guardian HRS impresses me with their capabilities. "They can do a lot of things internally, security being one of them, but they still had to buy the hardware. And then there are the service providers—the electricians, plumbers, HVAC specialists. They leave traces."

I pace a bit more, the puzzle pieces coming together in my mind. "We need to look at delivery logs and supplier lists. They might have used aliases, but there are always consistencies. Even fake identities leave patterns."

Mitzy kicks Ethan's foot, prompting him to switch places with me. "Swap with Carter. It's time to pick your detective's brain."

Ethan grins, shifting his chair. "Alright, Carter. Let's dig deeper. What about the surrounding area? Any chance neighbors or local businesses noticed something?"

"Absolutely." I appreciate the quick shift in gears. "We canvas the area. Talk to anyone who might have seen unusual activity. Delivery drivers, joggers, dog walkers. Everyone's a potential witness."

I take a seat, leaning over the table. "We also check for any unexplained surges in utility usage. Sudden spikes in electricity or water can indicate recent activity. Plus, we look at any unusual shipments. High-frequency deliveries of specific items can point to what was going on inside. I'm thinking booze. My guess is we'll find large purchases of top-shelf alcohol. Those kinds of requests spark questions and curiosity. If we can find who supplied alcohol to that place, flowers for events… Catering." My mind spins with possibilities.

Mitzy types rapidly, capturing every detail. "Got it. I'll start compiling the data and cross-referencing with what we have."

"Good." I feel a renewed sense of hope. We follow every thread, no matter how small. It's the meticulous work that breaks cases like this wide open. And if there's one thing I've learned, it's that patience and persistence always pay off.

I appreciate Mitzy's comment. I've felt a bit useless with the power and might of Guardian HRS. Their resources make me feel as if I have little to contribute to the case.

But the devil truly is in the details. That's where I thrive, and I know exactly where to look.

The next few days are a blur of activity. Sam, CJ, and Ethan pore over satellite images of the compound, looking for any signs of recent activity. Stitch and Jeb comb through financial records, scouring public records to trace back the construction of the compound as far as possible. Blake, along with Gabe, Walt, and Hank, pore over the few physical pieces of evidence we managed to collect, hoping for a fingerprint, a stray hair, or anything.

No stone is left unturned.

It's grueling, frustrating work, with each dead end and false lead chipping away at our resolve, but I refuse to give up, refuse to let Jenna or the girls down.

Mitzy and I work shoulder to shoulder, digging through the weeds, looking for anything that will tell us more about this organization.

But it's slow going, and as the hours tick by and the days pass, my frustration mounts. Every dead end and false lead feel like a personal failure.

It's late when I finally make it back to Jenna's apartment. She's curled up on the couch, Max's head resting comfortably on her lap. The goofball has definitely made himself at home.

His tail thumps lazily against the cushions, but he's too content soaking up all the attention Jenna's giving him to get up and greet me. I chuckle at the sight.

"Some guard dog," I mutter under my breath, finding it funny as hell, but then I notice the tension in the room, the way Jenna's shoulders are hunched.

She looks, her eyes shadowed and heavy with a haunted look.

"Hey." I sink down beside her, pulling her into my arms. "Rough day?"

"The memories… They're getting worse." She leans against my chest, her fingers curling into my shirt. "It's like, now that I've started remembering, I can't stop."

"I'm so sorry. I wish I could make it all go away." My heart aches for her, for the pain she's enduring.

"You being here helps." Her voice is soft, muffled against my shoulder. "Knowing I'm not alone."

We sit like that for a long time, just holding each other. Max whines softly, nuzzling Jenna's hand. Even he can sense her distress.

That night, the nightmares come again. Jenna thrashes in her sleep, whimpering and crying out. I hold her close, whispering soothing words, but it's like she's trapped in a place I can't reach. When she finally wakes, she clings to me, her body shaking with sobs.

"It was so real," she gasps. "I was back there, in that room…"

"You're safe now." I stroke her hair, trying to calm her, but words offer only so much comfort.

The next morning, I kiss her forehead and gently extricate myself from her grasp, leaving a note on the nightstand before heading out.

Back at Guardian HRS, my determination is renewed. I comb through every piece of information. Hours pass, and I finally stumble upon something—a tiny discrepancy, easily overlooked. A delivery of flooring materials for an addition to the estate.

I dig deeper, tracing the company to its source. It's a shell, of course, but every shell has an origin. I follow the paper trail, each step taking me deeper into the labyrinth of false leads and useless data.

I keep going, however, pulling threads that lead me through a tangled web of front companies and dummy corporations. It's tedious, frustrating work, but I refuse to give up.

And then, buried under layers of obfuscation, I find it—the banker who financed the construction. Marcus Levinson, of Levinson & Associates. His name is the key that unlocks the next part of the puzzle. I follow the money, each transaction pulling back another layer of the veil.

Blue Ridge Holdings, LLC. The official owner of the estate.

I lean back in my chair, the pieces finally fitting together. Now, I have a lead—an address, a name, a direction. It's not much, but it's a start.

The sense of victory is tempered by the knowledge that this is just one step in a long journey. I glance at my phone, where a picture of Jenna smiles at me. Her nightmares might be relentless, but so is my determination to bring those responsible to justice.

It's not a smoking gun, but it's a start. I feel we're closer now, but I also know the closer we get, the higher the stakes become.

My eyes blur from staring at screens and shuffling through papers. The hours melt away, each one blending into the next. My phone buzzes with a message from Jenna. Just a simple *'I miss you,'* but it warms me from the inside out.

I glance at the time and curse under my breath. I'm late once again. This case consumes me, and the hours fly by without me realizing it. Guilt gnaws at me as I try to call her back, but it goes straight to voicemail.

I send Jenna a text, letting her know I'll be late.

The trip back is a beast. The traffic is a snarl, and the minutes tick by with agonizing slowness. I drum my fingers on the steering wheel, impatience bubbling under my skin.

TWENTY-EIGHT

Jenna

My last customer lingers well past closing time. Thirty minutes pass, and Walt finally tells him it's time to pack things up and leave. Walt's imposing presence and stern tone make the customer uncomfortable.

Sensing the tension, I quickly fill a to-go cup and hand it to my customer with a smile and apology, hoping to smooth things over and ease some of Walt's intensity.

Fortunately, my tactic works, and my customer leaves after giving me a pretty nice tip. Once he's gone, however, I let out a heavy sigh.

My shoulders sag with exhaustion and the lingering unease that has become my constant companion. At least that one stranger who gave me the creeps is no longer in town. He must have been just a regular guy in town for some conference.

Totally innocent.

I move through the familiar motions of closing the café, wiping down tables, and switching off lights, but my mind is far away, tangled in the nightmares that seem to plague me.

As I'm finishing up, my phone buzzes. It's Carter letting me know he's running late. I send a quick reply, telling him I miss him.

I glance over at Walt, who stands by the door, his keen eyes scanning the street outside. He's supposed to be on a date with Malia tonight, but our last customer's extended stay made him late.

I bite my lip, torn. I don't want to ruin his night, not when he finally asked Malia out. They've been dancing around each other for days, their simmering attraction clear in every glance, every smile, and every lingering touch.

Making a decision, I walk over to where Walt stands. His brow furrows in concern as he looks down at me.

"Everything alright?" he asks.

"Yeah, I'm just about done here. You don't have to wait." I manage a small smile.

"Not leaving you alone, sweetie." He hesitates, glancing at his watch and then back at me. "I don't mind walking you home."

"You don't have to do that. You should go. Have a great time with Malia." I appreciate his concern, but it's clear how much he wants to be with her.

"Carter would have my hide if I left you unprotected." He shakes his head, but his wistful glance outside says he wants to be with Malia, not stuck guarding me.

"I won't be unprotected," I assure him. "Max is here, and he won't let anything happen to me. Plus, Carter just texted. He's on his way."

As if on cue, Max trots over, his tail wagging as he leans against my leg. I reach down, scratching him behind the ears, taking comfort in his solid, steady presence.

"I should wait until Carter gets here." Walt's gaze flicks between me and the street, but his eagerness is palpable.

"It's fine," I insist. "Carter will be here before you know it. Besides, you and Malia deserve some time together, and I don't want to be the one to make you late. I've got this. Nothing is going to happen to me. I'll lock the doors behind you and finish cleaning up. What could happen?"

He hesitates, but the lure of a night with Malia must be too strong to resist because he finally nods, a grin splitting his face.

"Alright, but you call if anything feels off, you hear? Call me when Carter gets here." His shoulders relax slightly, and a grateful smile spreads across his face.

"Aye aye, Captain. I'll report in promptly." I snap to attention and give a mock salute.

He chuckles, shaking his head. "Just make sure you do."

"I will. Now go before she thinks you stood her up."

With a ruffle of Max's fur, Walt heads out, the bell jingling cheerfully as the door closes behind him. When I don't immediately lock the door, he raps on the glass, making the entire door vibrate. I shake my head, roll my eyes, and turn the lock with an exaggerated flair. Walt, ever protective, checks to ensure the door is locked. I grin when the lock holds.

"Go. I'll be fine." I give a little finger wave followed by a shooing gesture.

Walt returns a flagrant eye roll, but there's a spring to his step as he leaves for his date with Malia.

I focus on the simple, repetitive tasks of cleaning, letting the familiarity soothe my frayed nerves. The hum of the refrigerator, the clink of mugs as I stack them, and the soft thump of Max's tail against the floor are the sounds of a normal day.

A normal life.

I glance at the clock, frowning. Carter should be here by now, but the minutes tick by, and there's no sign of him, no familiar silhouette outside the glass, and no comforting jingle of the bell above the door.

Not that there would be a jingle with the door locked.

I pull out my phone, checking for missed calls or messages, and see a message from Carter. He's running late.

I'm just about to call him when a sudden knock makes me jump.

Max is instantly alert. Instead of his tail wagging, a low growl rumbles in his chest as he stares at the front door. His body is tense and ready. Ready to protect.

I peer through the glass and see a ghost from my past.

"Sophia?" Her name falls from my lips, barely more than a whisper.

TWENTY-NINE

Jenna

SOPHIA LOOKS DIFFERENT; HER ONCE VIBRANT EYES ARE HAUNTED and hollow. Her cheeks are gaunt, the bones jutting out sharply, and her clothes hang loosely from her too-thin frame as if she hasn't eaten or rested properly in months. Once glossy and full of life, her hair lies limp and unkempt around her shoulders.

But it's her.

There's no mistaking it.

I rush to the door, my hands shaking as I fumble with the lock. A million questions race through my mind, but they all fall away as I pull the door open.

Sophia stumbles inside, collapsing into my arms.

"Jenna," she sobs, her voice ragged and raw. "Is it really you?"

I hold her close, feeling the way her body trembles against mine. The desperation in her grip is palpable, her fingers digging into my arms as if I were her lifeline. Over her shoulder, I scan the street, looking for any sign of pursuit, but it's empty; the only movement is the lazy drifting of leaves pushed across the pavement by a gentle breeze.

"It's me." I pull back to get a good look at her. "I should ask the same. Is it you? How…" The shock of seeing her after so many years makes my brain misfire. "I don't know what questions to ask."

She pulls back, her eyes searching mine, a flicker of hope amidst the despair. Dark circles are etched beneath her eyes, like permanent shadows. Her lips are chapped and cracked. There's a rawness to her that wasn't there before, a brokenness that makes my heart ache.

"I can't believe it's you. When I saw you through the window, I thought I was hallucinating. I've been running for so long; I don't know what's real anymore."

A pang of sympathy tightens my chest. I know that feeling all too well, the sense of dislocation, of being untethered from reality.

"Come." I guide her toward one of the tables. "Sit. Let me get you something to drink."

She sinks into a chair, her arms wrapped tightly around herself. I move behind the counter, going through the familiar motions of brewing a pot of tea. I choose soothing chamomile rather than a jolt of caffeine.

As the tea steeps, I watch Sophia out of the corner of my eye. She looks so tiny, so fragile, a far cry from the fierce, defiant girl I remember.

She's the only girl who stood up to Lucian, who refused to break, no matter how hard he tried. Now, she hunches over, her shoulders slumped and eyes hollow.

Her once vibrant spirit is extinguished, replaced by a vacant shell and trembling hands. Whatever wounds she carries, they're raw and deep.

Sophia is broken.

A shiver runs through me as memories rise unbidden, flashes of cruel smiles and rough hands, the bitter taste of fear on my tongue. I push them away, focusing on the present, on the girl in front of me who needs my help.

I pour chamomile tea into two mugs, the fragrant steam curling in the air, and carry them over to the table. Sophia takes one, cradling it between her palms as if trying to absorb its warmth into her bones.

"Thank you," she whispers, her voice thready and thin.

I sit across from her, my mug clasped in my hands.

"What happened? How did you find me?"

"I just saw you through the window and couldn't believe it was you."

"What happened to you?"

She takes a shaky breath, her gaze fixed on the swirling depths of her tea. "The night of the party, they took me. Locked me in a room, alone. I don't know how long I was there. Days, weeks maybe? Time lost all meaning."

Her words send a chill down my spine, the echo of my trauma resonating in every syllable. I reach across the table, laying my hand over hers, a silent offer of support, of understanding.

"I thought I would die there." Her voice is barely audible over the hum of the refrigerator. "But then, the door opened, and it was him."

"Him?"

"The man who bought me. He took me and told me I was part of his private collection."

"Private collection?"

"That's what he called it. Said he was the curator and I belonged to him."

Bile rises in my throat, hot and acidic. I know all too well the depravity that lies behind those words, the horror of being treated as nothing more than an object, a possession to be used and discarded at will.

"A little part of me died that day."

"Sophia…" I reach for her, my heart splintering as she tells me her story. It could've been me. "How did you survive? How did…"

Dear God, it could've been me.

It could've been me.

"I waited. I waited for him to become complacent." A flicker of her old defiance sparks in her eyes. "And when an opportunity finally came, I ran. I've been running ever since, never staying in one place too long, always looking over my shoulder."

She looks up at me, then, her gaze boring into mine, a desperate intensity burning in their depths.

"Tonight… I couldn't believe my eyes when I saw you through the window. I thought I was hallucinating, but I stood out there all day, watching you."

It wasn't my imagination. I *felt* her gaze on me.

Not Lucian.

Not the man who bought me.

But Sophia.

Scared and all alone, how long did it take her to work up the courage to come to me?

My heart clenches, tears prickling at the back of my eyes. I squeeze her hand, trying to convey everything I can't put into words. The solidarity, the shared pain, the fierce, unshakeable bond born of surviving the unsurvivable binds us together.

"I have friends, people who can help. You're safe here. I promise." My voice is rough with emotion.

A tentative smile ghosts across her lips, but it's fleeting, chased away by the shadows that haunt her eyes.

I know that look, the constant vigilance, the fear that the next moment will bring the nightmare crashing back down around you.

I glance at the clock, realizing how late it's gotten. Carter should be here by now, he should have arrived to walk me home as he does every night.

A flutter of unease stirs in my gut, but I push it aside. He's probably just caught up with the case and lost track of time.

He'll be here soon.

"Why don't you come home with me tonight? My place is just a few blocks away. We can get you cleaned up and get some food in you. Carter will be here soon."

"Carter?" Sophia's eyes widen at the mention of his name.

"It's okay," I reassure her. "Carter's a detective. He can help."

Sophia shakes her head, her gaze darting to the windows, to the darkened street beyond. "No police. I can't… I can't trust them. Not after everything."

I reach out, laying a hand on her arm. "Sophia, listen to me.

Carter's different. He knows what happened to me, to us. He's trying to bring down the people who did this."

She meets my gaze, her eyes frightened and uncertain. "I want to believe you, but I'm scared. I've been running for so long, I don't know how to stop." She gestures to the windows. "I don't feel safe with all the glass. Anyone can see us."

An idea strikes me: a way to ease her fears. "We'll leave now. My apartment is close, and the streets are quiet. We can be there in minutes, and then we'll be safe. Carter can meet us there."

Sophia hesitates, biting her lip. Her eyes dart around, filled with a tumultuous mix of desperation and fear, the desire for safety warring with the ingrained fear of trusting anyone.

"We'll be there before you know it. No one will know you're there."

Something in my words must reach her because she nods after a long moment, a single, jerky motion.

"Okay," she whispers. "But let's go now. Before I lose my nerve."

Relief floods me, mingled with a sudden, urgent need to get her out of here and somewhere safe. I turn back to the café, my hands shaking slightly as I finish locking up.

The night air is cool against my skin, and the silence is broken only by the distant hum of traffic and Max's soft breathing beside me. Sophia hovers close, her eyes wide and watchful in the dim light.

"This way." I set off down the alley. "It's not far."

We walk quickly, our footsteps echoing off the brick walls. Every shadow seems to hold a threat, and every corner hides a hidden danger. I glance over my shoulder repeatedly, my heart pounding in my chest.

Suddenly, a screech of tires pierces the silence. Harsh headlights flood the street, momentarily blinding us. A dark van barrels toward us and then comes to a screeching stop, blocking our path.

I reach for Sophia, meaning to pull her back and find another way, but before I do anything, the van's side door slides open, and men pour out.

Dark masks hide their faces.

Panic seizes me, cold and paralyzing. I try to run, to scream, but my legs won't move. My voice is locked in my throat. Beside me, Sophia goes rigid, a choked gasp escaping her lips.

Max leaps forward, a snarl ripping from his throat. He lunges at the nearest attacker, his powerful jaws clamping down on an arm. But there are too many of them. They swarm him, fists and feet striking, but Max doesn't relent, defending me with every ounce of his being.

Their hands reach and grab, tearing me away from Sophia's side.

I scream, struggling against their grip, kicking and clawing with every ounce of strength I possess. But it's not enough; their hold is too strong, and their determination too fierce.

A rough hand clamps over my mouth, muffling my cries. My heart races, fear flooding every inch of my body. I catch a glimpse of Sophia, standing still, not fighting back.

A gunshot cracks the air. Max yelps. His body thuds to the ground. A wail of anguish rips from my throat, raw and primal, as I watch his form go still, dark blood pooling beneath him.

"Max! No, Max!"

But there's no time for grief, no time for anything but the blind, animal terror that consumes me. The world spins as they drag me toward the van. I fight harder, desperation fueling my every move.

But it's futile.

They shove me inside.

Through the tangle of limbs and the blur of tears, Sophia climbs into the van of her own volition, her face a mask of shame and regret.

Betrayal, hot and sharp, lances through me.

The door slams shut, and darkness engulfs me. They force a hood over my head. The van roars to life, speeding away into the night.

I scream, a sound of rage and despair, until my voice gives out, and there's nothing left but the bitter taste of defeat on my tongue.

THIRTY

Carter

THE CITY LIGHTS BLUR AS I WEAVE THROUGH THE EVENING TRAFFIC, my fingers tapping an impatient beat on the steering wheel. A glance at the clock confirms what the crawling cars make painfully obvious—I'm late.

I press Jenna's speed dial for the third time, my heart quickening with each unanswered ring.

"Come on, pick up."

I will my plea to somehow reach her, to pull her to the phone, but the rings give way to her voicemail. The sound of her bright, recorded voice sends a chill down my spine.

Hey, it's Jenna! I can't come to the phone right now, but leave a message, and I'll call you back as soon as I can. Thanks!

The beep sounds, and I end the call with a harsh jab, a sick feeling twisting in my gut. It's not like her not to answer.

I drum my fingers on the wheel, my earlier excitement soured by a growing unease. The lead we uncovered today could be the break we've been waiting for, the key to unraveling the tangled web of Jenna's past and bringing the bastards behind it to justice.

I've been buzzing with impatience to share the news with her, to finally offer some hope after all the dead ends and dark revelations.

But now, as the minutes tick by and the traffic crawls, that urgency takes on a desperate edge. I try to rationalize her silence—she could be in the shower or on the other line. She could have left her phone in the other room, but each explanation rings hollow, drowned out by the alarm bells sounding in my head.

I think of the shadows that have haunted her eyes these past weeks, the weight of the memories she's had to dredge up. I think of the fear that's clung to her like a second skin, the nagging sense that her past is never far behind. It's a darkness I've sworn to protect her from, a burden I've vowed to help her carry.

But right now, stuck in an endless sea of taillights, I feel helpless.

"Damn it, Jenna, pick up."

I swipe to redial, pressing the phone to my ear as if sheer force of will can make her answer, but her voicemail greets me again.

I end the call and toss the phone onto the passenger seat. My stomach churns with a fear I can't name. This isn't right.

Something's wrong. I feel it in my bones.

I clench my jaw and grip the steering wheel until my knuckles turn white, urging the car forward through the gaps in traffic. The lead, the case, the justice we've been chasing—none of it matters now. All that matters is finding Jenna, holding her, and seeing for myself that she's safe.

I send up a silent prayer to a God I'm not sure I believe in, a desperate plea for the woman who's come to mean more to me than I ever thought possible.

The car leaps forward as the traffic finally breaks, but the sick feeling in my gut only grows.

I'm coming, Jenna. I'm coming.

And God help anyone who stands in my way.

I pull up to her apartment, my heart pounding in time with the rapid-fire rhythm of my fingers on the steering wheel. The building looms before me, dark windows staring down like accusing eyes.

I'm out of the car before the engine fully stops, and the slam of the door echoes in the quiet street. The cool night air does little to calm the heat of my anxiety as I take the stairs two at a time, my footsteps a discordant beat in the oppressive stillness.

At her door, I pause, my fist raised to knock. A sudden fear grips me, cold and sharp, lodging in my throat.

What if she's not here?

What if something happened?

Doubt swirls in my mind, a dizzying spiral of worst-case scenarios. I push them aside and knock, the sound harsh and loud in the silence.

"Jenna? It's me."

I strain my ears for any sign of movement, any hint of her presence, but there's nothing. Just the heavy stillness and the pounding of my own heart.

I knock again, louder this time, more insistent.

"Jenna? Are you there?"

My voice sounds hoarse, even to my own ears, rough with a fear I can't quite control. I press my ear to the door, hoping to catch a footfall, a rustle, anything, but the apartment remains silent, a tomb-like quiet that sends an icy shiver down my spine.

With fumbling hands, I pull out the key she gave me for emergencies. It feels heavy and cold in my palm, a physical manifestation of the dread settling in my gut. I hesitate for a moment, torn between respecting her privacy and the overwhelming need to know she's safe.

Need wins out.

I slide the key into the lock, the click of the tumblers sounding unnaturally loud in the silence. I push the door open, half expecting to see her standing there, a puzzled smile on her face, asking me what the fuss is about.

But the apartment is empty.

Dark.

The air feels stale as if it's been untouched for hours. I step inside, my footsteps muffled by the carpet, and flick on the light.

"Jenna? It's Carter. Are you home?"

I move through the apartment, a growing sense of wrongness prickling at my skin. There's no jacket draped over the back of a chair. No keys on the side table.

No Max.

The fear that's been building in my chest expands, seeping into every crevice of my being. I check the bathroom, the bedroom, and even the closets as if she might be hiding inside them.

As if this might all be some misunderstanding.

But she's not here.

The realization hits me like a physical blow, staggering in its certainty. Jenna is gone, and I have no idea where.

I stand in the middle of her living room, my mind racing, trying to piece together what could have happened. Did she leave of her own accord?

Was she taken?

The possibilities swirl in my head, each more terrifying than the last.

I pull out my phone and dial her number again, but it goes straight to voicemail. The sound of her recorded voice is a cruel reminder of her absence.

I end the call and look around, really look, trying to see the apartment through the eyes of a detective.

Is there a sign of struggle?

No.

Everything looks normal, undisturbed. Just an empty home. Which means—she never made it here.

I turn on my heels and head for the door, my mind already racing ahead to the next steps.

The café.

I'll check there. Maybe she's lost track of time? Maybe she's knee-deep in inventories or supply orders? Even as I cling to that shred of hope, I know it's a lie.

Something is wrong here.

Terribly, terribly wrong.

The night air hits me like a slap to the face as I exit the building, but I barely feel it. All I feel is the cold knot of fear in my stomach and the burning determination in my veins.

I peel out of the parking lot, my truck tires screeching against the asphalt. The sound is jarring, but it barely registers over the pounding of my heart and the rush of blood in my ears.

The streets are a blur as I speed toward the café. I push the speed limit, daring any cop to stop me.

"Please be there." My words are a fervent prayer falling from my lips.

I don't know who I'm pleading with.

God?

The universe?

Jenna herself?

All I know is I need her to be okay, need it with a desperation that borders on physical pain.

Each red light is agony.

Each stop sign is torture.

My fingers pick up their drumming on the steering wheel, an erratic beat that matches the racing of my thoughts. Scenarios flash through my mind, each one worse than the last.

Jenna hurt.

Jenna taken.

Jenna, beyond my reach.

I shake my head, trying to dislodge the images. I'm overreacting. She's fine. She has to be. I cling to that thought like a lifeline.

Marlowe's Café comes into view, but as I pull up, all hope withers and dies. The windows are dark; the usually inviting atmosphere is cold and forbidding.

The café looks wrong.

I'm out of the car in a flash, the night air cool against my skin. I rush to the door, my hand shaking as I fumble with the keys. The lock clicks open, the sound unnaturally loud in the stillness.

I push inside, the bell above the door jingling cheerfully, incongruously.

"Jenna?"

My voice echoes in the empty space, bouncing off the walls and coming back to me as if in mockery. I stride to the counter, my eyes scanning every corner, every shadow.

But she's not here.

The fear that's been building in my chest expands, seeping into my veins like ice water. This isn't like her.

I pull out my phone, my fingers numb, and dial her number—*again*.

The ringing fills the empty café, echoing off the walls, but there's no answer—just the cold, impersonal click of her voicemail.

I end the call, my hand clenching around the phone until the edges bite into my palm.

Think, Carter. Think. What's your next move?

I take a deep breath, forcing air into my lungs, and try to focus.

Okay. Okay. One step at a time. Retrace her steps. You're a detective, damn it. Detect.

I look around the café again, this time with a critical eye. Is there anything out of place? Any sign of a struggle, a clue to what might have happened?

No.

Everything is neat and orderly. Just as she left it. Just as she always leaves it.

Except for one thing.

Two mugs sitting on the counter.

They're both half-full of tea.

Someone else was here.

With uncooperative fingers, I fumble for my phone, scrolling through contacts until I find Walt's number. The call connects on the second ring, and Walt's voice fills my ear, a mix of surprise and confusion.

"Carter? What's up?"

"Jenna. Is she with you?" I force the words out, each one feeling like lead on my tongue.

There's a pause, a beat of silence that stretches for an eternity.

"No, she told me to head out early. Said you were on your way." Walt's tone shifts, concern bleeding into his words. "What's going on?"

The ground beneath my feet tilts as if the world is spinning off its axis.

"I can't find her." I rake a hand through my hair, trying to focus past the pounding in my head.

Walt is silent for a moment, the weight of the situation sinking in, and then he curses.

"Shit, Carter. I'm sorry. I didn't want to leave. She made me go. Said you'd be there in just a couple of minutes." His words tumble out in a rush, laced with panic and regret. "Fuck, I shouldn't have listened. I should've stayed with her."

I close my eyes, trying to steady my breathing. It's not Walt's fault. Jenna can be stubborn when she sets her mind to something.

"When was the last time you saw her? Did anything seem off? Out of the ordinary?"

Walt takes a deep breath as if trying to collect his thoughts.

"It wasn't that long ago. Ten, twenty minutes? She seemed fine. A little tired, maybe, but nothing unusual. She was closing up the café."

I should've gone to the café first, but with traffic delaying me, I assumed she had already gone home. I could have missed her between here and there.

My mind races with possibilities, each one more terrifying than the last.

"Where are you?" Walt asks.

"At the café. It's empty. No sign of a struggle, but…" I trail off, unable to voice the fears clawing at my throat. Walt seems to understand anyway.

"Fuck, Carter. I'm on my way. We'll find her."

It's a plan, a course of action. Something to focus on beyond the buzzing static of panic in my head.

"I'm going to retrace her steps. I'm assuming she walked home."

"I'll be there in five."

"Copy that." I end the call, my hand clenching around the phone like it's a lifeline.

Retrace her steps. Right. I can do that. I have to do that.

I push off from the wall and start walking, my feet moving of their own accord. The night air is cool against my skin, but I barely feel it. All I feel is the pounding of my heart and the sick, twisting fear in my gut.

Jenna's apartment isn't far from the café, a walk she's made countless times. I try to see the street through her eyes, to imagine her footsteps on the pavement.

Did she feel safe? Did she know something was wrong? The questions swirl in my mind, taunting and relentless.

I quicken my pace, my breath coming in short, sharp bursts.

Come on, Jenna. Where are you?

A cat slinks across the deserted road, disappearing into the shadows. A car passes, headlights cutting through the darkness, but there's no sign of Jenna.

No sign at all.

I round the corner, and my heart stops.

There. A shape on the pavement. Dark and unmoving. For a moment, my mind refuses to process what my eyes are telling me.

It can't be. It can't.

But as I draw closer, the shape resolves into a form I know all too well.

No. No, no, no.

I break into a run, my feet pounding against the pavement.

THIRTY-ONE

Carter

Max. My loyal companion, the dog who's been by my side since he was a pup, isn't moving. He's on his side; his fur matted and dark with something I don't want to acknowledge staining the cold concrete.

I drop to my knees beside him, my hands shaking as I reach out to touch him.

Please. Please, don't let him be…

"Max?" My voice is a broken whisper, a plea, and a prayer all in one.

His fur is sticky, warm, and wet beneath my fingers. The coppery scent of blood fills my nostrils, and bile rises in my throat.

"Max, buddy. Come on. Look at me."

But his eyes are closed, his body still.

Too still.

I press my fingers to his neck, searching for a pulse, praying for any sign of life.

And there, beneath my fingers, a weak flutter. It's thready, but there.

He's alive.

Hurt but alive.

Relief crashes over me like a wave, staggering in its intensity, but it's short-lived, chased by a fear colder and sharper than before.

If Max is here, hurt and bleeding, then where is Jenna?

What's happened to her?

I look around, desperate for any sign of what might have transpired.

And then… Right there, her phone on the ground. Its screen cracked.

Shit.

I fumble for my phone again, my fingers slick with Max's blood. I hit Walt's number. The line clicks, and I don't wait for a greeting.

"I found Max. He's hurt. Bleeding. Jenna's not here, but her phone is. She's gone."

Walt is silent for a beat, and then he sucks in a sharp breath. "Shit. Okay. Where are you?"

I give him the cross streets, my eyes never leaving Max's still form. The line goes dead, and my phone falls from my hand. I cradle Max's broken body against my chest. Hot blood seeps through my fingers, the coppery scent turning my stomach.

Quickly, I pull off my shirt, rip it into long strips, and do my best to bandage his wound. I gather Max into my arms and wait help-lessly for Walt's arrival.

"Hold on, buddy. Help's coming. Just hold on." I press my fore-head to Max's, my tears mingling with his blood.

A few minutes later, Walt's vehicle screeches to a halt beside me. He leaps out. Malia is hot on his heels.

"Jesus Christ." Walt's eyes widen as he takes in the scene.

"Is he…?" Malia lets out a choked sob, her hand flying to her mouth.

I shake my head, not trusting myself to speak. I gather Max closer, trying to shield him from their horrified gazes.

"We need to get him to a vet. Now." Walt crouches down beside me, his hand on my shoulder.

I nod, my movements feeling slow and clumsy. Together, Walt and I lift Max. A whimper escapes him, protesting the movement, suffering and in pain.

It's a sound I'll hear in my nightmares.

We ease Max into the backseat of Walt's vehicle. I slide in beside Max, cradling his head in my lap while applying pressure to his wound.

The tires squeal as Walt peels away from the curb. The force of it slams me back against the seat. Malia gives Walt directions to a twenty-four-hour emergency vet, then calls ahead to let them know we're on our way.

We race through the night, the city lights blurring past in a kaleidoscope of color. Max's labored breathing fills the car, each ragged gasp a ticking clock, a countdown to the unthinkable.

With a shaking hand, I pull out my phone. The screen is smeared with blood, the keypad slick beneath my fingers.

I call my brother.

"What's up?" Blake's voice turns sharp, alert.

He knows me.

He knows I wouldn't call at this hour unless something was very, very wrong.

"I need you." My voice sounds foreign to my own ears, hoarse and strained. I'm surprised my phone hasn't shattered in my white-knuckled grip. "Jenna's missing. Max has been shot."

The words feel like glass shards in my throat, jagged and cutting. Saying them out loud makes it real, makes it something I can't pretend isn't happening.

"Where are you now?" Blake's sharp intake of breath crackles across the line.

"I'm with Walt. We're heading to the emergency vet on Fifth."

"I'll rally the team." There's steel in his voice, a promise and a vow.

Walt makes good time. Before I know it, the emergency vet looms ahead, a beacon of harsh fluorescent light in the darkness. Walt barely has the car in park before I throw open the door and stumble out with Max in my arms.

"I need help. My dog's been shot," I call out as I enter the emergency room.

Vet techs in scrubs rush to meet me, their faces grim and

focused. They have a stretcher, and they load Max onto it with practiced efficiency. When I try to follow, the vet puts out her hand.

"I'm sorry, sir. You can't go back there."

I want to argue, to push past her and stay with Max, but I'll only be in the way. He needs their help more than he needs me right now.

"He's lost a lot of blood." I choke on the words and bite back a very unmanly sob.

But dammit.

It's Max!

"We'll take care of him, Detective Jackson." The vet recognizes me, but I barely register her name.

She leaves me standing in the waiting room, hands hanging uselessly by my sides, as she rushes to save Max's life.

The adrenaline that's been fueling me ebbs, leaving me feeling hollowed and empty.

Jenna's absence is a gaping wound in my chest, a physical ache that steals my breath. She should be here, pacing this room with me, worrying about Max, waiting for news.

But she's not.

She's gone, taken, and I don't know how or why or by whom. I don't know who to worry about more.

Max?

Jenna?

I can't take care of both of them.

The not-knowing is a special kind of torture, a nightmare I can't wake up from.

Time loses meaning in the harsh light of the waiting room. Minutes bleed into hours, marked only by the relentless ticking of the clock on the wall.

I pace the linoleum, my boots clicking against the floor in a staccato rhythm. It's a poor substitute for the pounding of my heart and the blood rushing in my ears.

Memories of Jenna flash through my mind, a slideshow of moments I'd give anything to have back. Her smile, warm and bright as the sun. The feeling of her hand in mine, her skin soft and cool. The trust in her eyes, the way she looks at me like I can do no wrong.

Each memory is a twist of the knife in my gut, a reminder of what I've lost.

What I've failed to protect.

If I'd been there...

If I'd gotten to her sooner...

The thoughts chase themselves in circles, a never-ending loop of guilt and recrimination.

I should have been there.

I should have kept her safe.

But I wasn't, and I didn't.

Now she's gone, and Max is fighting for his life.

And I'm here.

Useless.

Helpless.

The weight of it presses down on me, a physical force that drives the air from my lungs. I feel like I'm drowning, like I'm being crushed under the weight of my own failure.

I lean against the wall, my head falling back against the cold plaster. The fluorescent lights buzz overhead, a mocking counterpoint to the silence of the waiting room.

Please, Max. Please pull through. I can't lose you.

It's a prayer and a plea, a desperate bargain with a universe that feels cold and uncaring. I'll do anything, give anything if it means Max survives.

Hang on, Max. Just hang on. And Jenna, wherever you are, whatever is happening... I'm coming. I'll find you. I'll bring you home.

It's a promise I make to the empty air and to the uncaring walls of the waiting room. A promise I seal with blood and tears and the shattered pieces of my heart.

Blake suddenly appears in the doorway, his face etched with worry. He takes one look at me and strides over, his hand coming to rest on my shoulder.

"How's Max?" His voice is steady, sure. An anchor in the storm.

"In surgery. If I'd been any later..."

"Max is in good hands, but Jenna needs you now. Every second counts in a kidnapping. You know this."

I do know it. It's a knowledge that sits heavy in my gut, a certainty that chills me to the bone.

"I can't leave Max on some operating table. He's my best friend." My voice breaks on the last word, the admission of just how much Max means to me.

"The best thing you can do for Max is find Jenna." Blake's tone leaves no room for argument. His grip on my shoulder tightens, forcing me to meet his gaze. "He'd want you out there, fighting for her. Can you do that?"

It's the truth, hard as it is to hear. Max is a fighter, a protector. He'd never forgive me if I abandoned Jenna to sit vigil at his bedside.

I'm torn, the need to be there for Max warring with the desperate urgency to find Jenna.

Blake is right. I know he is.

Just then, Malia steps forward, her face streaked with tears but her eyes fierce with determination.

"I'll stay with Max." Her voice is steady, resolute. "I won't leave his side. I promise. You need to go. Find Jenna."

I look at her, really look, and see the strength beneath her fear.

"Thank you." With a last glance at the operating room doors, I square my shoulders and turn to my brother.

"I don't know where to begin."

"Well, thank fuck we've got that covered."

"We?"

"Yeah, dude. The whole team is here. Charlie team. Sam, CJ, and Mitzy with her magic."

"How…" I can't even formulate the words.

It's different being on this side of a person's disappearance. It's as if I've suddenly forgotten years of training. Fortunately, I've got Blake, and Blake has the might of Guardian HRS behind him.

"We're all here. Waiting on you. Mitzy's on support. CJ and Sam are standing by. Come on. Time to get your girl."

We burst out of the clinic like soldiers going to war, a grim determination settling over us, but I pause, glancing back at the doors leading to the operating room.

It feels wrong to leave Max.

Walt places a hand on my shoulder, his grip firm and reassuring. "He's in good hands. Malia will call the moment anything changes."

I swallow past the lump in my throat. "I know. It's just—he's always had my back. Leaving him behind, it feels…"

"Wrong," Walt finishes, his voice soft with understanding. "I get it. But Max would want you out there, finding Jenna. He knows you've got his back, even from a distance." Walt repeats the very same words Blake said not moments before.

And damn if they aren't right.

There are two vehicles in the parking lot, both filled with the members of Charlie team. With Walt's truck covered in blood, Walt and I climb into a vehicle with Ethan and Blake while Hank, Gabe, and Rigel stay in the other.

Mitzy's voice fills the cab of the SUV via speaker.

"I'm pulling traffic cam footage from around the café and surrounding streets." Her words are clipped and focused. The rapid-fire clatter of her keyboard fills the background, a staccato beat that matches the pounding of my heart. *"If someone took her, we'll find them."*

Her voice is a lifeline, a glimmer of hope. I cling to it, to the certainty in her skills. She's the best there is. If anyone can find a lead, it's her.

"I've got something," Mitzy says, her tone urgent. *"Jenna's leaving the café with another woman. Max is with them. There's no sign of distress from Jenna or Max. Switching to the next camera… They're on the sidewalk."*

The tension in the vehicle is palpable as we hang on Mitzy's every word. It's like watching Jenna's final moments.

"A van just pulled up. They grabbed Jenna and shot Max. Oh, Carter, I'm so sorry. Is he…"

"Max is in good hands. What about Jenna?" I don't have time for side commentary.

"They forced Jenna into the van. I'm tracking it now. Umm…"

"What?"

"The other woman…" Mitzy pauses. *"She's not fighting and she just*

climbed into the van on her own. I'm sorry, Carter, but it looks like Jenna was set up."

"Fuck!" I'm going to kill the motherfucker who took my girl.

She feeds us information as she finds it. Each new lead is a puzzle piece slotting into place. Meanwhile, we're on the move, heading to intercept.

"The van is headed north on the 101, toward the coast. Her words are punctuated by the relentless clatter of her keyboard. *"They're moving fast, but they won't shake us."* Mitzy's voice cuts through the tension. *"I'm switching to the next set of cameras."*

Before long, we're on a coastal road, a winding ribbon of asphalt cutting through the rugged landscape. The ocean is a black expanse to our left, and the cliffs rise steep and jagged to our right.

Ethan drives with focused intensity, his hands steady on the wheel. I keep my eyes glued to the GPS, watching the blinking dot that represents the van.

Mitzy's voice crackles through the speakers, a constant presence guiding our path. Then, suddenly, we lose the tiny red dot.

"Mitzy?" My voice is tight, strained. "Mitzy, do you copy?"

"I lost visuals on the van."

THIRTY-TWO

Carter

Mitzy's words make my heart clench, but her calm voice continues, *"Hold on a moment. I'm analyzing the area where we lost the van."*

The tension in the vehicle is palpable as we wait.

"Alright, from where the van disappeared, there are two potential routes," she says finally. *"One heads inland to a private estate. The rest of the land in the area is government-owned and empty."*

She pauses for a breath before continuing, *"The other road heads toward the coast and ends at another private estate right on the water's edge. Both are worth checking out."*

Ethan nods, taking charge. "We'll head toward the private estate with the boat launch. Gabe, Hank, Rigel, you guys take the inland estate."

"Copy that," Gabe confirms. "Let's move."

I lean back in my seat, my hand tight around my phone. The GPS blinks, and the estate coordinates are seared into my mind.

This is it.

The final stretch.

Somewhere ahead, Jenna is waiting, counting on us to bring her home.

I close my eyes for a moment, sending a silent prayer to God, to the universe, and to anyone who might be listening.

Please. Please let her be okay. Let us find her in time.

When I open my eyes, the road is a blur of motion. Ethan presses down on the accelerator, and the car surges forward.

Mitzy sends technical information to each of our cell phones, mine included. The private estate is a sprawling compound of manicured lawns and towering fences. Security cameras glint in the moonlight, motion sensors blanketing the perimeter.

"Perimeter is hot," Blake mutters, assessing the defenses. "We're gonna need a way in that doesn't trip the alarms."

"The woods?" I point to a scraggly tree line skirting the property. It's more scruff and grass than trees, but there is some cover. "We can use the cover to approach. Or approach by water."

"I don't like the look of that surf." Ethan's gaze is cold and calculating. "Too rough, and I don't want us getting bashed on the rocks. Mitzy?"

"Yes?"

"We need intel on that wall and its security systems."

"Already on it. Looking for blind spots as we speak. If not, then we'll try something different."

Blake grabs a tablet streaming intel from Command and Control. He pulls up scans of the camera placements.

"There's a blind spot in the northeast corner. If we time it right, we can slip through undetected."

"No-go," Walt chimes in. "There are motion sensors inside. We'll trip one the moment we're over that wall."

Mitzy's voice comes through the comms. *"You have two Rufi units with you. Their armor is invisible to the motion sensors. Send a Rufi in to disable the sensors long enough for you to make it past the wall."*

"Alright, let's deploy the Rufi." Ethan gives the signal.

We stand just outside the tree line, watching as the Rufi units move into position. One Rufi approaches the ten-foot wall, placing its paws against it. It stretches up, extending to its full height on its hind legs. The second Rufi uses the first as a springboard, leaping over the wall with a fluid, mechanical grace.

Ethan turns to us as we wait for the Rufi units to complete their tasks.

"We have a few options. The main house, the guest house, the garage, and the boathouse. We need to decide where to start." Ethan's voice cuts through the tension, grounding us. "Since there are four of us, we can split into two teams, each taking a Rufus."

"If we locate the van, we'll know where to focus our search." I rub my temples, trying to piece everything together.

"The main house is the most obvious. It's secure and has plenty of places to hide someone." Blake paces, his eyes scanning the perimeter.

"But it's heavily guarded. If we go in guns blazing, we might alert them before we confirm Jenna is there." Walt shakes his head, glancing at the main house.

"The guest house and garage are smaller targets. Easier to secure, but they might not keep her there if they're expecting a quick getaway." Ethan folds his arms, his brow furrowed in thought.

"The boathouse makes the most sense," I say. "If they need to move her quickly, they'll want access to the water. They can't defend this house well, but it's harder to track her if they get her on the water."

"I agree with Carter, but we can't ignore the possibility that she's in the main house." Ethan looks to the others, looking for feedback. "We need to be smart and think this through. We've only got so long before they realize we're here."

"The sensors are down. The patrol unit is scanning the area." Mitzy's voice cuts through the discussion.

"Send the patrol unit to check for any evidence of the van. Focus on areas with the highest probability of activity." Ethan nods.

We watch the feed as the Rufi move swiftly and silently across the grounds. Their sensors scan for signs of the van. The tension is palpable, each second stretching into an eternity as we wait for an update.

"The patrol unit just picked up something," Mitzy announces. *"Fresh tire tracks lead to the boathouse down by the water."*

"Guess you were right." Ethan gives me a nod of respect. He

thumps me on my shoulder. "Let's move out. We check out the boathouse first." Ethan makes the call.

All four of us approach the ten-foot wall, the imposing barrier looming before us. Blake examines the structure, his fingers brushing against the rough surface. Without a word, he kneels down, lacing his fingers together to create a foothold.

I step onto Blake's hands, feeling the firm support as he boosts me. Ethan and Walt stand ready, their eyes sharp and vigilant. I reach the top and pull myself over, landing softly on the other side.

Walt follows quickly, his movements just as fluid. He swings his leg over the top, landing softly beside me. Ethan is the last; his ascent is smooth and efficient. He reaches the top, hanging there momentarily to assist Blake.

Their teamwork is seamless, a fluid dance of precise actions and silent communication. They move as one, each anticipating the other's needs without a single word spoken. It's clear they've done this countless times before. The fluidity and coordination of their actions speak volumes about their training and camaraderie.

The estate grounds are eerily quiet as we make our way toward the boathouse, our movements precise and coordinated. Hand signals pass between Ethan and his team, a silent language honed through years of training. Language I barely know, but I get enough to follow Ethan's lead.

The boathouse looms ahead, a dark silhouette against the glimmering water. The scent of salt, brine, and seaweed fills the air, mingling with the droning of distant waves.

Following Ethan's commands, we fan out, each taking a position around the boathouse. The water around it is calm, barely a ripple. The soft ground muffles our footsteps.

I spot fresh tire tracks, the ground disturbed and small rocks scattered. The tracks lead straight to a set of large double doors.

"Someone's been here." I point out the deep grooves in the gravel.

Blake kneels down, his keen eyes examining the ground around the tire marks. His fingers brush over the disturbed earth, tracing the edges of a footprint.

"Footprints, scuff marks. Multiple individuals." He looks up, his face grim in the shadowed light. "They were in a hurry."

My heart pounds faster, adrenaline surging through my veins. We're close. I feel it in my bones, a prickling sense of anticipation mixed with dread.

Ethan signals us to move in, his hand cutting through the air like a blade. We approach the boathouse cautiously, our weapons drawn and ready. The weight of my weapon is familiar in my hands, a cold comfort in the face of the unknown.

But as we draw near, Ethan raises a fist, signaling us to stop. Another quick succession of gestures explains the rest.

We're getting wet.

We move to the edge of the water, the cool breeze hitting our faces like a slap. The water is dark and murky but calm.

I take a deep breath before slipping into the water. The cold shocks my system like a thousand icy needles pricking my skin, but I push through, focusing on the mission.

On Jenna.

Blake and Walt follow, their movements smooth and controlled. They cut through the water like shadows, leaving barely a ripple in their wake.

We swim silently, the water muffling our movements as we approach the rear of the boathouse. The structure looms above us. Large doors hang above the waterline.

Ethan gestures for us to line up, preparing to enter simultaneously. We position ourselves beneath the doors, treading water as we wait for the signal.

With a sharp nod, Ethan gives the go-ahead. As one, we slip beneath the doors and into the boathouse. The water is inky black, the only light coming from the faint moonlight filtering through the cracks in the walls. From the night vision in my HUD, I see it all in shades of gray and green.

The boathouse is silent and empty.

Ethan signals the all-clear, and we move forward, pulling ourselves out of the water and onto the wooden planks. Our clothes cling to our bodies, the fabric heavy, cold, and wet, but the discomfort is a distant thought.

My mind is focused solely on the task at hand.

We move cautiously, our footsteps light and measured. We keep our lights off, not wanting to alert anyone who might still be in the area. The darkness is thick, broken only by the faint gleam of moonlight through the dusty windows.

The walls are lined with shelves, hooks, boating equipment, and coiled ropes scattered haphazardly. The air is thick with the scent of gasoline and salt water, a heady mix that makes my head spin.

We fan out, each of us taking a section of the boathouse to investigate. I move toward the dock, my eyes scanning the water for any sign of the launched boat.

Blake moves to the edge of the slip, his keen eyes taking in the details. He points to the fresh scrapes on the dock, the wood pale and raw.

"They launched a boat," he says, his voice low and grim. "Recently, by the looks of it."

My heart sinks, a cold dread settling in my gut. We're too late. They've taken her by water, putting even more distance between us.

"Mitzy," I say, my voice rough with emotion. "Please tell me you have eyes on that boat."

There's a beat of silence, a moment that stretches into eternity. Then, Mitzy's voice crackles over the comms.

"Drones are in the air. I've got a visual. It's heading toward a large yacht, moving fast. And…" She pauses and static hisses in my ear. *"Carter, I've got a positive ID on Jenna."*

Relief crashes over me, so strong it nearly brings me to my knees.

She's alive.

She's there.

We found her.

But the relief is short-lived, chased by a renewed sense of urgency. She's not safe yet. Not until she's back in my arms.

"We need a plan." Ethan's voice cuts through the static in my head, calm and focused. "A water rescue, extraction by air or sea.

We need to coordinate with the Coast Guard and local marine units. Mitzy, I need ideas."

"Already working on it. Go ahead and retreat. Sending coordinates. Hank, Gabe, and Rigel will meet you there."

"Copy that," Ethan commands us to move out with a swirl of his finger overhead. We exit the way we came in, silently and through the water, then hump it back to the vehicle.

I send up a silent prayer. *Hold on, Jenna. Just a little longer. I'm coming for you. I'll always come for you.*

THIRTY-THREE

Jenna

THE VAN DOORS SLAM SHUT, PLUNGING ME INTO DARKNESS. I SCREAM until my voice gives out, rage and despair mingling with the bitter taste of betrayal on my tongue.

The image of Max lying in a pool of his own blood burns behind my eyelids. My faithful protector callously gunned down without mercy.

"Max," I choke out, my voice a broken whisper. "Oh God, Max."

The van lurches into motion, throwing me against the cold metal wall. Pain explodes across my back, but it's nothing compared to the agony in my heart. I curl into myself, sobs wracking my body.

"Sophia." My voice breaks. "How could you?"

Her betrayal hits like a physical blow, stealing my breath.

"I'm sorry." Sophia's voice comes from the darkness, thick with emotion. "I had no choice. I'm sorry."

Rage flares hot and bright within me. I lunge toward her voice, but strong arms hold me back. My hands claw at the air.

"How could you? I trusted you."

"Settle down," a gruff voice warns.

We take a turn at dizzying speed, and I'm thrown against the cold metal wall again. The impact jars my teeth, the taste of blood sharp on my tongue. I twist and squirm. Kick and buck.

"Don't fight." Calloused hands grab my wrists.

Zip ties bite into my skin as they're cinched tight. The plastic digs in deeper as I struggle, panic clawing at my chest.

"Please." I hate the desperation in my voice. "You don't have to do this. Let me go. I won't tell anyone, I swear."

A dark chuckle is my only response.

The van speeds on. The drive is endless. Each turn and bump send fresh waves of fear through me. The van reeks of sweat and fear, the air thick and suffocating.

My heart pounds so hard I fear it might burst from my chest. Time loses all meaning in the darkness. It could be minutes or hours before the van finally slows.

Finally, we stop.

When the doors open, the sudden influx of cool night air makes me gasp.

The cool air should be a relief, but it only heightens my terror. The hood is removed. We're at a boathouse, dark water stretching endlessly before us.

Ocean water.

Hands grab me, dragging me out. My legs, numb from the long ride, buckle beneath me. I'm hauled upright, forced to stumble forward.

"Move," one of the men grunts, shoving me forward.

I dig my heels in, a futile gesture of defiance. It earns me a sharp slap across the face, the sting bringing tears to my eyes.

They half-drag, half-carry me to a waiting speedboat. I'm tossed in like a sack of potatoes, my bound hands making it impossible to break my fall. Pain shoots through my shoulder as I land hard on the deck.

The boat rocks beneath my feet, and for a moment, I consider making a break for it. But as if reading my mind, Sophia shakes her head, her eyes wide with warning.

The boat's engine roars to life, and we shoot out into the open water. Spray stings my face, mingling with my tears.

I curl into myself, trying to make sense of what's happening.

This can't be real. It has to be a nightmare.

The bite of the zip ties, the ache in my body, and the terror coursing through my veins—it's all too real. I'm back in the world I thought I'd escaped. The world of men who see women as things to be bought and sold.

I risk a glance over the side, gauging the distance to shore. It's too far. Even if I could swim with my hands bound, I'd never make it. They'd just fish me out of the water.

Sophia huddles in the corner, her arms wrapped tightly around herself. The guilt etched on her face does nothing to ease the ache of her betrayal.

The lights of a massive yacht loom ahead, growing larger with each passing second. My heart pounds, fear clawing at my insides. My stomach churns, equal parts seasickness and fear.

As we pull alongside the yacht, hands reach down, roughly hauling me onto the deck.

This is really happening.

I'm dragged to my feet, forced to stand before a man whose very presence makes my skin crawl.

I remember him all too well.

He's handsome in a conventional way, but his eyes—they're cold, predatory. He looks at me like I'm a prized cow at auction.

"Welcome aboard." His eyes might be cold and calculating, but his voice is as smooth as silk and twice as slippery. "This has been a long time coming."

I try to speak, but my voice fails me. He circles me slowly, his gaze raking over me like I'm a prized animal.

"You were mine. You escaped, but now my property has been returned," he continues, his tone matter-of-fact. "You will be with me for the rest of your life. How long that is… Well, that depends on you." The threat in his words is unmistakable.

"I'm not property." Bile rises in my throat. I spit at his feet, a small act of defiance. "You don't own me."

His hand moves faster than I can track. Pain explodes across my cheek as his backhand connects, the force nearly knocking me off my feet. Stars dance in my vision, the metallic taste of blood filling my mouth.

"Tsk, tsk." He clicks his tongue, grabbing my chin roughly. "We'll have to work on that attitude. Won't we?"

"Go to hell," I spit out, summoning what little defiance I have left.

"It's best if you obey." Sophia steps forward, her eyes downcast. "Please, don't fight. It won't go well."

"You see," he runs a finger down my jaw, "it took Sophia some time to learn her place, but she's come around. Haven't you, pet?"

He pulls Sophia to him, crushing his lips against hers in a sickening display of dominance. She doesn't resist, doesn't even flinch. It's like watching a doll being manipulated, lifeless and compliant.

When he releases her, Sophia's eyes meet mine briefly. The emptiness in her gaze chills me to my core. Is this what awaits me? To be broken down until there's nothing left?

"Now then." His attention returns to me. "Let's get you settled in, shall we?" He snaps his fingers and men seem to appear from the shadows. "Take her below. Let her contemplate her new reality."

The men grab me, their fingers digging in hard enough to bruise. I'm dragged down narrow stairs and through opulent corridors that mock my situation. They throw me into a small, bare cabin.

"Please," I try to reason with the men, hating the tremor in my voice. "You don't have to do this. I won't tell anyone. Just let me go."

They shove me into a chair, efficiently securing me with more zip ties. Each one feels like another nail in my coffin, sealing away my freedom.

"Property doesn't get to make demands." One of the men laughs at me as he slams the door shut, leaving me alone in suffocating darkness.

My breath comes in short gasps as panic sets in.

Time passes in a haze of fear and pain. My wrists bleed from struggling against the zip ties. Every creak of the boat sends fresh waves of terror through me.

Many hours pass, and when the door finally opens again, my nightmare's silhouette fills the frame. "Come," he says. "It's time you understood your place here."

"You're a madman." I spit in his face.

He rewards me with another backhand to the face, causing me and the chair to topple to the floor.

"I see you haven't had enough time. I'll leave you to think about your new situation," he says, moving toward the door. "We'll continue this discussion when you're in a more cooperative mood."

The door slams shut, and the lock sliding into place echoes in the small space. I strain against my bonds, but it's useless. The zip ties only dig deeper, drawing blood.

Alone in the darkness, the reality of my situation crashes over me. Tears stream down my face as sobs wrack my body.

Time loses all meaning. I drift in and out, exhaustion warring with terror. Every creak of the boat and every distant sound sends fresh waves of fear through me. At times, I hallucinate, hearing my sobs through the deck, pitiful cries full of fear.

What will happen when that door opens again?

When it finally does, the man who claims to own me fills the narrow frame. The light from the hallway casts sinister shadows across his face.

"Have we had time to reconsider our attitude?" He steps into the room.

I gather what little courage I have left.

"Go to hell," I spit out.

His eyes narrow, a dangerous glint appearing. "I was hoping you'd be smarter than this." He reaches for me. "But some lessons have to be learned the hard way."

His hand tangles in my hair, yanking my head back. Pain lances through my scalp as he forces me to look at him.

"You will learn obedience." His face is inches from mine. "One way or another. The question is, how much will it hurt before you submit?" He leaves the room with a gentle click of the door handle, but it may as well be as loud as a gunshot.

Terror claws at my insides, but I refuse to let him see it. I steel myself for whatever comes next, praying for a miracle. I know he's trying to break me mentally by leaving me by myself.

An hour passes, maybe more, before he returns. There's more of that phantom sobbing, making me question my sanity.

We go through the same routine, only this time, I don't answer. I glare at him but then lose my nerve and look away.

"Ah, my pet. You're beginning to understand."

I'm untied from the chair but kept bound as he leads me through the yacht. We enter a spacious suite in the bow, all gleaming wood, polished steel, and plush fabrics.

"Sophia," he says. She appears from an adjoining room, her eyes downcast. "Show Jenna what it means to be obedient."

What follows is a nightmare I can't wake from. Demonstrating his complete dominance, he uses Sophia. She doesn't resist, doesn't flinch. It's like watching a doll being manipulated, lifeless and compliant.

"This will be you soon." His eyes gleam with sick pleasure. "You'll learn to love it, just like Sophia does."

"Never," I snarl, earning myself another stinging slap.

"Tie her to the chair," he orders, gesturing to an ornate armchair. "She needs to watch and learn."

Secured once more, I'm forced to witness his continued abuse of Sophia. I try to look away, but rough hands grab my hair, forcing me to watch.

Tears stream down my face, a mix of rage, fear, and utter help-lessness.

Finally, the man tires. He forces Sophia into the massive bed, climbing in after her. "Sleep now, my pet. Tomorrow, we begin your training in earnest."

The lights dim, but sleep is impossible. I strain against my bonds, my mind racing.

How long will it take before Carter realizes I'm missing?

Does he know where to look?

What about Max? Oh, poor Max! What if he is dead? Will Carter blame me?

The night stretches endlessly, each second an eternity of fear and despair. I think of Max. I hear his yelp of pain. I see blood. So much blood.

My heart breaks.

THIRTY-FOUR

Carter

As we gather for our final briefing, the night air is thick with tension. CJ, the commander of the Guardian teams, stands before us, his face etched with determination.

"Alright, people," CJ begins, his voice low but commanding. "We've got one shot at this. Let's make it count." He outlines the plan with military precision, each word sinking into my bones.

"Three teams." CJ turns to Brady, leader of Bravo team. "Bravo's on distraction. Draw attention away from the main assault. Create enough chaos to give Alpha and Charlie the opening they need."

"We're on it." Brady gives a sharp nod.

"Alpha team—Max, your team will handle hostile suppression. Neutralize the guards on deck. Clear a path for Charlie team." CJ turns to us.

"Ethan, you have the most critical job—hostage rescue. Go in. Rescue Jenna. No mistakes, no second chances. Since stealth is key, you'll be equipped with tranquilizer guns in addition to your standard kit. Ethan, you have tactical command of the mission as a whole." CJ claps his hands, bringing an end to the briefing. "This is it, people. Let's bring her home."

Her.

My Jenna.

My heart clenches at the thought of her trapped on that yacht.

I don't know how, but Guardian HRS procured three RIBs somehow. We do a final check of our gear, and then we load up.

The small boats cut through the water. Salt spray stings my eyes, and the taste of brine is sharp on my tongue. An hour later, the mega yacht looms like a fortress, a sleek silhouette against a star-strewn sky.

As we near the yacht, its true size becomes apparent. It's at least 300 feet long and a behemoth of steel and luxury—lights shimmer along its hull, reflecting off the obsidian water. Armed guards patrol the decks, their silhouettes impossible to make out with the naked eye against the night sky.

Fortunately, our enhanced night vision reveals the world in vivid shades of green.

Jenna's there.

So close.

Every cell in my body screams to reach her.

"One minute out," CJ's voice crackles in my earpiece. *"Alpha and Charlie team, prepare for approach and be ready for boarding. Bravo team, standby for distraction."*

I grip my weapon tight. The familiar weight grounds me. Around me, tension radiates from my teammates.

We're ready.

We have to be.

"All teams, this is Command," Mitzy's voice comes through, clear and focused. *"Satellite imagery shows minimal movement on the yacht's upper decks. Thermal scans indicate most heat signatures are below deck. We cannot see below the waterline. Proceed with caution."*

"Bravo team, you're up," CJ's voice commands. *"Initiate distraction."*

In the distance, a series of small explosions light up the night. Flares arc across the sky, drawing the guards' attention on deck.

"Alpha and Charlie teams, move in," CJ orders. *"You've got a small window to board without being seen. Make it count."*

We kill the engine, gliding the last few yards in eerie silence.

Walt secures the RIB to the yacht's hull on the port side, near the stern. Alpha team does the same on the opposite side of the vessel.

We board the vessel one by one, our movements fluid and practiced.

Jenna. Jenna. Jenna.

Her name pulses with each beat of my heart.

We creep onto the deck, lethal shadows in the night.

Two guards, alerted by some sixth sense, turn. Before they can raise the alarm, Blake and Gabe fire tranquilizers. The darts find their marks, and the guards crumple silently to the deck.

Ethan directs us with hand signals. Hank and Gabe go to the bridge, Rigel and Walt head below to the engine room, and Blake and I remain with Ethan to sweep the cabins.

And find Jenna.

We move into the yacht's interior. The opulence is staggering—marble floors, gold-plated fixtures, priceless art adorning the walls. It reeks of money and power. Of men who think they can buy and sell lives.

A guard comes up a set of stairs. Blake moves like lightning. His dart finds the man's neck.

Another silent takedown.

So far, we've yet to raise any alarms.

We penetrate deeper into the interior, past luxurious guest cabins and lavish lounges. Each closed door is a possibility.

Is she behind this one?

No.

This one?

No.

As we round a corner, we come face to face with another guard. He's big, easily six-foot-four, with fists like hams. He doesn't hesitate, swinging a meaty fist at my head.

I duck the punch. His fist whistles over my head. Blake moves in, landing a solid hit to the guard's solar plexus. The big man grunts but doesn't go down. My elbow connects with the guard's jaw.

It's a brutal, silent dance.

We can't risk using our weapons in the enclosed space. Can't alert the entire yacht to our presence. The guard fights like a cornered animal, all brute strength and desperation.

Finally, I see an opening. Blake keeps the guard distracted. I slip behind him. My arm loops around his thick neck. He thrashes, trying to throw me off, but I hold on and jab a tranquilizer dart into the meat of his neck. Slowly, his struggles weaken, and he slumps to the floor, unconscious.

We pause, catching our breath.

Too close.

We continue our methodical sweep of the yacht, clearing room after room. Guest cabins, lounges, a state-of-the-art gym—all empty.

The tension builds with each cleared space.

Where is she?

Mitzy's voice comes through again as we move deeper into the yacht's interior. *"Charlie team, thermal imaging suggests three heat signatures in the master suite, starboard side of the bow. They could be our targets."*

"Copy that," Ethan responds.

As we approach the master suite, I take a deep breath, steadying myself.

This is it.

"On my mark." Ethan reaches for the door handle. He counts down silently. *"Three. Two. One."*

The door flies open, and we surge inside, our movements synchronized. The room is massive and dripping with luxury. A California king bed dominates one wall, its silk sheets rumpled, and there, tied to a chair on the side, is Jenna. A bruise mars her cheek, and fury rises in me like a tidal wave.

A man leaps from the bed, grabbing for a knife on the nightstand. Blake's tranquilizer dart catches him mid-leap. He crashes to the floor, the knife clattering away.

"How are you?" I rush to Jenna, my hands shaking as I untie her bonds. "Are you okay? Can you walk?"

"Sore, but okay." She collapses against me, her body wracked with sobs. I hold her tight, breathing in her scent. For a moment, the chaos fades away.

She's here.

Alive.

In my arms.

Her body trembles against mine, and she pulls back, eyes wide with fear. "Max. They shot Max. I'm so sorry, but I think he's… I think he's…"

"Max is alive." I cup her face, forcing her to meet my eyes. "I found him. He's in surgery. He's going to be okay."

Relief floods her features, and she collapses back into my arms, her sobs quieter now but still shaking with the aftershocks of fear and worry.

Movement from the bed catches my eye. A woman, her face pale and drawn in the dim light, sits up in bed. Her hair is a tangled mess. Dark circles under her eyes speak of sleepless nights and unending torment.

"Jenna, I'm so sorry." Her eyes fill with tears. "I had no choice. I was forced to…" A sob chokes her. "I never meant to—you have no idea how hard it's been." The woman looks like a ghost, her spirit crushed under the weight of unspeakable abuse.

Jenna looks at me, then back at the woman. In a move that surprises me, she breaks from my embrace and rushes over, enveloping her in a fierce hug.

"I don't blame you, Sophia. I know how these men can be, how they can force us to do things we wouldn't otherwise."

"Time to go," Ethan urges us to move.

"We can't leave yet," Sophia's voice is urgent. "He's got documents in a safe." She points to a painting on the wall. "It's all there. Names, dates, locations—everything. It's important… And there are others."

I share a look with Blake.

Could it be?

I dare to hope.

"Sophia, four girls are missing. Teenagers. Do you know anything about them?"

"Yes." She takes a shaky breath, her eyes darting nervously. "They're here."

THIRTY-FIVE

Carter

"Here?" Blake approaches Sophia. "Where?"

"Down below somewhere." She shakes her head. "But the safe. The information—it's all in there. Where they're to be taken, who buys them. Everything."

"Carter," Ethan warns, "we're on a clock here."

"We need what's in that safe," I say. "It's got intel on God knows how many others."

"Do it fast." Ethan activates his comms. "All units, listen up. We've got a new development. Carter's four missing girls are on the yacht, sequestered somewhere below. Gabe and Hank abandon the bridge and prioritize locating those girls. Alpha, assist as able. Time is critical, people. Move out."

After weeks of dead ends and false leads, I finally have a chance at saving those girls. My heart races with excitement, but my mind remains focused.

As a detective, I understand the gravity of what's in that safe. The information could be critical to rescuing so many other girls.

We can't afford to leave it behind. I trust the team to find the missing girls. They're the best at what they do and won't disappoint me. I turn my attention to Sophia.

"Show us the safe. Quick."

Sophia leads us to a massive abstract painting that probably sells for more than I make in a year. Blake and I carefully remove it, revealing a sleek, high-tech safe built into the wall.

"Shit." Blake's eyes widen as he examines the safe. "Retinal scanner. We can't crack this."

"Maybe we can." I glance at the unconscious man on the floor, an idea forming in my head.

"Do it." Ethan nods grimly, understanding dawning on his face.

Blake and I move to the unconscious man. On Ethan's signal, we grip his arms and hoist him up. His body is dead weight, his limbs flopping like spaghetti, and it takes all our strength to maneuver him.

"Christ, he's heavy," Blake grunts as we awkwardly maneuver the body toward the safe.

We prop him up against the wall, his head lolling to one side. Ethan grimaces as he gently pries open the man's eyelid with his thumb and forefinger.

"Little more." Ethan struggles, trying to angle the man's head toward the scanner, but nothing happens. "Shit. Blake, hold his other eye open."

Blake complies, his face a mask of concentration. We must look ridiculous—three grown men wrestling with an unconscious body like some macabre puppet.

"Steady." Ethan tries to position the man's face as I bear the brunt of the man's weight.

The scanner beeps once, twice, then flashes green. A soft hiss sounds as the seal breaks.

We lower the man back to the floor, and I turn to the safe. Inside, we find stacks of documents, hard drives, and bundles of cash.

"Holy shit." I flip through pages of names, dates, and locations.

"Grab it all." Ethan's eyes harden as he surveys the contents. "Every last scrap."

The scale of this operation is bigger than I ever imagined.

A crackle comes through the comms. *"Gabe here. We found all four girls. They're in rough condition, but alive."*

Relief floods through me.

We have Jenna.

We have the girls.

We have intel.

This mission is turning out better than I dared to hope.

"Good job," Ethan replies. "Get them ready for extraction."

"Copy that," Gabe responds.

"Exfil in five," Ethan's voice crackles over the comm. "Wrap it up. Let's move. Time to get out of here."

We stuff everything into waterproof bags.

"There are thumb drives and external drives—you need to take those, too." Sophia points to the desk.

We sweep through the room, gathering every scrap of potential evidence. It's a goldmine of information, and I can only imagine what it will reveal about the scope of this operation.

"Rigel," Ethan speaks into his comm, "status on the engines?"

"Almost there," Rigel's voice returns through the comms. Seconds later, the vibrations from the engines stop. *"Disabled. This yacht isn't going anywhere."*

"Good. Meet us at the stern."

Gunfire erupts from above.

"Time to go." Ethan makes a circling gesture, telling us to wrap things up. Blake grabs Sophia, and Ethan grabs the waterproof bags full of the safe's contents. I fold Jenna into my arms.

"Ready?"

"No." She tucks her head beneath my chin, hugging me tight. "But I trust you."

"Stay close." I take her hand and place it on my belt at the small of my back. "Don't let go."

We move through the yacht, our progress slower now with Jenna and Sophia. As we near the deck, we encounter two more guards. This fight is quicker, our urgency lending speed to our blows.

Finally, we emerge onto the rear deck and swim platform. The night air is thick with salt spray and tension. Our inflatable boat bobs below. Bravo team closes in and continues to provide cover from their position away from the boat.

Moments later, the other four members of Charlie team arrive with the four missing teenagers. The girls are beaten, battered, and bruised, their eyes wide with fear, filled with a glimmer of hope, yet they're also in shock, their expressions vacant and bodies trembling.

Alpha team appears next, moving with precision and urgency.

We gather at the stern, the two RIBs waiting below are barely able to contain our numbers.

"Max, you take the four girls," Ethan gives commands. "It's going to be cramped, but we need to get everyone out safely."

"Ladies first." I help Jenna and then Sophia into the boat.

Once they're safely aboard, the rest of us follow. I keep Jenna close, trying to shield her from the wind and spray. Blake does the same for Sophia.

The teenagers are helped into the second RIB, and Alpha team ensures they're as comfortable as possible given the circumstances.

"Go, go, go!" Ethan yells once we're all onboard.

The engines roar to life, and we speed away from the yacht. Bravo team's RIB pulls up alongside Alpha team's boat.

"We've got space if you need it." Brady's voice carries over the noise of the waves and the engines. Two of the men from Alpha team transfer over.

As we head toward the shore, I allow myself a moment to breathe. I look down at Jenna, huddled against my chest. Her eyes meet mine, filled with exhaustion, relief, and something else—something that makes my heart skip a beat.

"I knew you'd find me." Her voice is barely audible over the roar of the engine and the splash of waves. I tighten my grip and take a breath.

She's safe.

The shore looms ahead, and the lights of emergency vehicles are visible even from this distance. As we near the beach, several figures wait for us: Guardian HRS personnel and local law enforcement.

We slow as we approach the shallows. The moment the bottom

of the boat scrapes against the sand, I scoop Jenna into my arms and leap into the knee-deep water. Behind me, there are splashes as the others follow suit.

Paramedics rush to meet us, blankets at the ready.

Not paramedics but medical personnel from Guardian HRS. Skye Summers takes Jenna from my arms.

"We're going to take good care of her." Skye soothes with her calming voice. "I promise."

I watch as they wrap her in a blanket and guide her toward a waiting ambulance. Sophia receives the same treatment. Blake hovers protectively over Sophia and, like I was with Jenna, doesn't appear to want to let her go.

"Carter." CJ pulls me away. He stands with a group of stern-faced men and one woman in suits—FBI, if I had to guess.

He introduces the agents. "Carter, meet Special Agent Lawson, Agent Harris, and Agent Reynolds from the FBI. This is Detective Carter, lead on this case."

Lead? I stand straighter, a swell of pride and gratitude washing over me. Guardian has been a powerhouse, and to have CJ acknowledge me in front of these federal agents is a significant validation of my work.

"We've been briefed on your situation," Agent Lawson says. "And we're here to help in any capacity." He turns toward CJ. "We understand this case has significant ties to—other ongoing investigations."

I haven't a clue what those are, but know better than to turn down help of any kind. Fortunately, CJ speaks up. "If you would accompany us to Guardian Headquarters, it would be best to debrief as a group."

"What about the yacht?" I look to CJ. "We need to send people out and apprehend them."

CJ and the Federal agents exchange a look. CJ clears his throat. "Unfortunately, they're in international waters. We don't have authority…"

I look to the team from the FBI, who nod.

"Well, shit." I run a hand through my hair.

"Don't worry. Mitzy will track them."

I cast one last glance at Jenna, realizing I won't be able to ride back with her.

She's safe.

That's what matters.

Everything else can wait.

Before joining the others in a van to head back to Guardian HQ, I make my way to the rescued girls. Seeing them here, safe, after working their cases for weeks, fills me with an overwhelming sense of relief and responsibility.

I clear my throat, drawing their attention. "Hi, I'm Detective Carter. I've been working on each of your cases for some time now, trying to find you and bring you home. You don't know me, but I know each of you. I've been staring at your pictures every day, hoping for this moment."

Emma Collins, Sarah Turner, Emily Hayes, and Grace Bennet, the smiling photos I've memorized don't match the haunted faces before me. The girls look at me with wide eyes, their expressions a mix of shock, exhaustion, and lingering fear. Their bodies are battered, bruised, and visibly shaken, their eyes wide with the terror they've endured and a glimmer of hope that it might finally be over.

I kneel to their level, my voice soft and steady. "First and foremost, we're going to take care of you. You'll be taken to a secure facility to get medical attention and rest. After that, we'll talk. I'll contact your families or whoever you want."

All four come from broken homes. They may not want their families notified—at least not at first. Severe trauma can often be a catalyst for repairing broken bonds, but I understand that they need time to process.

Tears well up in their eyes, and a few of them nod, the reality of their rescue slowly sinking in.

"You've been through so much, but it's over now." I reach out, gently touching Emma's shoulder. "You're safe with us. We'll make sure you're taken care of."

What I don't say, or maybe I did in my tone, is that they're far from safe. Jenna's abduction proves that the men who took them are still out there, and they might try to take them again. Their safety isn't guaranteed, but at least for now, they're out of immediate danger.

I stand, casting one more reassuring look at each of them before approaching the ambulance where Jenna and Sophia sit, both wrapped in blankets. My heart clenches seeing Jenna so worn out yet safe. I take her hand in mine.

"I have to debrief with the team," I say softly. "But I'll see you as soon as I'm free."

"Be safe." Her fingers tighten around mine.

"I will." I lean in, gently kissing her and pulling her into a tender embrace. "I'll be back soon."

She nods, her eyes glistening with unshed tears. As I pull away, the warmth of her touch lingers on my skin. With one last glance, I join the others, ready to finish what we started.

I follow Ethan toward a waiting van. My mind is already racing ahead. The information we recovered from the yacht could be the key to bringing down this entire trafficking ring. I'm eager to get my hands on it and dig in.

But it's not over—not by a long shot. Whoever is behind this is still out there. The fight isn't over. It's only just begun.

THIRTY-SIX

Carter

The clock on the dash flips to 0500 hours when we pull into Guardian HRS headquarters. My eyes burn with exhaustion, but there's no time for rest. Not with what we've uncovered.

"Let's move." Ethan's voice is gruff as he kills the engine.

We pile out, our footsteps echoing in the empty parking lot. The weight of the waterproof bags feels heavier than it should, laden with secrets we've yet to uncover.

Inside, the command center hums with activity. Screens flicker with data streams; the air is thick with tension and the acrid scent of stale coffee.

Mitzy, Stitch, and Jeb huddle around a central console while CJ and Sam confer in low voices nearby. Forest Summers stands at the helm, his presence commanding even in the early hours.

"What have you got for us?" Forest's eyes lock onto the bags we're carrying.

I upend the first bag onto a nearby table. Documents spill out, along with several hard drives. "Everything we could grab from the yacht."

Mitzy rifles through the papers, her brow furrowed in concentration. "This is going to take some time to sort through. I'm sure it's heavily encrypted."

"Start cataloging everything." Forest's expression is grim. "We need to know exactly what we're dealing with."

For the next few hours, we meticulously document each item. The team works in near silence, the gravity of what we uncovered weighing on us all.

"Look at this." Mitzy holds up a document, her finger tracing a series of symbols. "These keep repeating. Nine distinct markers."

Forest leans in, studying the page. "Interesting. Could be some kind of organizational structure."

More silence follows.

As noon draws near, CJ steps forward. "Alright, people. You've done good work. Get some rest. We'll pick this up again later."

Blake catches my eye. "You should see Jenna. She's probably waiting in medical."

"Yeah. Let's go." My bones ache with exhaustion, but the thought of seeing Jenna adds a spring to my step.

When we arrive, the medical wing is quiet. Jenna and Sophia sit together on a bed. Jenna has her arm around Sophia, who looks pale and vulnerable. The sight of them together, survivors supporting each other, tugs at something in my chest. When we enter, Jenna's eyes light up. She disentangles herself from Sophia and rushes into my arms.

"Carter." Her voice cracks with relief and exhaustion.

I wrap her in my arms, holding her as tightly as I dare. She buries her face in my chest, her shoulders shaking with silent sobs. I stroke her hair, murmuring soothing words into her ear, trying to calm the storm of emotions raging inside of me.

"How are you holding up?" My voice thickens with emotion.

"Better now that you're here." She clings to me like a lifeline, her fingers digging into my back and her tears soaking my shirt. I don't mind. It means this is real, and she's no longer in danger.

Sophia pushes back on the bed, drawing her knees up to her chest, curling into a tight ball. Blake hovers near the door, his gaze fixed on Sophia. His hand twitches at his side as if he wants to reach out, but he holds himself back.

"How are you *really* feeling?" I pull back just enough to examine the bruises marring her face.

"Like I've been hit by a truck." She manages a weak smile through her tears. "But I'll live. How's Max?"

"He's stable." Fortunately, Malia called me with an update a few hours ago. I brush a stray lock of hair from Jenna's forehead. "Lost a lot of blood, and the surgery was successful. He'll need time to recover, but he's going to be okay."

"Thank God. I want to see him." Relief washes over Jenna's face.

"We'll arrange that soon. We found a lot of stuff on the yacht, but most of it's encrypted. They haven't figured anything out yet, but I'm hopeful something will lead to Sentinel."

At the mention of Sentinel, Sophia's head lifts. Blake takes a half-step forward, reaching out before catching himself. I hold Jenna closer, feeling her heartbeat against mine, and press a gentle kiss to her forehead.

"I'll make them pay for this." My fingers brush her cheek, tracing the outline of a particularly dark bruise.

I kiss her again, softly, tenderly, then pull her even closer, holding her as if I could shield her from all the pain she's endured. After a long moment, I gently take her hands in mine, turning them over to look at her wrists. My thumb brushes over the hidden tattoo, barely visible under the UV light.

"Jenna," I say, my voice softer now, "do you know anything more about this? About *shàobīng* or if the number nine means you were his ninth?"

"Do you have something like this?" Jenna turns to Sophia.

"Mine's a bit different." Sophia nods slowly, her voice barely above a whisper. "But—it doesn't mean what you think."

"What do you mean?" Blake steps closer, his eyes narrowing.

"It's not about the number of women. It's Nine…"

"I get that." I lean in, confusion and annoyance flickering across my face.

"It's something else. Something bigger." Sophia's gaze shifts between Jenna and me, and then she looks down at her wrists.

"He's a Sentinel. There are nine of them, all with different roles." Sophia takes a shaky breath. "It doesn't mean you were the ninth slave he owned. It means he's the Ninth Sentinel."

"Ninth Sentinel?" Blake's eyebrows shoot up. "I thought Sentinel was an organization."

"No." Sophia shakes her head. "There are nine Sentinels. He was the Ninth."

"What does that mean?" I ask, my mind racing.

"Each one has a different role." Sophia uncurls slightly, her eyes distant. "The Ninth, he deals in human trafficking. The others... I don't know all of them, but I heard things. One deals with weapons, another with money... They're..." She grasps at the air as if struggling for an explanation.

"They're, what?" I ask gently.

"Disruptors. With a capital D. Their entire purpose is to disrupt the normal state of things." Sophia curls in on herself as if trying to disappear; her voice is low but clear.

"How do you know all this?" Jenna shifts closer, her hand resting gently on Sophia's arm.

"Jonathan—got complacent." Sophia's fingers twist in the blanket, her gaze distant.

"Jonathan?" Blake steps closer, his expression hardening.

"Jonathan Greaves." Sophia's voice trembles as she looks at Jenna, a mix of fear and regret in her eyes. "The Ninth Sentinel."

"That's his name? Jonathan Greaves?" I look to Blake, not needing to state the obvious. Sophia is a wealth of information.

"He thought I was broken, that I had no fight left in me. That I didn't matter anymore. He left me in rooms during meetings or talked on the phone like I wasn't there. I heard things I shouldn't have."

Blake's jaw clenches, his body angling toward Sophia as if to shield her from an unseen threat.

"There's more," Sophia whispers. "There's someone above

them all. Jonathan was terrified of him. I heard him begging for more time once, telling Malfor he'd fix it. No matter what."

Blake and I exchange another glance at the mention of Malfor. We know that name, but now isn't the time to discuss it.

"Fix what?" Blake asks.

"I don't know, but it was important, and he was scared."

"Thank you, Sophia," I say gently. "This is incredibly helpful."

Sophia nods, curling back into herself. Blake takes another half-step toward her before stopping, his hand clenching and unclenching at his side.

The weight of this new information settles over us. We've uncovered something massive, something that goes far beyond what any of us imagined.

Nine Sentinels.

Not Sentinel, but nine of them.

An organization so vast and complex it makes my head spin.

"How are *you* holding up?" Blake's gaze fixes on Sophia, his posture shifting subtly. There's a protectiveness there I've never seen before.

"Managing. Thanks for asking." Sophia glances up, her eyes meeting Blake's briefly before darting away. "It doesn't feel real."

There's so much I want to say and need to know, but now isn't the time to push.

I think of the document Mitzy showed us, the nine repeating symbols. "The tattoos," I breathe. "They're designations?"

"In so much, to say that we belong to the Ninth Sentinel. That's what our tattoo means." Sophia nods, her eyes haunted.

"Is there more?" Blake's voice is gentle and encouraging. "Other girls who belong to other Sentinels."

"Yes." Sophia swallows hard. "Lots more. Jonathan took extensive notes and records on inventory and transactions. He took private notes as well. Things he didn't share. Things he wasn't supposed to keep track of. That's why you had to take the stuff from the safe."

Sophia's words have severe implications. Blake and I exchange a look, realizing the gravity of what we've just learned.

"Sophia," I say gently, "I know this is difficult, but we must debrief you. The information you have is crucial."

"We need to know everything you've heard, every detail you can remember." Blake finally moves to stand beside Sophia. He places a hand on her shoulder, touching her as if she'll break.

Just as Sophia begins to respond, the door swings open. Dr. Skye Summers steps in. Her keen eyes take in the scene. "I came to check on our patients," she says, her voice calm but authoritative. "What's going on here?"

I briefly explain the information Sophia has shared, emphasizing its potential importance to our investigation.

"Absolutely not." Skye's expression hardens. "These women have been through a traumatic ordeal. They need rest and time to process, not an interrogation."

"Doc, the information Sophia has—" Blake steps forward, his protectiveness for Sophia evident.

"Can wait," Skye cuts him off firmly. "Their mental and physical health comes first. Period."

A tense silence falls over the room. Jenna's shoulders sag. Dark circles accentuate her eyes, and her movements are sluggish. As much as I want answers, Skye is right.

"I'm okay. I want to help." Sophia looks up, her voice steady despite her fatigue.

"I agree with the doc. You need to decompress and recover," Blake says. "We can debrief you later."

Once that is settled, I turn to Jenna and gently grasp her hand, feeling the weight of everything we've been through.

"What do you think about heading home? You could rest better there, and we can check on Max on the way."

"I don't want to leave her alone." Jenna hesitates, glancing at Sophia.

"She won't be alone." Blake steps in. "I'll watch over her and make sure she gets whatever she needs."

"Thanks." Sophia's gaze lingers on Blake, a faint blush coloring her cheeks. "Go check on Max. I feel safe with Blake. I'll be fine."

"Thank you, Blake." Relief fills Jenna's expression.

"Thanks, Doc. We'll head out now." I turn to Skye, gratitude in my eyes.

"Just make sure she gets some rest, and I'll want to check in on her."

"Promise." I take Jenna's hand, eager to get her out of here and someplace private.

Blake pulls me aside as we prepare to leave. "I'll keep you updated on anything Sophia shares, but…" His voice drops to a whisper. "Whatever's going on here, it's big. We need to be careful."

"I know."

With a final glance at Sophia, who watches with wary eyes, I lead Jenna out of the medical wing. I can't shake the feeling we've scratched the surface of something much larger and more dangerous than we ever imagined.

Nine Sentinels.

Malfor at the head.

An organization that spans the globe.

Disruptors.

My arm tightens around Jenna's waist, a fierce protectiveness surging through me.

Yeah, this is far from over.

THIRTY-SEVEN

Jenna

THE HUM OF THE CAR ENGINE FILLS THE SILENCE BETWEEN US. Carter's hand envelops mine, his thumb tracing gentle circles on my skin. The familiar streets of our town blur past the window, but I barely register them.

My mind races, replaying the events of the past few days in a never-ending loop.

The van.

The yacht.

Jonathan's cruel smile.

Sophia's betrayal and subsequent redemption.

It's all too much.

"Do you want to talk about it?" Carter's voice is soft—careful.

I shake my head, then pause. The weight of everything I've been through presses down on me, threatening to suffocate me.

"I can't stop thinking about Max."

"He's a fighter. Just like you." Carter's hand tightens around mine. His jaw clenches, a muscle twitching beneath the skin.

"He was so brave." My voice cracks. The memory floods back, vivid and painful. "When those men grabbed me, he just… He leaped at them. No hesitation."

The scene plays out in my mind: the snarl ripping from Max's throat, the flash of his teeth, the deafening crack of the gunshot. His yelp of pain was so sharp and sudden it felt like a knife to my heart.

"I saw him fall." My free hand clenches into a fist, nails digging into my palm. "There was so much blood. I thought... I thought he was gone."

"Max would do anything to protect you." Carter lifts our joined hands, pressing a gentle kiss to my knuckles. His eyes flick to mine, full of concern and love.

"How did you find him?" My voice trembles with lingering fear.

"I didn't know where to look at first." Carter's jaw tightens, his eyes darkening with the memory. "But I had to find you. I searched your apartment, then your shop. I knew something was wrong; I just felt it. When I couldn't find you, I retraced the path you take when walking home. That's when I found Max and your phone. I called Walt and he, of course, called Guardian HRS. That place is beyond incredible. By the time we took Max to the emergency vet, Guardian HRS had already mobilized Blake's team. Mitzy was on the traffic cameras. She saw you being taken, then told us where to go. I couldn't stop thinking about you." He trails off, swallowing hard.

I squeeze his hand, encouraging him to continue.

"Walt helped me get Max to the vet. Malia stayed behind. She kept me updated while we were..." His knuckles whiten on the steering wheel. "While we were looking for you."

The car falls silent again. I stare out the window, watching the world rush by. My mind drifts back to Sophia's pale face and trembling hands.

"How did Sophia play into this?" Carter glances at me, his brow furrowing.

"She just—appeared. Out of nowhere." I take a deep breath, the memory washing over me. "Walt was supposed to be on a date with Malia. She left early to get ready. I told him to leave, but he didn't want to. Please don't blame him for what happened. I made him go."

"I don't blame him."

"Well, I was closing the café, and suddenly, there she was, looking like a ghost."

"What do you mean?"

"She was so frail. Her clothes were rumpled and loose like she hadn't changed in days. And her eyes…" I shudder, remembering the hollow, haunted look in Sophia's gaze. "They were empty. Like all the life has been drained out of her." My voice wavers, and I wrap my arms around myself, mirroring the way Sophia held herself.

"Her hands trembled. Her entire body shook. Her fingernails dug into her arms like she was trying to hold herself together. She looked so fragile." Looking back at Carter, I see a mix of sorrow and determination in his eyes. "When she talked to me, it was like she was searching for something, anything to anchor her. Her entire body seemed to curl in on itself like she was trying to disappear."

"What did she say to you?" Carter's hand tightens on mine.

"She begged me for help. Said she'd escaped, that she needed somewhere to hide." My voice cracks. "God, Carter, she looked so scared. I couldn't turn her away."

"You let her in."

I nod, shame and anger warring inside me. "I thought I was helping her. I made her tea and tried to calm her down. She kept looking over her shoulder like she expected someone to burst in at any moment."

"Then what happened?"

"She asked if we could go somewhere more private. Said she was afraid they'd find her if we stayed in the café." I close my eyes, remembering the moment everything went wrong. "I suggested we go to my place. We were halfway there when—"

"The van," Carter finishes softly.

"Yeah." I swallow hard. "I never saw it coming. One minute we were walking, the next—chaos. And Sophia, she just—changed. It was like a switch flipped. She went from terrified victim to… I don't know. Resigned? Defeated? Ashamed? She knew what was coming. I thought I was helping her, you know." The words tumble out before

I can stop them. "Sophia. She looked so scared, so vulnerable. I never imagined…"

Carter's thumb resumes its gentle circles on my hand. "It wasn't your fault."

"I was so angry when I realized." Hot tears prick at my eyes. "When I saw her climb into that van. I wanted to hate her."

"But you don't?"

"How can I? After seeing what he did to her. How he used her. She didn't have a choice." I shake my head. The memory of Sophia's broken expression on the yacht is seared into my mind.

I squeeze my eyes shut, trying to block out the images, but they flood back with brutal clarity. "I saw fear in her eyes, the way she flinched whenever he came near. His touch was a weapon. His words poison. He didn't *just* hurt her physically. He shattered her spirit, piece by piece."

My voice breaks, and I clutch my arms tighter around myself as if trying to hold my own pieces together. "He paraded her in front of me, a twisted display of his control. Of what he would do to me. Sophia's eyes were vacant. Like she'd given up hope. She didn't fight; she just accepted what he did. It was terrifying."

Tears sting my eyes, but I blink them back, refusing to let them fall. "How can I blame her for anything, knowing what she went through? He turned her into a shadow of her former self. She didn't have a choice. She was as much a victim as I was, maybe even more."

Carter's grip on my hand tightens.

The memory of Jonathan's cold eyes and cruel smile makes me shudder. Carter notices and pulls over to the side of the road. He turns to face me, both hands now holding mine.

I lean into him, burying my face in his chest. His arms wrap around me, solid and secure. For a moment, we just breathe together.

"Is Max really okay?" I mumble into his shirt. I don't want to talk about Sophia anymore. My heart can't take the brutality she endured.

"He's tough, just like you." Carter pulls back, his hand coming up to cup my cheek.

"Can we see him? Before we go home?" A watery laugh escapes me.

"Of course." Carter starts the car again, pulling back onto the road. "He'll be happy to see you." As we drive toward the vet clinic, I lean my head against Carter's shoulder. For the first time since this nightmare began, I feel safe.

Max is alive.

I'm safe.

We're together.

Carter's voice breaks the silence. "Maybe we stop at home first?" His thumb still traces circles on my hand, a gentle, soothing motion.

"Home?" I lift my head to look at him.

Home.

The way he says it, like it's his too, sends a warm flutter through my chest. I want that.

I want us to have our home.

"Yeah," he says softly, his eyes flicking between me and the road.

"But I want to see Max."

"Max is still recovering from surgery." Carter's eyes flick toward me before returning to the road. "Malia's with him, keeping an eye on things. I think you should take a warm shower and put on some fresh clothes. It might help you feel human again."

I open my mouth to protest, but Carter continues, his voice soft but firm.

"That way, we can spend more time with Max without having to leave for these things. He'll be more alert later too."

Reluctantly, I nod. As much as I want to see Max right now, Carter's right. I'm exhausted, sore, and probably look a mess. I nod slowly, the thought of a shower and clean clothes suddenly incredibly appealing.

"We'll check on Max right after, I promise." Carter squeezes my hand, a small smile tugging at his lips.

"Okay," I whisper. "Home first."

"It won't be long, I promise. Just a quick stop, then we'll go see our boy."

Our boy.

The words settle in my chest, warm and comforting. As Carter turns the car toward home—our home—another spark ignites in my heart.

The rest of the drive passes in a blur of streetlights and the rhythmic hum of the engine. Carter's presence beside me is a steady anchor, keeping the lingering fear at bay. I'll need to deal with my trauma, but I'll do that—later.

The apartment door clicks shut behind us. The familiar surroundings are both comforting and surreal. Everything looks the same, yet nothing feels the same. Carter's hand on the small of my back guides me gently forward.

"Let's get you cleaned up." His voice is low and soothing.

I nod, suddenly aware of how heavy my limbs feel and how every movement takes effort. Carter leads me to the bathroom, his presence steady and reassuring.

The hiss of the shower fills the small space as Carter turns the knobs, adjusting the temperature. Steam begins to rise, fogging the mirror and wrapping around us like a warm blanket. I stand there, swaying slightly, as Carter turns to me.

His hands are gentle as he helps me out of my clothes, his touch reverent, careful of my bruises and scrapes. My energy seems to evaporate with each layer removed until I'm standing bare, vulnerable, barely able to keep my eyes open.

Carter sheds his clothes quickly before guiding me into the shower. Hot water cascades over us, and I lean my forehead against the cool tiles, letting out a shaky breath.

Carter's hands are on me again, gentle and sure, as they work shampoo through my hair. His fingers massage my scalp, and some of the tension in my body melts away. He works methodically, washing away the grime and fear infusing every pore.

The last of my strength fades as he runs the washcloth over my skin. A sob escapes me, then another, until I'm shaking with the force of them. Carter's arms encircle me immediately, pulling me against his chest.

Holding me.

"I've got you," he whispers into my hair. "I've got you."

I cling to him, my face buried in the crook of his neck as the water beats down on us. Slowly, the sobs subside, replaced by bone-deep exhaustion and something else—a need to be closer, to feel alive.

I lift my head, meeting Carter's gaze. His eyes are dark with concern, with love, and with a hunger that matches my own. Slowly, giving me every chance to pull away, he lowers his lips to mine.

The kiss is gentle at first, a reaffirmation of life and love.

His kiss is tentative as if he's afraid I might break, but as the warmth of his body seeps into mine, something ignites within me—a hunger and desperate need to feel alive.

My hands slide up his chest, feeling the strong beat of his heart beneath my palms. I tangle my fingers in his hair, pulling him closer. Carter responds instantly, his arms tightening around me, molding my body to his.

The kiss deepens, becoming more urgent, more passionate. Carter's tongue traces the seam of my lips, and I open to him with a soft moan. The taste of him, the feel of his skin against mine, it's intoxicating. I lose myself in the sensation, in the heat building between us.

His touch is both soothing and arousing, and a familiar heat pools in my stomach. His lips brush against my neck, trailing feather-light kisses that send shivers down my spine.

"You're so beautiful." His voice is rough with desire.

Carter's hands roam my body, leaving trails of fire in their wake, fanning the flames of my desire. He traces the curve of my spine, the swell of my hips, his touch both reverent and possessive. I arch into him, craving more, needing to be closer.

My nipples harden under his touch, and I can't restrain the moan that escapes my lips. His touch sends electricity coursing through my veins, straight to my core, where the heat between my legs grows more insistent with each passing second. I need him—need to feel him inside me.

I reach for him, but Carter's warm hands stop mine.

"Slow down." He breathes into my ear, sending shivers down my spine. "I want to savor every inch of this body, but we can stop at any time."

His fingers continue their agonizingly slow exploration of my body. His eyes never leave mine as he caresses the sensitive skin of my stomach before making his way up to cup my breasts.

My breath catches in anticipation as his thumbs tease my swollen nipples, causing me to arch my back, silently begging for more.

"I don't want to stop."

His response is a wicked grin before he lowers his mouth to my cleavage, nipping and sucking where he'd just been touching. He trails kisses down my stomach until my whole body is on fire.

Carter kneels in front of me, his eyes locked with mine. A shiver of anticipation runs down my spine, sending my heart racing. His breath is hot against my skin, each kiss more deliberate and tantalizing than the one before. I arch, offering myself to him.

With a gentle touch, he presses a kiss right where I'm most sensitive—that spot between my thighs that feels like it's on fire with desire. The soft heat of his lips causes me to gasp again, and this time, it's more of a moan than anything else.

He takes his time exploring with his tongue, dancing around my clit before finally circling it slowly and deliberately.

I throw my head back in pure ecstasy, feeling like I might explode from the sheer pleasure coursing through me. My fingers find their way into his hair as he devours me with his mouth, each lick and suck driving me further over the edge. I beg him without words, pleading for more as he works his magic on me.

Carter doesn't disappoint; he slides two fingers inside of me and strokes in time with his tongue. The sensation is overwhelmingly intense but in the best way possible. I feel every stroke, as well as each swirl around my clit, as he continues to lavish attention on both areas simultaneously.

The shower fills with muffled noises of pleasure escaping from between my parted lips and gasping breaths while Carter feasts on me like a delicacy prepared just for him alone.

Carter works his magic between my legs, and my moans turn into cries when he finally brushes his thumb over my clit. The sensation causes undulating sensations throughout my entire body. I come apart, screaming out his name before crashing into an orgasm so powerful it leaves me shaken.

On his feet, he pushes me against the shower wall. His fingers dig into my hips. Carter lifts me, pinning me gently against the cool tiles. The contrast of temperatures—the heat of his body, the coolness of the wall—sends shivers down my spine.

I wrap my legs around him, feeling every ripple of his hard abs beneath my fingers. I draw him closer, needing him with an intensity that takes my breath away. My heart drums a rapid beat, each thump echoing the thrill and anticipation coursing through me.

He presses our bodies together, chest to chest, his hardness pushing against my curves. My breath hitches in my throat as he looks down at me with lust and adoration in his eyes. The water pours around us, adding to the steam as we stand entwined under the hot spray.

His hands grip me firmly, holding me close as he gazes into my eyes with a look that makes my stomach flutter. His lips press against mine while he eases into me, thrusting deeper with each pulse of his hips.

Every inch of his thick length stretches me open. He takes it slow at first—savoring every moment—until he's completely buried inside me.

We move together, creating sparks of electricity. I lose myself in the sensations—the slide of wet skin, the taste of him on my lips, the sound of our mingled breaths, and my soft moans echoing in the small space.

It's overwhelming, all-consuming, and exactly what I need.

The tension builds, a coiling heat in my core that grows with each passing moment. Carter's movements become more urgent, his grip on me tightening. I cling to him, my nails digging into his shoulders as I teeter on the edge of oblivion.

He shifts his angle, pressing deeper still, hitting that spot inside of me that sends waves upon waves of pleasure coursing through my body for the second time.

When I fall, it's with Carter's name on my lips, a cry of pleasure and release. He follows me over the edge, burying his face in my neck as he shudders against me.

The musky scent of arousal fills the air around us, mixed with the clean smell of soap—it's intoxicatingly sensual and addictive all at once. We're completely lost in each other—two souls connected by nothing but raw passion and primal desire for more than just physical release.

Each thrust, each caress, each whispered endearment is a promise. A vow that we're here, we're alive, and we're together. It's as if we've never been apart—every touch, every caress feels so right, so perfect.

Afterward, we stand together under the cooling water, our foreheads pressed together, just breathing. Carter's hands stroke my back in soothing circles as I nuzzle into his chest, listening to the steady thump of his heartbeat.

For the first time since this nightmare began, I feel whole again, safe and loved. The horrors of my capture seem distant now, washed away by the strength of our connection and the depth of our love.

Carter's hands continue their gentle exploration, no longer urgent with passion but tender with care. His fingers trace the outline of my face, brushing away stray droplets of water. I lean into his touch, savoring the warmth of his palm against my cheek.

"You're beautiful," he murmurs, his eyes roaming my face as if memorizing every detail. "I'm absolutely and totally captivated by you."

Warmth creeps up my neck, heating my cheeks. Even after everything, he still has this effect on me. I stretch up on my toes, pressing a soft kiss to the corner of his mouth.

"Thank you," I whisper. "For everything. For finding me, for saving me, for being here for me. And I'm absolutely and totally captivated by you, as well."

"I love you." Carter pulls me closer, enveloping me in his strong arms.

"I love you more." I rest my head on his chest, listening to the steady thump of his heart.

We stand like that for a long moment, the cooling water cascading over us, neither willing to break the peaceful bubble we've created.

Eventually, Carter reaches behind me, shutting off the water. He grabs a towel, wrapping it around me before quickly drying himself off. His hands are gentle as he pats me dry, careful of the bruises that mar my skin. When he's done, he pulls me into another embrace, pressing a kiss to the top of my head.

"We should get dressed," Carter murmurs eventually, pressing a soft kiss to my temple. "Max is waiting."

THIRTY-EIGHT

Carter

THE ANTISEPTIC SMELL OF THE VET CLINIC HITS ME AS SOON AS WE walk through the doors. Jenna's hand tightens in mine, her anticipation palpable. The receptionist recognizes me immediately, offering a warm smile as she leads us to Max's room.

My heart clenches as we enter. Max lies on a large, padded bed, various tubes and monitors attached to his body, but as soon as he sees us, his tail thumps weakly against the bed.

"Hey, buddy," I say, my voice thick with emotion. I kneel beside him, gently stroking his head. "You gave us quite a scare."

Jenna joins me, tears streaming down her face as she carefully hugs Max.

"My brave boy," she whispers, burying her face in his fur.

"He's doing remarkably well." The vet enters, clipboard in hand. "The bullet missed all vital organs, and he's responding well to treatment. With some rest and care, he should make a full recovery."

Relief washes over me. I look at Jenna, seeing my own emotions mirrored in her eyes. We're all going to be okay.

We spend the next hour with Max, talking to him softly and showering him with gentle affection. Jenna pulls out some treats she made special for him. His eyes never leave us, as if he's afraid we'll disappear if he looks away.

"I'm so sorry, Max," Jenna murmurs, her fingers tracing the bandages on his side. "You were so brave."

I wrap an arm around her shoulders, pulling her close. "He protected you. Just like he always has. Just like he always will."

Max's tail wags a bit stronger at that as if he understands my words. He manages to lift his head enough to lick Jenna's hand. She laughs softly, the sound like music after everything we've been through.

As we sit there, the three of us reunited, a sense of peace settles over me. Despite everything that's happened, this moment feels perfect.

The vet returns, informing us that Max needs his rest. We say our goodbyes, promising to return every day until he can go home. As we walk out, hand in hand, I realize how lucky I am to have Jenna by my side and Max on the mend.

We're halfway to the car when my phone buzzes. I pull it out, seeing Ethan's name on the screen. My stomach tightens—this isn't a social call.

"Everything okay?" Jenna asks, noticing my hesitation.

I nod, squeezing her hand reassuringly before answering. "Ethan, what's up?"

"Carter, we need you back at HQ." His voice is tense, urgent. *"Mitzy and Jinx have cracked some of the encryption. It's big."*

"Jinx?" I frown, the unfamiliar name catching me off guard. "Who's that?"

"Right, sorry," Ethan says quickly. *"Jinx is a former DEA codebreaker. Forest brought her in to help with the decryption. She's good. Really good."*

"How soon do you need me there?" I process this new information, my mind already racing with possibilities.

"Now, if possible. Sorry, I know you're with Jenna and Max, but..."

"No, I get it. I'll be there soon." I hang up, turning to Jenna with an apologetic look.

"Duty calls?" She smiles sadly, understanding in her eyes.

"I'm sorry." I pull her in tight, loving the feel of her in my arms.

"Don't be," she interrupts, her voice muffled against my chest. "Go. Do what you need to do. Max and I will be here when you get back."

"I'm not leaving you alone." I kiss her deeply, trying to convey everything I'm feeling—love, gratitude, determination. As I pull away, I rest my forehead against hers. "You're coming with me, where I can protect you."

"Carter—you don't have to…"

"I love you, and I'm not leaving you alone." I'll repeat myself as many times as it takes. After almost losing her, there's no way I'm leaving her without protection.

"I love you more." She lifts on tiptoe for a kiss. "Now go save the world."

We head back to Guardian HQ. I drop Jenna off at the medical center to visit Sophia.

The familiar hum of activity greets me as I stride into Guardian HRS headquarters. The command center is a hive of focused energy, screens flickering with data streams and analysts hunched over keyboards. I spot Ethan near the central console and make my way over.

"What's up?" I ask, diving straight in.

"Mitzy and Jinx are about to brief us." Ethan's face is grim.

As if on cue, Mitzy approaches. Her rainbow hair contrasts sharply with the seriousness in her eyes. Beside her is a woman I don't recognize—Jinx, I assume. She's tall and lean, with sharp features and eyes that seem to take in everything at once.

"Glad you could make it, Carter," Mitzy says. "We've got a lot to cover."

We gather around the main display as Mitzy pulls up documents and diagrams. The encryption symbols I remember from earlier are there, but now they're partially decoded, revealing a complex web of information.

"Alright, listen up," Mitzy begins. "Thanks to Jinx here, we've managed to crack a significant portion of Sentinel's encryption. What we've found is… Well, it's not good."

"The nine Sentinels aren't just an organizational structure." Jinx steps forward, her voice crisp and professional. "They're individuals, each with a specific role in Sentinel's global operations."

She taps a few keys, and nine silhouettes appear on the screen, each labeled with a number and a title. Only the ninth one has a name and a face.

"Sentinel One: Strategy and Leadership. Two: Finance and Money Laundering. Three: Weapons Development and Distribution. Four: Cyber Operations. Five: Intelligence and Counterintelligence. Six: Recruitment and Training. Seven: Logistics and Transportation. Eight: Research and Development. And Nine: Human Trafficking and Exploitation."

My stomach churns as I stare at Jonathan Greave's face, the Ninth Sentinel. The man who took Jenna and hurt so many others. He's just one part of this monstrous organization.

"Each Sentinel operates independently," Jinx continues, "but they're all connected through a centralized communication network. They report to a single individual known only as Malfor."

"Tell me more about Malfor."

"We know more than we'd like, but not nearly enough." Mitzy's expression darkens. "Stitch, you want to take this one?"

Stitch steps forward, her usual confident demeanor tinged with unease. She takes a deep breath before speaking.

"Malfor isn't just a name in encrypted files. He—or she, or they… It's personal." Stitch's voice is tight with suppressed emotion. "Malfor was my mentor, back when I was just a kid with a keyboard and too much curiosity. Taught me everything I know about hacking. Well, almost everything."

She pauses, her eyes distant. "Malfor's the one who got me arrested. Dared me to hack the NSA, then abandoned me when I got caught. I thought my life was over after that, but Mitzy recruited me. I joined Guardian HRS and was immediately assigned to the Citadel case." She shakes her head. "After the Citadel incident, I received a text from Malfor. Telling me to back off and stay away from Sentinel."

The room falls silent as I process this information.

"Malfor's not just the head of Sentinel," Ethan says slowly. "He's a master hacker, on par with, or better than, Stitch."

"And they're not afraid to play the long game." Mitzy nods grimly. "Grooming Stitch from childhood, setting her up years later… This is someone with patience, resources, and a frighteningly strategic mind."

"But we still don't know who he is?" Frustration colors my voice.

"No," Stitch admits. "Malfor could be anyone. Man, woman, a group of people… Hell, for all we know, it could be an AI. Whoever or whatever Malfor is, he/she/they are incredibly good at staying hidden."

As the briefing continues, I can't shake the feeling we've just scratched the surface of something far more complex and dangerous than we ever imagined. The fight against Sentinel isn't about bringing down criminals anymore. It's a chess game with the highest stakes imaginable, and we're playing against a grandmaster we can't even see.

After some discussion, the room falls into a tense silence as we all grapple with the implications of what we've learned. CJ finally breaks the silence, his voice cutting through the heavy atmosphere.

"It's time we hear from someone who's been on the inside." His eyes scan the room.

"Agreed. Let's bring Sophia in." Mitzy nods, her expression grim. "Our hope is she will be able to fill in some of the gaps."

THIRTY-NINE

Carter

We all know how fragile Sophia is and how traumatized her experiences have made her, but we also know that her insights could be crucial.

"I'll get her," Blake volunteers, his voice tight with barely concealed protectiveness.

I do a double take because I've never seen Blake act like this before.

As he leaves to fetch Sophia, the rest of us rearrange ourselves, preparing for what promises to be a difficult debriefing. I can't help feeling a twinge of guilt, knowing we're about to ask Sophia to relive her worst nightmares.

I did that to Jenna and experienced the fallout firsthand.

Minutes later, the door opens. The briefing room falls silent as Sophia enters. Blake is close behind, protecting her.

Her shoulders are hunched, and her gaze darts nervously around the room. Blake's posture is rigid, and his eyes scan each person as if assessing potential threats.

The tension in the room ratchets up another notch as Sophia sits at the table. We're all acutely aware of the delicate balance we're trying to strike—between getting the information we need without further traumatizing a victim of Sentinel's cruelty.

Ethan speaks first, his voice gentle but probing. I steel myself for what's to come. Whatever Sophia has to tell us, I have a feeling it's going to change everything.

"Sophia," Ethan begins gently, "can you tell us more about the Ninth Sentinel's operations? You mentioned he allowed you to stay in place during business dealings."

"He—he thought I was broken. Harmless." Sophia's hands tremble slightly as she speaks. "He'd leave me in the room during meetings, on phone calls. I heard—so much."

Blake's hand comes to rest on her shoulder, a gesture of support and protection. Sophia draws strength from it, sitting up a little straighter.

"There were frequent calls about shipments. Girls, mostly, but sometimes weapons or drugs. He used code words, but I started to understand them over time."

Sophia pauses, her eyes meeting mine for a brief moment. "A few weeks ago, there was a call about a new acquisition. It was a new order for four girls. Jonathan seemed—excited about them. Said they were perfect retribution."

"Retribution?" I lean forward. "Retribution for what?"

"I don't know, but he was really excited." She pauses for a moment, darkness hooding her eyes. "Not in a good way. He's a sadist. A wicked man. If he said *retribution*, he meant that he wanted to hurt someone. I don't know how, but those girls are somehow connected. I'm sorry, but I don't know anything more than that."

"Why wait?" A sudden thought strikes me.

"Excuse me?" Sophia blinks slowly, shifting her attention to me.

"He abducted the girls weeks before putting them on the yacht."

"No. They were there the whole time."

The whole time? I didn't see where the girls were kept, but it was on one of the lower decks. I couldn't imagine their terror.

"Why didn't he move them sooner? They're a liability."

She looks up at Blake, then curls into herself. The entire room waits, giving her breathing room and time to think. She finally takes a deep breath, her fingers twisting together nervously, and looks at me.

"He was waiting." Her voice trembles. "He had orders to hold. Malfor… Malfor told him to wait."

"Wait for what?" Ethan leans in, his brow furrowing.

"For Jenna," Sophia whispers, her voice barely audible. "Jonathan didn't know the exact reason at first. Malfor just ordered him to wait. He found out later that it was because of Jenna. Capturing her would be a huge win for him, a personal vendetta against the one who got away."

A chilling picture emerges.

"He was waiting for Malfor's go-ahead. It was all about timing and making the most of his *prize*. He spent a week watching her café, establishing her routines. Who knew her, and who would care if she disappeared. He hated you." Sophia once again stares at me. "And then he noticed she was being guarded—and protected." She sniffs. "That's when he devised his plan and told me what I had to do." Tears fall, and she swipes absently at her cheeks. "I couldn't refuse. I had no choice."

"No one is blaming you, Sophia." Blake places a hand on her shoulder, giving a reassuring squeeze. "We understand you were forced."

"That's right." I step in, needing to reassure Sophia that none of us blame her for what happened to Jenna.

A heavy silence fills the room as we process Sophia's revelation. The Ninth Sentinel's cruelty and meticulous planning are more horrifying than I imagined.

"I just want it to be over." Sophia's eyes flicker with relief, and her shoulders sag with exhaustion.

"I wish we had taken him when we rescued the women." My mind races with this added information. "We should've taken him during the rescue."

"We would have." CJ pushes back in his chair. "But we weren't prepped for that, and by the time we could, they'd already fixed their engines and powered into international waters."

The Ninth Sentinel's strategy is clear—he's a predator, waiting for the perfect moment to strike.

"I wouldn't worry about him," Sophia speaks up.

"Why not?"

"Malfor doesn't tolerate failure. He'll be taken care of, one way or another." Silence falls over the room as we absorb Sophia's words.

"Thank you, Sophia. You've been incredibly brave and given us crucial information," Ethan finally breaks the silence. "Blake, do you mind escorting her back to medical?"

"Sure thing." Blake offers a hand to help Sophia out of her chair, then hovers protectively beside her as they exit the briefing room. Once the door closes, Forest clears his throat.

"This is bigger than we thought." Forest's voice is grave. "Nine Sentinels, each controlling a different aspect of global criminal operations. Disrupters. That's what she called them. We're talking about an organization with unprecedented reach and resources."

"Not to mention Malfor," Mitzy adds. "A master pulling all the strings."

The discussion continues with plans being formed and discarded as we grapple with what we're facing.

"If Malfor's going after the Ninth Sentinel," Forest says, "we need to act fast. We can't let him get to Jonathan Greaves before we do."

"Agreed," Ethan's voice remains steady. "If we offer Greaves protection, maybe we can get him to flip on Malfor and the entire operation. It's a long shot, but it might be our best chance to understand this network and how it works."

A lull settles over the conversation, the weight of the discussion hanging in the air. Sam and CJ break off from the briefing and approach me, their expressions serious.

"Carter, got a moment?" Sam's voice breaks the silence.

"Sure, what's up?" I shift my focus to them.

"We're impressed with how you handled yourself with Charlie team." Sam crosses his arms, a hint of a smile playing on his lips.

"Thanks, but I was just doing my job." I straighten, feeling a surge of pride.

"You did more than just your job," Sam insists, his gaze unwavering. "You kept a cool head under pressure, and that's not something everyone can do."

"Thanks." I pause, glancing around at the impressive setup. "I've been grateful for the opportunity to be part of this."

CJ steps forward, his eyes steady on mine. "Carter, your detective skills are exactly what we need. Your instincts and your ability to think on your feet—those are invaluable. Training can be provided, but what you bring to the table is something special. You'd make a great addition to our team."

"I appreciate the offer, but I'm not trained like the others." I shake my head, cutting him off. "It was great to be included, but I lack essential skills. Plus, I want to be there for Jenna."

I've always felt like I've lived in Blake's shadow. He became a US Navy SEAL while my life got sidelined by a pregnancy scare for a baby that wasn't even mine. I did the right thing: stepped up, got a job, missed my chance with the Navy, and then found out it was all for nothing.

But I landed well.

I love being a detective. I've never regretted the path I landed on, and I'm good at my job—damn good. My brain loves the challenge of putting the pieces of a puzzle together and breaking a case. Being included in these missions with Blake was eye-opening. I saw what he does, and it's incredible, but that's not the life I want for myself.

Sam and CJ exchange a look, a silent conversation passing between them.

"What about joining as a Protector?" Sam's voice is earnest.

"A Protector?" I frown, confused.

CJ leans in, his tone serious. "Protectors are our personal protection specialists. The threat to Jenna is still out there, and after what Sophia said and your reaction, it's clear there are unresolved pieces to your investigation surrounding why those girls were chosen. You could be Jenna's Protector and continue to work on this case. It's a way to stay involved without the intensive combat training our field operatives undergo."

"You mean I'd get access to all this amazing tech? I've been wanting that since I saw your setup." I smirk, a thought crossing my mind.

"We've got great tech, the best in the world, and our operatives are top notch." Sam chuckles, glancing at CJ before turning back to me. "What we struggle with is finding good men—and women. Please don't tell Mitzy I said *men*, she'll have my hide. What I mean is we can always use strong operatives. We need you on our team."

The idea hangs in the air, and I weigh it carefully. Being close to Jenna, ensuring her safety, and continuing to work on the case—it's tempting. I look between Sam and CJ, searching their faces for any sign of doubt. They both seem confident, and their belief in my abilities bolsters my own.

"The Ninth Sentinel is still out there. As long as he's alive, Jenna's at risk. But if Malfor gets to him first and kills him, the risk to Jenna remains."

CJ nods, his voice grave. "Malfor offered Jenna as a prize to the Ninth Sentinel. Until Malfor is brought down, her life will always be in jeopardy."

"So, what are you saying?" The weight of their words hits me like a ton of bricks. "That she needs to go into protective custody?"

"Exactly," Sam says, his tone somber. "Her life isn't going to be able to continue the way it is. She needs protection, and that's where you come in. As her Protector, you can ensure her safety 24/7."

The thought of Jenna having to live her life under constant guard makes my heart ache. She's already been through so much.

"And you think I'm the right person for this?"

"You've got the training and the skills." CJ steps closer, his hand resting on my shoulder. "You've already proven yourself, and you care about her. That's what she needs right now—someone who's not just doing a job but truly invested in her well-being. Not to mention, we get the added benefit of your detective skills. You want access to our tech? It's yours."

"Okay. I'm in." I take a deep breath, letting their words sink in.

"I'll do whatever it takes to keep her safe, but who's going to break the news to Jenna?"

"Sounds like the perfect job for her Protector." Sam huffs a laugh. "But seriously, we'll walk you through the program. She's going to have questions."

"Welcome to the Guardians and Protectors." CJ extends a hand. Relief is evident in his voice.

The thought of being Jenna's Protector, of being there for her in every way, stirs something deep within me. Maybe this is the path I'm meant to take, but it's a big step, one that will change everything.

As they walk away, I shake my head, pushing thoughts aside for now. Right now, I have more immediate concerns—plans to make, operations to coordinate, and Jenna to protect.

Speaking of, I need to tell Jenna her life's about to change.

FORTY

Carter

When I pick Jenna up from medical, she's curled up in a chair, a book forgotten in her lap. Her face lights up, and she jumps up, racing into my arms. She wraps her arms around my neck, pulling me into a tight embrace, her body warm and soft against mine.

Without hesitation, she presses her lips to mine in a big, fat kiss, pouring all her relief and love into it. Her fingers tangle in my hair, and I hold her close, the weight of the world momentarily lifting. When we finally pull back, she rests her forehead against mine, her eyes searching mine.

When we arrive at her apartment, it feels different. The weight of Guardian HRS's offer is heavy on my mind.

"It's good to be home," she whispers, her voice filled with emotion.

"Agreed," I reply, my heart swelling with gratitude for this incredible woman in my arms. I guide her to the couch. "I've got some things to tell you."

"What?"

"We uncovered a lot of information, but there's something you need to know."

"What?" Jenna pulls back slightly, her eyes searching mine.

"They offered me a position as a Protector." I take a deep breath.

"Protector? What's that?"

"The official title is Personal Protection Specialist. It's like a bodyguard for people who need to disappear."

"Disappear?"

"Yeah, people with active threats against them."

Jenna frowns, a flicker of concern crossing her face. "Who would you be protecting?"

"I would be your Protector."

She looks at me, shocked. "Me? Why would I need protection? The threat against me is gone. Isn't it? I thought it was gone."

I sigh, taking her hands in mine. "Greaves is still out there. Malfor and his network don't tolerate failure. He's a loose end they won't ignore. Even though we rescued you, the danger hasn't passed. They might come after you again."

Her eyes widen, and she takes a step back, her hand covering her mouth. "What does that mean?"

I struggle to find the right words. "It means you'd have to change your entire life. New identity, new location... Everything. And I'd be your Protector, ensuring your safety."

She looks at me, shocked. "Change my life? Again? But what about my café? What about everything I've built?"

"It's a huge change, and it's not fair. But I promise we'll find a way to make it work. Your safety is the most important thing."

"And if I don't do this?" She's silent for a moment, processing the weight of my words.

I take a deep breath, my heart aching at the thought of what I have to say next. "If you don't, you'll always be at risk. You'll always have to look over your shoulder, never feeling safe. You could never be alone, never relax. They'd find you eventually. But if you do this, I'll be right there by your side. We'll figure out a new life together. You won't be alone in this. I promise."

"I thought it was over. That I was finally free." She buries her face in my chest, her body trembling. "I don't want to live in fear, but it's a lot to give up."

"I know." I hold her tighter.

She's quiet for a long moment, her fingers absently tracing patterns on my back. "What do you think about it?"

"There's more work to be done. This is a chance to make a real difference, to be part of something bigger. But it's not about me."

"You've always been my protector." She cups my face in her hands, her gaze steady. "This would just make it official." Her words wash over me, easing some of the tension I've been carrying.

"I love you," I murmur, pulling her in for a kiss.

"I love you more." She breathes out a sigh, her eyes shimmering with emotion.

Our lips meet, and the world fades away.

The kiss starts slow and tender, a gentle exploration that deepens with every passing second. Her hands slide from my face to my shoulders, pulling me closer. I feel her warmth, her heartbeat echoing in time with mine.

Her taste is intoxicating, a blend of sweetness and desire that makes my pulse race. I lose myself in her, in the sensation of her lips moving against mine, her breath mingling with mine.

The kiss is long and languid, unhurried, a dance of tongues and whispers that leaves us both breathless.

When we finally part, our foreheads rest together.

"We'll build a new life where you can be safe and happy."

"As long as we're together, I can face anything." Her fingers gently brush my hair.

My phone rings. "It's the vet."

"What is it?" Jenna leans close. "Is something wrong with Max?"

"No." I brush a strand of hair from her face, my heart swelling with love for this incredible woman. "He's ready to come home."

"Then what are we waiting for?" Jenna jumps with excitement. "Let's bring him home."

When we arrive, the vet clinic is bustling. The receptionist greets us with a warm smile.

"He's ready." She leads us to the back.

Max sits in his kennel, his tail thumping hard against the floor the moment he sees us. Despite the shaved patches and healing wounds, his eyes are bright and alert.

"Hey, buddy." I kneel down to his level. "Are you ready to go home?"

His answer is an enthusiastic lick to my face, drawing laughs from both Jenna and me.

After a final check and care instructions from the vet, we help Max into the car. He settles in the backseat, his head resting on Jenna's lap as she sits beside him.

The drive home is quiet, but it's a comfortable silence. I help Max out of the car, supporting him as we make our way inside. Once in the apartment, he makes a beeline for his favorite spot by the window, settling down with a contented sigh.

Jenna and I stand there for a moment, arms around each other, watching him. Despite everything we've been through, despite the looming threat of Sentinel, this moment feels perfect.

"We're going to be okay, aren't we?" Jenna asks softly.

I pull her close, pressing a kiss to her temple. "Yeah, we're going to be just fine."

Max lets out a soft woof as if in agreement. Jenna laughs, the sound music to my ears, and moves to sit beside him. I join them, completing our little family circle.

Tomorrow, I'll give Guardian HRS my official answer.

Tomorrow, we'll continue the fight against Sentinel.

But for now—in this moment—the three of us are home.

We're safe.

We're together.

And really, that's all that matters.

With one last lingering kiss, we hold each other tightly, savoring the moment. This is our beginning, a fresh start filled with love.

Enjoyed Carter and Jenna's story?

Come join us for an exclusive bonus scene with Carter and Jenna.

You can read Carter and Jenna's bonus scene here.
elliemasters.com/JennasProtector_BonusScene

Ready for the next book in thc Charlie team series?
elliemasters.com/RescuingSophia

YUP! We're checking out Carter's twin brother, BLAKE, and his fascination with SOPHIA. It's going to be a wild ride!

Book Description:

In a world of secrets and lies, how far would you go to protect the ones you love?

BLAKE: My Navy SEAL training never prepared me for someone like Sophia. She's not just enigmatic and alluring—she's a magnet for danger. Recently freed from the brutal world of human trafficking, she's haunted by shadows I can barely comprehend. I'm used to high-stakes missions and life-or-death decisions, but the moment she entered my life, I knew I was in over my head. The closer I get, the more I realize her past isn't just a threat to her—it threatens everything I hold dear.

SOPHIA: Blake doesn't know the half of it. He can't. My secrets are the only thing keeping everything I've fought so hard to protect safe. But Blake's strength, his fierce protectiveness, draws me in, making it harder to keep my distance. I want to trust him, to let him in, but the price might be too steep. One wrong move, one moment of weakness, and everything I've fought to protect could be lost forever.

Rescuing Sophia is a heart-pounding ride of suspense, passion, and impossible choices. If you crave protective alpha males, fierce heroines, and sizzling romance woven into high-stakes action,

Rescuing Sophia is for you. **Don't wait—grab your copy today and dive into this unforgettable story of love, danger, and sacrifice.**

Don't Miss Out
Get Rescuing Sophia today:
elliemasters.com/RescuingSophia

Please consider leaving a review

I HOPE YOU ENJOYED THIS BOOK AS MUCH AS I ENJOYED WRITING IT. If you like this book, please leave a review. I love reviews. I love reading your reviews, and they help other readers decide if this book is worth their time and money. I hope you think it is and decide to share this story with others. A sentence is all it takes. Thank you in advance!

CLICK ON THE LINK BELOW TO LEAVE YOUR REVIEW
Goodreads
Amazon
Bookbub

ELLZ BELLZ

ELLIE'S FACEBOOK READER GROUP

If you are interested in joining the ELLZ BELLZ, Ellie's Facebook reader group, we'd love to have you.

Join Ellie's ELLZ BELLZ.
The ELLZ BELLZ Facebook Reader Group

Sign up for Ellie's Newsletter.
Elliemasters.com/newslettersignup

Books by Jet Masters

If you enjoyed this book by Ellie Masters, the LIGHTER SIDE of the Jet & Ellie writing duo, and aren't afraid of edgier writing, you might enjoy reading BDSM themed books written by Jet, the DARKER SIDE of the Masters' Writing Team.

The DARKER SIDE
Jet Masters is the darker side of the Jet & Ellie writing duo!

Romantic Suspense
Changing Roles Series:

THIS SERIES MUST BE READ IN ORDER.
Command Me
Control Me
Collar Me
Embracing FATE
Seizing FATE
Accepting FATE

HOT READS

A STANDALONE NOVEL.

Down the Rabbit Hole

Light BDSM Romance
The Ties that Bind

EACH BOOK IN THIS SERIES CAN BE READ AS A STANDALONE AND IS ABOUT A DIFFERENT COUPLE WITH AN HEA.

Alexa

Penny

Michelle

Ivy

HOT READS
Becoming His Series

THIS SERIES MUST BE READ IN ORDER.

The Ballet

Learning to Breathe

Becoming His

Dark Captive Romance

A STANDALONE NOVEL.

She's MINE

About the Author

Ellie Masters is a USA Today Bestselling author and Amazon Top 15 Author who writes Angsty, Steamy, Heart-Stopping, Pulse-Pounding, Can't-Stop-Reading Romantic Suspense. In addition, she's a wife, military mom, doctor, and retired Colonel. She writes romantic suspense filled with all your sexy, swoon-worthy alpha men. Her writing will tug at your heartstrings and leave your heart racing.

Born in the South, raised under the Hawaiian sun, Ellie has traveled the globe while in service to her country. The love of her life, her amazing husband, is her number one fan and biggest supporter. And yes! He's read every word she's written.

She has lived all over the United States—east, west, north, south and central—but grew up under the Hawaiian sun. She's also been privileged to have lived overseas, experiencing other cultures and making lifelong friends. Now, Ellie is proud to call herself a Southern transplant, learning to say y'all and "bless her heart" with the best of them.

Ellie's favorite way to spend an evening is curled up on a couch, laptop in place, watching a fire, drinking a good wine, and bringing forth all the characters from her mind to the page and hopefully into the hearts of her readers.

FOR MORE INFORMATION
elliemasters.com

Connect with Ellie Masters

Website:
elliemasters.com
Purchase Direct:
elliemasters.com/shopify
Amazon Author Page:
elliemasters.com/amazon
Facebook:
elliemasters.com/Facebook
Goodreads:
elliemasters.com/Goodreads
Bookbub:
elliemasters.com/Bookbub
Instagram:
elliemasters.com/Instagram

Final Thoughts

I hope you enjoyed this book as much as I enjoyed writing it. If you enjoyed reading this story, please consider leaving a review on Amazon and Goodreads, and please let other people know. A sentence is all it takes. Friend recommendations are the strongest catalyst for readers' purchase decisions! And I'd love to be able to continue bringing the characters and stories from My-Mind-to-the-Page.

Second, call or e-mail a friend and tell them about this book. If you really want them to read it, gift it to them. If you prefer digital friends, please use the "Recommend" feature of Goodreads to spread the word.

Or visit my blog https://elliemasters.com, where you can find out more about my writing process and personal life.

Come visit The EDGE: Dark Discussions where we'll have a chance to talk about my works, their creation, and maybe what the future has in store for my writing.

Facebook Reader Group: Ellz Bellz

Thank you so much for your support!

Love,

Ellie

Dedication

This book is dedicated to you, my reader. Thank you for spending a few hours of your time with me. I wouldn't be able to write without you to cheer me on. Your wonderful words, your support, and your willingness to join me on this journey is a gift beyond measure.

Whether this is the first book of mine you've read, or if you've been with me since the very beginning, thank you for believing in me as I bring these characters 'from my mind to the page and into your hearts.'

Love,
Ellie

THE END